"I ____ __ ____ ____ ____ ____ ____ ctive
fic ___ ____ ____ ____ ____ __ ar—
tha ____ ____ ____ ____ ___enre.
Th_ ___ ____ ____ ____ the ____ Rice
bo__ ____ ____ ____ ____ ___ sonnets
of Shakespeare, some of the odes of Swinburne, and
practically all of *The Faerie Queen*. But I cannot
imagine myself skipping a line of Craig Rice.

—Louis Untermeyer

Novels by **CRAIG RICE**
available in Crime Classics® editions

Featuring Malone and the Justuses
8 FACES AT 3
THE CORPSE STEPS OUT
THE WRONG MURDER
THE RIGHT MURDER
TRIAL BY FURY *
THE BIG MIDGET MURDERS
HAVING WONDERFUL CRIME*
THE LUCKY STIFF*
THE FOURTH POSTMAN*
MY KINGDOM FOR A HEARSE*

attributed to CRAIG RICE
CRIME ON MY HANDS by GEORGE SANDERS

by STUART PALMER and CRAIG RICE
PEOPLE VERSUS WITHERS AND MALONE
*forthcoming

Series Consultant: William Ruehlmann

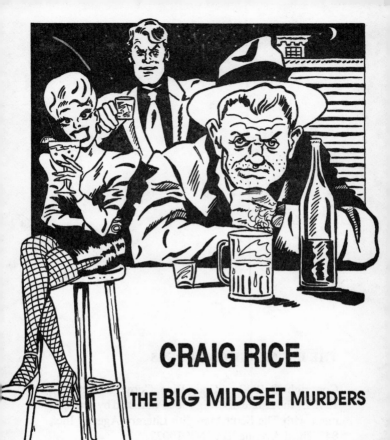

CRAIG RICE

THE BIG MIDGET MURDERS

LIBRARY OF CRIME CLASSICS®

MISTER E'S™

INTERNATIONAL POLYGONICS, LTD.
NEW YORK CITY

THE BIG MIDGET MURDERS

Library of Congress Card Catalog No. 91-73851
ISBN 1-55882-112-0

Printed and manufactured in the United States of America
First IPL printing October 1991.
10 9 8 7 6 5 4 3 2 1

There are night clubs like The Casino, and there is a city called Chicago, and perhaps by now Jake Justus, Helene, and John J. Malone are as real as other people. With these exceptions I'll have to admit that the characters and events in this book were all dreamed up. If they resemble any actual persons or parties I wouldn't be surprised.

CRAIG RICE

Chapter One

"TAKE HIM AWAY—he scares me!"

The short, stocky man with the red face put one hand over his eyes and peeked around his finger.

Jay Otto had just appeared on the stage of the Casino. There was a sudden roar of applause from the crowd at the tables. Now he stood there, in top hat and tails, not uttering a sound, just standing there looking over the audience with a mocking smile, swinging a miniature walking stick in one hand. The handsome band leader had hushed his men and was watching for his next cue.

John J. Malone, Chicago's famous criminal lawyer, mopped his brow with a slightly soiled handkerchief and looked away. "He scares me," he repeated stubbornly.

Jay Otto performed some antic with the walking stick and stood still again, while the audience howled appreciatively.

"Shame on you, Malone," said the blonde girl at the same table. "Afraid of a little midget!"

"Especially," her tall, red-haired companion added, "when that midget is going to pay our rent." He paused and added piously, "I hope!"

Another wave of laughter went over the audience and Malone looked back at the stage in spite of himself. Jay Otto, in wordless pantomime, had begun his famous imitation of a slightly boiled after-dinner speaker. The orchestra began to play, very softly.

The entertainer, less than three feet high, was a perfect travesty of a human being. Unlike so many of his kind, his proportions were almost exactly the same as those of a full-sized man; his head was not too large for his body; his arms and legs were proportionately the right length. Because of that, and of the fact that he handled his tiny body with such consummate skill, he made it appear that the rest of the world had suddenly swelled out of all proportion. Looking at him and then at the audience, it seemed to Malone that he was in a roomful of people all nine or ten feet tall, with enormous, grinning faces. He shuddered.

"Marvelous," the red-haired man breathed. He reached out for one of the blonde girl's hands. "One more week, and we can pay off the mortgage."

"It's either that," she said, "or we're out on the street without a night club to our name."

"The old homestead!" Malone murmured, without the faintest trace of sympathy in his voice. He relit his cigar, leaned back in his chair, tried to ignore Jay Otto, and looked about him.

There had been a time when the Casino was so exclusive that only socialites, celebrities, and better-class gangsters could get in. That had been before Jake Justus, ex-reporter, ex-press agent, ex-amateur detective, had won it on a bet from a Chicago millionairess who'd wagered that she could commit a murder without being caught at it, and lost.*

Not that Jake had needed to own a night club. His bride, *née* Helene Brand, was heiress to more money than Malone cared to count. But Jake had that funny old-fashioned notion about earning his living and supporting his wife.

Malone rolled an eye over the remodeled Casino and shook his head. No, its best friends wouldn't know it now. "I'd rather have a thousand customers at a buck a head than a hundred at ten bucks a head," Jake had declared. "It's just as much dough and ten times as much fun."

Now, the Casino was half night club, half theater, and two halves circus, Malone reflected. Walls had been knocked down, balconies constructed, the dance floor doubled in size, and a stage—where Jay Otto was now pretending to be a football coach between halves of the big game—built at one side. "The big-best little night club in the world," Jake had announced modestly on the billboards.

* Mona McClane, in *The Right Murder* and *The Wrong Murder*. Sensitive readers will be happy to know that Mona and the law parted friends.

Malone sighed and hoped it would begin to crawl out of the red before the banks got nasty about the money borrowed to pay for the remodeling.

There was a sudden roar from the audience, and Malone instinctively looked toward the stage.

The midget's walking stick had suddenly shot up to twice its length, and a gesture from him had turned it into a microphone. Now the midget had become Lou Holtz, clinging to the microphone and shrinking coyly from the applause.

He tossed the stick into the wings, and in the same instant a man appeared carrying a piano. Malone blinked. After watching Jay Otto for a few moments, the man with the piano looked like a giant, at least ten feet high, while the piano he carried seemed to be of only normal size.

"A man carrying a piano is always funny," Jake murmured. "A man carrying a little piano is even funnier. But when a man carries a piano under one arm—"

The man with the piano—an ugly, lowering brute with a surly face and thick, tousled brown hair—put down the piano with exquisite care. It was exactly the right size for Jay Otto. Malone saw that the big man had been carrying a tiny piano stool in the other hand. Now he placed it with mathematical precision before the keyboard. Then Jay Otto sat down and rested both hands on the keys, assuming so soulful and faraway an expression that it was a moment or so before Malone realized that the big man had disappeared into the wings.

"He really is huge," Helene commented. "He's six foot six if he's an inch. But he looks twice that beside his boss. I think he really loathes Jay Otto."

"So do I," Malone said in a low growl. "Give me Angela Doll any day."

Helene sniffed. "You don't need to tell anybody," she said, "that you'd rather watch Angela Doll do her strip than a sneak preview of the Day of Judgment."

"Angela Doll," Malone said stiffly, "is a great artiste."

"All of that," Jake agreed. "And she's cute, too."

Jay Otto, seated at the keyboard, imitated a series of famous pianists, from Rachmaninoff to Hazel Scott. Neither he nor the piano made any sound at all. The crowd howled, and at last became thunderous when the big man ran out from the wings, picked up the piano under one arm and Jay Otto under the other, and carried both off stage.

"I still don't like him," Malone said.

Jake sighed. "I didn't ask you here to like him. I asked you here to help me fight out that tricky clause in his contract. We'll go back and see him in a few minutes."

Two curtain calls later the orchestra suddenly began to play Angela Doll's music. The crowd quieted immediately, wondering what was coming. Jake stiffened.

It was Jay Otto who appeared through the maroon-colored curtains, adopting the pose Angela Doll had made famous with her entrances.

"Damn it, he's always changing his act," Jake said. "This never was in it before."

Starting from top hat and tails, the midget began going through the familiar strip routine of Angela Doll. The crowd giggled, then laughed, and then roared and clapped its appreciation. It was a biting, merciless travesty, and watching it Malone suddenly realized that all of Jay Otto's imitations were cruel, hateful, even brutal. He found himself laughing uproariously as the midget skipped off stage waving a tiny pair of shorts through the curtains in a parting gesture—and immediately wished he hadn't.

"My God," Jake gasped, catching his breath and wiping his brow, "Angela'll kill him for that."

"I'd defend her for nothing," Malone said, "on the grounds of justifiable homicide."

The crowd began to quiet down. The members of Al Omega's orchestra had slipped away from their places and the relief band had started a fast Cuban rhythm. The dance floor slowly began to fill.

To Malone all the dancers seemed to be giants. He shuddered again.

"Tell that waiter to bring me a drink before a noted lawyer drops dead in the world-famous Casino," he said. "And when we go back to talk to this guy, put him behind a screen. I've got a phobia about midgets." He lit a fresh cigar and said, "At least, I've got a phobia about that midget."

Jake signaled to the waiter, and said, "He's a mean, hateful little cuss. But the customers are insane about him, and in this corner tavern the customers are always right. Anyway, until we get the decorations paid for."

"All right," Malone said. "I'll try to love him for your sweet sake."

He took a quick glance at Jake. The lean, pleasantly homely face under the shock of red hair was pale with fatigue and lined with worry. He reminded himself that this meant a lot to Jake, more than just the successful re-opening of a night club. If the Casino should go down the river, it meant back to the press agent grind again: dance bands, fan dancers, mind-reading acts; hotel rooms in Dayton and Lansing and Milwaukee and Keokuk; getting along with radio singers and theater managers and cowboy yodelers and city editors, stretched clear from hell to breakfast and back again. It wasn't what Jake had wanted for Helene.

"Remember the girl who wanted to be married to a man who owned a jewelry store?" Helene asked happily, lighting a cigarette. "Well, imagine being married to a man who owns a saloon."

Malone sighed almost imperceptibly, and looked over the cash customers. What he saw promised well for the future of the remodeled Casino. It had been designed to draw the crowd, and the crowd was there. But not only the crowd. There was a dancer from the visiting ballet, dropped in to catch the late show. There was a table of slightly aging North Shore socialites. There was Betty Royal, a bright-eyed youngster with shining hair, surrounded by her usual football team of admirers, and there was half the cast of a Loop hit show.

There was Lou Goldsmith, the slot-machine king, a tall, barrel-stomached, unhappy-looking man, with his restless glittering young wife, who had, surprisingly, stayed on in the Casino chorus after her marriage. As Malone watched them, the couple rose from their floorside table, waved cordially at Jake and Helene, and moved toward the door leading backstage, Lou a step or two in the rear, protest showing in the very set of his bulky shoulders. Malone wondered if there was anything to the stories about Lou Goldsmith's wife and Al Omega, the orchestra leader.

There was Frank Ferris, the city hall reporter, squiring a dowdy little woman with glasses. There was the handsome, distinguished-looking business man whose presence was the accolade to any night club. There was a table of radio people.

Yes, Malone decided, the Casino was over its first hurdle. He smiled cheerfully around the room, then abruptly stiffened to sharp attention.

At a secluded table in a shadowed corner there was an immense, grinning man in a tuxedo that was—

Malone blinked and squinted once or twice before he was sure—a deep, jungle green. His pink face was scrubbed, powdered, and beaming, in one plump hand he held a rose-quartz cigarette holder in which burned (Malone remembered) a slim, perfumed, and probably tinted cigarette. The men who hovered behind him, out of range of the floor lights, were black, immovable shadows. Malone sensed that every one of them had a tense hand in his right-hand coat pocket.

The little lawyer felt a chill flow over him, as though ice had suddenly been rubbed against his bones. He reached for his glass, coughed into it, dropped his cigar and caught it halfway down his vest, and said, "I never saw Max Hook in a night club before."

There was a little, almost uneasy silence before Helene said lightly, "After all, Malone, even a gambling czar has to have a little relaxation."

"Besides," Jake said, "he probably wanted to drop in and see what kind of decorations his money had paid for."

Ramon Arriba's Cuban Band suddenly let loose a blast of impassioned music that drowned out all speech and almost all thought. It was a good three minutes later before Malone could say, between cold lips,

"You didn't borrow the money for the remodeling from Max Hook! Because if you did, he—"

Jake said fast, "Listen, Malone, this is no time to talk business." His grey eyes signaled, "Shut up!" and he added, "Relax and enjoy yourself."

Malone caught the signal, nodded, sipped his drink, and relit his cigar.

A couple of lively youngsters from Northwestern had started a conga chain. The Goldsmiths were back at their table, apparently quarreling. Frank Ferris was writing down the cigarette girl's name. Max Hook had clasped one of his rosy, puffy hands over the wrist of one of his weasel-eyed young bodyguards.

"Hold your breath," Helene said, without moving her lips. "Here comes Ruth Rawlson."

Malone immediately forgot the Casino, the rhumba band, Jake and Helene, and even Max Hook. He knew now what it would feel like to have an electric eel lie alongside of his spine.

Ruth Rawlson. Had it been 1921 or 1922? Malone wasn't sure. He only knew that he'd gone to the Follies three nights out of five during their stay in Chicago. Maybe it had been 1926. Oh Lord no, not later than 1924. Who the hell cared about the date, anyway. There had been that tall, slim, devastating girl with the lush, reddish-gold hair rippling to her waist, the face, the throat, the shoulders, the—Malone closed his eyes. For just that moment he was in his twenties again.

He heard a faint murmur of voices saying something about wanting a drink, and ordering one, and then Helene was kicking him under the table as she said, "Miss Rawlson—Mr. Malone."

"How delightful!" said the deep, throaty voice of Ruth Rawlson.

Malone braced a hand against the table edge and opened his eyes.

They'd always said Ruth Rawlson had good bones. Sculptors, indeed, had raved about them. But you could really appreciate them now. In fact, with a reasonably searching eye, Malone realized, you could probably identify every one of them.

She had been tall, graceful, swan-like. Now she was only tall, and thin as a haddock-bone. There was a streak of face powder down the front of her shabby and remodeled black satin evening dress. Her face, that had been the most pictured face of the decade, was still beautiful, in a haggard, picturesque way, like a famous ruin, Malone thought. The red-gold hair was grey now, and, at the moment, more than a little disheveled. And she was staggering like a camel on ice-skates.

Malone said, "I've always wanted to meet you," and meant every word of it.

Ruth Rawlson turned an engaging smile on him and breathed, "You charming man!" She pushed an empty glass toward Jake and said, "How stupid of me! I didn't mean to drink it that fast!" Beamed at Helene and said, "My dear, how exquisite you look." Turned back to Jake to whisper, "When the waiter comes around again——" And then informed them all, in a torrid murmur, that she'd turned down a Broadway offer over a little matter of price.

Jake obligingly hailed the waiter. Ruth Rawlson downed a drink, delicately pressed the drops off her chin with a corner of the tablecloth, rose to her feet by taking a firm grip on the edge of the table, flashed her still dazzling smile impartially at them all, and careened off toward the door leading to the dressing rooms.

"Isn't she wonderful!" Helene breathed. "She's lived for years on cheap whiskey and vitamin pills!"

Malone remembered a poem he'd learned in grade school about Titania vanishing into the heart of a flower, and said crossly, "She probably drinks to forget something."

"Sure," Jake said, lighting a cigarette, "her future." He blew out the match and added, "She'll probably have us into bankruptcy yet. Helene left messages with all the bartenders that any drinks Ruth Rawlson bought should be charged to the house." He snapped the burnt match between his lean brown fingers. " 'I wouldn't dream of taking five hundred,' " he mimicked. " 'Ruth Rawlson never got less than seven-fifty.' " He snorted loudly, and added, "Not as long as the twenty-five bucks per week pension holds out."

"Jake," Helene said sternly, "you're a very rude man."

Malone watched the ex-Follies girl vanishing

through the door and said, "Well anyway, I never saw a finer pair of shoulder blades. How much longer do I have to sit around here waiting to go back and bulldoze your midget? My nerves are beginning to knit themselves up into doilies."

Jake glanced at his watch, finished his drink, and said, "We might as well go back now. He'll have his make-up off by this time and be ready to leave. That was his last show tonight."

Helene rose, wrapped a glittering white-and-silver cape around her smooth shoulders, and said, "I'm coming too. To keep Malone's courage up."

There was a long corridor back of the stage of the Casino. One end of it led toward the kitchens, and one toward the service entrance. Just at the end of the stage, a flight of unpainted wooden stairs went down to the dressing rooms.

Jake led the way, warning the other two to watch where they stepped. At the foot of the stairs a door was marked, "J. OTTO. PLEASE KNOCK."

Jake knocked twice, heard no answer, and said, "Hell, I'm the boss of this joint." He opened the door.

Malone drew a slow breath. He wasn't looking forward to the session ahead of him. From all he'd heard, and from what some secret place in the back of his brain told him, the famous midget was going to be a nasty customer to deal with, even over a little matter of a difficult clause in a contract.

The door slammed behind him. Hard, and loud.

He didn't really see, at first: he felt. There was a

strange, muffled, half-strangled sound from Jake's throat. There was a smothered "Oh!" on an indrawn breath, from Helene. A delicate and suddenly cold hand clutched his wrist.

Then he saw.

To the left of the dressing table there was a narrow closet, its door open. Above the doorway was a hook. And suspended from the hook was the body of Jay Otto, the Big Midget, its face blackened and discolored, hanging in a noose that seemed to Malone's swimming eyes to be made of gleaming, skin-colored, long silk stockings.

Chapter Two

I T WAS probably a purely reflex action. Malone had shut the door behind him, shot back the bolt, and hissed, "Keep quiet," before he realized that he'd even moved.

The "Keep quiet" was entirely superfluous. Neither Jake nor Helene showed the slightest intention of making a sound. Indeed, they appeared not to have heard it at all.

After that first, instinctive move, Malone stood still, looking not at the tiny body hanging in that singular noose, but at Jake and Helene. One of the most wonderful things about Helene, the lawyer reflected, was that you could always count on her not to scream, regardless of the provocation. She was staring at Jay Otto with eyes that had suddenly grown wide and dark, and her face had turned a ghastly white, but for all her horror, she wasn't moving a muscle nor uttering a word.

Jake's face was pale too, but Malone realized it was the pallor of indignation, almost fury. For a moment he stood there, while the shocked surprise in his grey eyes turned slowly to a suppressed rage. Then he strode across the room, still speechless, and made a quick examination of the midget's body. The look on his face when he turned round again told everything Helene and the lawyer wanted to know.

"Well," Malone said quietly, "I hope you can get another star act on a moment's notice."

It was a good thirty seconds before Jake drew a long, profane-sounding breath, and whispered between his teeth, "The son of a bitch!"

Helene gasped. "Jake," she whispered. "He's—" She looked toward what had been Jay Otto.

"All right," Jake said, bitterly, "so he's a dead son of a bitch. And just like him to go and hang himself on opening night, with a four weeks' contract left to run."

Malone had been looking around. "What makes you think he hung himself?"

Jake glared at him. "I suppose you're trying to tell me it's an optical illusion."

"No," the lawyer told him, "but maybe it was intended to be." He scowled. "Not a very successful one, though, because something essential was left out."

"This is no time to play games," Jake said. "Do you know what you're talking about?"

"What did he jump off?" Malone asked.

"It's no time to ask riddles, either," Jake said.

Malone sighed and pointed toward the doorway where the body was hanging. "He'd have had to have a chair, or a table, or something to jump from, or to kick out from under him. But nothing of the sort is there. What's more, nobody but a contortionist could tie a knot exactly like that at the back of his own neck." He strolled nearer, took a quick look, and turned away again. "No," he repeated, "he didn't hang himself."

"Oh, *no!*" Helene said unexpectedly, in a strange, gasping voice. She had turned a shade more pale. "It can't be." Her lips were stiff and trembling; soundlessly they formed the word, "Murder!"

"Evidently," Jake said. He looked at her for a moment, lit a cigarette, and put it between her fingers.

"Stop looking as though you'd never heard of it before," Malone said crossly. "There's nothing so surprising about a mere murder." He glanced toward the midget and added, "You might even say this was only half a murder."

"That's just it," Helene said, shuddering. "It isn't murder that's horrible. But this—" She caught her breath. "It isn't like the murder of a human being. Because he never seemed to me like one. More like something—" She paused, biting her lip.

"The word," Malone told her, "is leprechaun." A new look came into his eyes, far away, and almost dreamy. "So that's it," he said very softly. "The little men."

Jake stared indignantly at them both. "I suppose in another minute you'll try to tell me a band of elves came in and murdered my star act. First it's an optical illusion, and now it's done with magic."

"It was done with something almost as unusual," Malone said, in the same thoughtful voice. "What the devil kind of a rope is that? It looks like a bunch of silk stockings."

Jake examined it. "That's exactly what it is. Long silk stockings, twisted together." He reached toward the hook.

"Don't!" Helene said sharply. "Don't touch it!" For just a moment she closed her eyes. "In another minute I'll have the first fit of hysterics I ever had in my life."

"I hope to Heaven you have it quietly then," Malone said, "because it sure would scare hell out of the cash customers out front."

Jake started; stared at the lawyer. "Malone, what are we going to do?"

"In these cases," Malone said, "it's customary to call a cop."

"And have the Casino closed up tight as a drum for days?" Jake said. "It's bad enough as it is, but if that happens, right now—" His voice trailed off.

"Yes," Malone said, looking at him gravely. The look of quiet desperation in Jake's eyes had to do with the remodeling of the Casino, with the newspaper ads and the twenty-four sheet billboards, with the crowd that had turned out for opening night, and with what it would mean to have other crowds turned away for even two or three nights. "Yes," he repeated, "I know exactly what you mean. But what can you do? When you have a murder on your hands, you can't just walk off and leave it."

"No, but you can walk off and take it with you," Jake said hoarsely. "Look, I'm a law-abiding citizen. But—"

"The words," Malone told him, "are law-abiding, tax-paying citizen. A citizen," he repeated, "who happens to own a night club with a murdered midget in one of its dressing rooms."

"Who could have murdered him?" Helene asked. Her voice was calmer now.

"We'll take that up in an advanced course," Jake snapped. "Right now, we've got to get him out of here."

For a moment there was silence. Helene crushed out her half-smoked cigarette in the saucer on the dressing table. Malone took out a cigar, started to unwrap it, then put it back in his pocket. Jake stared miserably at the opposite wall.

"I don't mean to dispose of the body, or anything like that," Jake said at last. "The fact that an entertainer from the Casino has been murdered mightn't do any harm. Maybe the reverse. But I can't afford to take the chance. Just so he isn't found here, on the premises. If his body should be discovered up an alley somewhere—" His voice trailed off on a questioning note.

"But—" Malone paused, scowling. "I hate to bring up such a subject as justice at this point, but you'd be making it tough for the police if you moved the body from here. It might make the difference between their finding—or not finding—the murderer."

Jake said, "Frankly, from all that I've heard about Jay Otto, I don't think I care whether his murderer gets caught or not. There's more than one kind of justice in the world."

"Besides," Helene said slyly, *"we'd* know the truth."

"If you're hinting *I* find out who murdered him," Malone said in an indignant voice, "you can go jump off a kite."

Helene sniffed. "You mean 'go fly a lake', don't you?"

He pretended he hadn't heard her. "I don't even want to know who murdered him," he said in a suppressed roar. "The last time I mixed up in anything like that I was blown up by a bomb, nearly drowned in a river, trapped in a burning insane asylum, and all I got out of it was a lousy thousand bucks." * He paused and looked thoughtfully at the late Jay Otto. "I'll probably be sorry for this, but have it your way. How shall we carry him out of here?"

Helene frowned. "The corridor at the top of the stairs leads to a rear entrance. But until closing time there's always people coming and going in it."

* *Trial by Fury.*

"Then we can't take him out until closing time," Malone said. "And we can't just stay here keeping curious people out, or later somebody'll be bound to remember we were missing for an unaccountably long time. Is there a lock on the door?"

Jake shook his head. "Only the bolt on the inside."

"Well then," Malone began. He stopped suddenly, staring at Helene. "What's the matter with you?"

Her eyes flickered with excitement. "Look!"

Malone looked in the direction she pointed. In the corner of the room, leaning against the wall, was a bull fiddle case. Jake looked.

"Yes," he said breathlessly, "yes, it would fit."

Malone blinked. "What in the name of all that's impossible did he want with a bull fiddle?" he demanded.

"It wasn't his," Jake explained. "One of Al Omega's boys was fired yesterday at rehearsal. He owed the midget money, and had to leave this for security." He crossed the room at a bound, reached for the fiddle case and suddenly paused. "Hell, that's no good. There wouldn't be room inside it for the midget and the fiddle too."

"No," Helene agreed, "but there's a closet here where we can store the fiddle."

Jake nodded slowly, and swung the big, unwieldy case down to the floor.

"This is all very fine," Malone said, "and a lot of good clean fun, I've no doubt. But if you think you

can walk through a crowded corridor carrying that"
—he pointed to the case—"without being conspic-
uous—"

Jake sat back on his heels and looked up at Helene.
"Malone's right." He frowned, and looked back at
the case. "But this thing locks. The key is probably
in the corpse's pocket. We can lock the case and lean
it back against the wall, exactly the way it was, and
then when the joint is empty, come back and get it."

"Now you're talking." Helene said enthusiastically.

Malone suppressed a sigh. He had an uncomfortable feeling that no good would come of this. But he
knew better than to argue with Jake and Helene.

"Give me a hand," Jake said. "We'll take him down
and then go through his pockets." He reached up
toward the hook. "Hell, I can't reach it." He looked
around for a chair. There was none.

"For the love of Mike," Malone growled. "Didn't
the little guy ever sit down?"

"Not in here," Jake said. "He had to stand up to
the dressing table, and he couldn't bear it for anybody else to be sitting down when he was standing up.
Hence, no chairs. But wait a minute." He went out
into the hall, closing the door quietly after him.

Helene waited a moment before she said, "Jake's
right about this? About moving the body out of here,
I mean?" Her eyes were wide and dark and anxious.

"Of course he is," Malone reassured her, hoping his
voice sounded more convincing than hers.

Jake returned with a chair filched from the next-door dressing room, and set it down beside the dangling body. "We'll get this over with in a hurry," he said between his teeth, "and then—" He climbed up on the chair and unhitched the peculiar rope from the hook by which it had been suspended.

"It looks like a big doll," Helene said. She glanced quickly at the tiny body on the dressing room floor, and turned away.

Jake looked up at her from his task of searching for the key. His jaw was set in a grim line. "I know just how you feel, but we've got to do this."

Malone spotted a quart bottle of Scotch, nearly full, on the dressing table, and reached for a glass. He couldn't remember a time in his life when he'd needed a drink more acutely. He unscrewed the cap, started to tilt the bottle, stopped himself suddenly in the middle of the motion and stared at the top of the bottle.

"If you've found a jinn in the bottle," Jake said, "I don't want to hear about it." He heard a faint giggle from Helene and added hastily, "And this is no time for bad puns."

Malone ignored him. He was holding the bottle directly under the electric light and staring at it intently.

"Maybe it doesn't mean a thing," he said at last, "but there's a little line of white powder on the rim." He screwed the cap back on the bottle, set it on the dresser again, and stood looking at it suspiciously.

Helene gasped. "He may have been poisoned first, and then—" She paused.

After a moment Jake said, "I thought it was funny he didn't put up a struggle. Even a midget might make a fuss if somebody was trying to hang him. Thank God, here's that key."

He unlocked the case, lifted out a big, shining bull fiddle, stowed it in the closet, and closed the door.

"But why?" Helene demanded. "Why not just poison him and let it go at that? Why go to all the bother of hanging him afterwards?"

"Never mind why," Malone growled. "This is no time to ask foolish questions. Let's get this over and get out of here."

Jake had unfastened the noose, and tossed the shimmering strand aside on the floor. Helene picked it up half curiously, and began examining and unwinding it.

"There must be a dozen stockings here," she reported, "just twisted and knotted together. Why on earth use stockings, when it's so easy to find a rope?"

Jake had closed the fiddle case and was preparing to lock it. Now he paused and opened it again.

"Give me those stockings and I'll put them in here too. We can't just leave them lying around."

"Wait a minute," Helene said. Her eyes were blazing. Then suddenly she tossed the stockings to Jake, and looked up.

"There's exactly eleven stockings here," she reported.

"Well?" Jake said. "What of it?" He locked the fiddle case and stood it up in the corner, exactly as it had been. "We all know you can count."

"Eleven stockings," she said slowly. "The funny thing about it is that none of them were exactly the same size!"

Chapter Three

"THE IMPORTANT THING," Jake said, lighting Helene's cigarette for her, "is to stay out here where everybody can see us, and act as though everything was perfectly normal."

Malone nodded, gazing out over the still crowded dance floor of the Casino. From some long buried place in his memory came the picture of an Irish grandmother telling him how to cope with the strange and horrible things that might appear in the dark of night. "Just look at them and pretend they aren't there at all, and keep very still, and afore long they'll go away of their own accord."

Perhaps if he kept very still, and pretended the tiny corpse of Jay Otto wasn't concealed in the bass fiddle case, the whole horror would go away of its own accord, as though it had never been there at all.

It wasn't just that a man had been murdered. He'd encountered murders before. Nor that Jake and Helene might be in a devilishly tight spot. They'd get out of it, as they always had in the past. Indeed, it wasn't even the fact that the murdered man was a midget. No, it went deeper than any of those things. It was just that the little lawyer felt that all of them were skirting the edge of something strange and dark and terrible, something he couldn't describe or explain, but that he knew was there.

"Stop looking as if you saw ghosts on our lovely new dance floor, Malone," Helene said sharply.

Malone sighed, began slowly unwrapping a cigar, and tried unsuccessfully to pretend that he was having a wonderful time.

Al Omega's band was back at work again, and the dance floor was jammed. Max Hook and his bodyguards had gone, the lawyer noticed with relief, and a party of noisy young people occupied what had been his table. The Goldsmiths were still there, the big, homely man looking worried and unhappy, his blonde wife's lips set in a thin, cross line. Betty Royal was still at her table, entirely oblivious of the wistful and curious glances cast in her direction by the pretty young stenographers in their five-ninety-five formals, equally oblivious of the attention she was drawing from her tableful of handsome young men. She was gazing at Al Omega like a kitten gazing at a can of sardines.

Malone glanced up at the orchestra leader. "How does he do it?" he growled under his breath.

Most of the early evening crowd had gone, and

their places had been taken by a later, noisier crowd, who would not remain long. It would only be a little while before the Casino would begin to empty. The lawyer drew a long, almost sighing breath, and leaned across the table to Helene.

"I don't get it about those stockings," he said in a low voice. "You said there were eleven of them, and all different sizes."

She nodded her sleek blonde head. "I measured them. I happened to pick up two and they didn't look alike, so I measured them all."

Malone scowled at her. "I'm not calling you a liar," he began slowly, "but I've paid for a lot of silk stockings in my lifetime. And there aren't eleven different sizes. There's eight and a half, nine, nine and a half, and so on up. I think the largest size made is twelve, but I never knew a girl with bigger feet than that. You couldn't have had a hallucination, could you?"

"I could," she whispered indignantly, "but I didn't. Those were specially made stockings, and besides being different foot sizes, they were different lengths. There weren't any two of them alike." She crushed out her cigarette. "They were the kind of stockings the chorus here wears in that South American number, and all those girls are different heights. *Jake!*"

"I heard you," Jake said, "and shut up!" He glanced around quickly to see that no one was in hearing distance before he spoke again. "All I need now is to be told that the midget was murdered by the best night club chorus in town." He paused, frowned, and added, "Not that they wouldn't have liked to."

Malone relit his cigar. "Now that we're on the subject, who might have wanted to murder your midget?"

"I don't know," Jake said thoughtfully. "Nobody really liked him, and a lot of people downright hated him, but not murderously, as far as I know. I can't imagine anybody hating him that much."

Helene nodded. "It would take twice as much motive to make someone murder a midget as an ordinary person. You'd think it would be just the other way, but it isn't."

"I know exactly what you mean," Malone told her. Before he could say anything more, he caught sight of the huge figure of Jay Otto's assistant in the doorway leading backstage, and felt a sudden cold shiver run up and down his spine.

Jake saw him in the same instant, and whispered in what he hoped was a reassuring tone, "He can't possibly know anything about it."

Seen at close range, the big man appeared even more massive than on the Casino's stage. Malone peered at him for a moment, trying to place a resemblance, until at last he realized he was remembering the pictures in the early pages of *The Outline of History*.

Jake introduced him as Mr. McJackson—Allswell

McJackson—and invited him to join them. Mr. Mc-
Jackson shook his head, ruffling his mane of thick,
brown hair.

"I've got to hurry to the hotel, or Mr. Otto'll be
in a frenzy." He spoke in a beautifully modulated
voice that had a very definite Harvard overtone. "I
went to take Angela Doll home the minute I left the
stage, and if I'd dreamed Mr. Otto would leave before
I got back, I'd have hurried more than I did."

Jake and Helene looked at each other, each signaling the other to speak first. Malone had trouble
with cigar smoke that went down the wrong way, and
by the time he'd downed half his drink in order to
stop strangling, Mr. McJackson had gone on talking,
apparently oblivious of the interruption.

"I hope Mr. Otto isn't angry," he said.

"For the love of Mike!" Malone exploded. "He's
only a midget." He'd been within a hairsbreadth of
saying, "He was."

Mr. McJackson smiled wryly. "You don't know Mr.
Otto."

Malone downed the other half of his drink. "Now
I'd have been glad to take Miss Doll home for you,"
he said gallantly, "if it would have saved you any
trouble."

"I wanted to get her away from the Casino before
Mr. Otto did his impression of her," the giant said.
"Not that she won't hear about it anyway."

Jake said, "He could have picked out someone else
and saved me a lot of trouble."

"Yes," Mr. McJackson agreed. "But he doesn't enjoy doing an impression unless it makes somebody mad." He sighed.

"It must be a lousy job," Malone said. "Why don't you quit him?"

Allswell McJackson shook his head, and a wistful look came into his eyes. "I'd do it tomorrow," he said unhappily, "if I could only get a professorship. Even in some little jerk-water college." He sighed again. "But it appears to be impossible." He sighed again, said goodnight, and began shoving his way toward the exit.

Malone waited till he was out of earshot before growling, "And *you* wouldn't believe in *leprechauns!*"

"Poor Allswell," Helene said feelingly. "He has a degree in chemistry, and nobody'll give him a job as a professor because he looks like a wrestling champion. All he could do was be a stooge for Jay Otto."

"And now," Jake said, "that's shot. Or hanged, rather."

Malone scowled. "I don't suppose, then, that he'd have murdered his way out of a good job."

"He might have," Jake said. "I imagine one could stand just so much of Jay Otto."

"But," Helene pointed out, "he couldn't have. Because he was taking Angela Doll home at the time."

"How do you know?" Malone demanded. "You don't know what time Jay Otto was murdered, except that it was after the last performance, and before we went backstage. This guy could have taken Angela Doll home and gotten back in time. As a matter of fact," he added thoughtfully, "just who could have gotten into that dressing room during that time and murdered the midget?"

"Any one of Al Omega's band," Jake said, "or any one of Ramon Arriba's band, or any one of the twelve chorus girls, or Angela Doll, or Allswell McJackson, or any one of the stage hands, electricians, waiters, bartenders, and kitchen help, or any member of the audience who might have strayed backstage."

"Or Ruth Rawlson," Malone added, looking toward the door that led backstage.

Helene said, "Now that we've limited the suspects so brilliantly!"

Jake's eyes narrowed momentarily. "None of this is any of our business. We've gone and fixed it so that probably no one will ever know who murdered the midget. Now, let's not talk about it."

Malone was silent, watching the tottering figure of Ruth Rawlson as it moved toward their table. Save that she had unfastened her high-heeled sandals, leaving the straps dangling, the ex-beauty looked, at first glance, exactly as she had earlier in the evening. As she came closer to the table, however, the lawyer noticed that she was a shade more pale, and several degrees unsteadier. He rose hastily and pulled out a chair for her.

She slid into it, beaming, and braced her elbows on the table. "Thank you so much, darling. Yes, I will have one drink. Just an itsy-bittsy one, though. Ruthie does have to get home early and get her sleep." She opened her still lovely eyes to their full width and turned them on Malone. "You've no idea, really, what a responsibility it is to be a professional beauty. Early to bed—diet—plenty of exercise—" She rolled her eyes skyward with a martyred expression. "Just one little teensy-weensy drink, remember." She picked up Jake's glass and began sipping from it while waiting for her own to arrive.

"I'm sure," Malone said, with perfect composure, "your beauty is worth all the care you have to take of it."

Helene flashed him a grateful look across the table, turned to Ruth Rawlson, and said innocently, "Been backstage?"

Ruth set down Jake's glass, picked up her own, and nodded. "I've just come from the loveliest long chat with Angela Doll. You wouldn't believe it, but I knew her mother. We were in the Follies together. Of course Angela is very young—it really wasn't so long ago." She sighed noisily. "Those dear, dead days! Sometimes, you know, sometimes I think I'll go back to them after all. But I do enjoy private life so much." She finished her glass, yawned, and closed her eyes. Malone had a sudden horrible notion that in another moment she would begin to snore.

Jake rose. "Get your wrap, Ruth," he said gently. "I'll buy you a taxi home."

She opened her eyes again, smiled at him, and let

him help her to her feet. "Been so nice meeting you," she said to Malone. "Must meet again sometime."

Jake aimed her toward the checkroom, and turned back to whisper, "I think by the time I get back it'll be safe to leave. And stop worrying." His face looked very tired, and a trifle pale.

"Damn Jake," Helene said affectionately, after he was gone.

"I know what you mean," Malone said, nodding. "But he's got to make a success of the Casino."

"While I'd be just as happy married to a press agent," she told him gravely. "Malone, let this be a lesson to you. Never marry a woman with money."

"Hell," the lawyer growled, "I've never even been able to meet a woman with money." He gazed thoughtfully into his cigar smoke. "Did I hear her say she'd just come from a long chat with Angela Doll?" As Helene nodded, he went on, "But that Man Mountain the Second said he'd taken her home right after he left the stage."

"You don't understand Ruth Rawlson," Helene said. "She just happened to pick on Angela Doll. She'd have made it Queen Victoria if she'd happened to think of her first."

Malone blinked. "I can see she's a souse," he said, "but the insanity doesn't show."

"Ruth is sane," Helene said. "She just lies by some kind of instinct, I think. It comes natural to her. If she's been shopping in Marshall Field's, and you ask

her where she's been, she says she's just come from
Mandel Brothers. Or if she went to the movies the
night before, she'll tell you she was home reading the
most fascinating book. The chances are this time she
was back chinning with the chorus girls while they
dressed."

"I'd love to be able to use Ruth on the witness
stand sometime," Malone said.

"Ruth," Helene said gravely, "is stranger than fiction."

The little lawyer pretended not to have heard. "She
couldn't have strayed into the midget's dressing room
and murdered him, could she?"

"She could," Helene said, "but she wouldn't have
done it that way. Malone, who did murder him?"

"I've mislaid my tea leaves at the moment," the
little lawyer said gloomily. He was silent a minute,
lost in thought. "The hell of it is, I have a hunch
I'll never be able to find them, now."

The late crowd had begun to thin out by the time
Jake returned. Betty Royal and her admirers had
paused to speak to Helene and then gone home; the
Goldsmiths had departed, not looking at or speaking
to each other; the tables were emptying fast. Al
Omega's musicians were beginning to cast hopeful
glances at their watches.

"Ruth must be losing her grip," Jake announced,
sitting and lighting a cigarette. "Usually she puts
away enough cheap whiskey to kill a horse, and keeps

right on navigating. Tonight when I put her into the cab, she was practically paralyzed. I told the driver to see her all the way in her door."

"It isn't every night one of her friends opens a night club," Helene reminded him.

"Or closes one," Jake said wearily. He blew out his match and stared at its charred end. "Let's go back and take the midget out of his fiddle case, and call the cops."

Helene stared at him. "Have you lost your mind?"

"I'm just getting it back," Jake said. A thin line had appeared in his forehead, between his eyebrows. "I don't mind breaking the law—or anyway, bending it a little—in a good cause, but murder is murder."

Malone drew a long breath. "I thought you didn't like the little guy."

"I didn't," Jake said, "I detested him. And the cops will probably close up this joint for a week while they horse around trying to find out who killed him, and in the meantime Max Hook will want his dough back and decide to take the Casino instead. And I'll end up with a job press-agenting an ice-skating troupe."

"Never mind," Helene said, "I adore traveling."

He leaned across the table and kissed her.

"Damn it," Malone said crossly, "never cross your bridges until the horse is stolen. Remember, things never seem as bad as they are. I can stall off Max Hook, and in the meantime, maybe I can find out who killed your midget. What's more," he added, "I'll bet you even money I can have your joint open for business by tomorrow night. I don't have three guys in the sheriff's office owing me money for nothing."

"Hooray for Malone!" Helene said enthusiastically.

Jake grinned. "As I've said before, what the hell do I have a lawyer for? Let's go."

He led the way back to the dressing room. The backstage of the Casino was deserted now, no light showed under the doors of the dressing room, save under the one that had been Jay Otto's.

Jake paused at the door, one hand on the knob.

"We couldn't possibly put him back the way we found him," he said thoughtfully, "and we probably left fingerprints all over everything. We'll just have to admit we took him down before we called the cops."

"Just say you thought he might be still alive," Malone advised.

Jake swung open the door. Helene stepped in ahead of him and switched on the light. Then she stood stock-still in the center of the floor, reaching for Jake's arm.

"Well," she said at last, "the marines evidently got here ahead of us."

The fiddle case that held the body of Jay Otto, the Big Midget, was gone.

Chapter Four

M ALONE STARED at the spot where the fiddle case had been, rapidly added up the events of the evening in his head, and privately resolved he would never take another drink, not as long as he lived.

For a moment Jake appeared to have been petrified. Then, without a word, he strode across the room to the closet where the bull fiddle had been stored and flung open the door. The bull fiddle was still there. He stared at it for an instant, then kicked the door shut again.

"It's nonsense," he said at last. "I don't believe it."

Malone leaned against the dressing table and stared bewilderedly around the room. There wasn't a place where the fiddle case could have been concealed, not another closet nor cupboard, not so much as a curtain.

"How—" he began.

"The question isn't 'how'," Jake told him. "It's 'what'. What the devil are we going to do now?"

"Search the rest of the place," Helene suggested.

Jake snorted indignantly. "I suppose you want to go around asking everybody you meet if he's seen a bass fiddle case with a dead midget in it."

"No," she said calmly, "but we can search the place from end to end for a pair of gloves I mislaid somewhere before the show." And while he stared at her admiringly, she went on, "After all, it's your night club, and you can search it if you want to."

"So it is," Jake said. "I keep forgetting that. Come on, then."

Half an hour later they returned to the midget's dressing room. By that time, save for Al Omega's boys packing up their instruments and preparing to leave, the Casino was deserted. And the fiddle case was definitely nowhere in the building.

Malone unwrapped a cigar and stared at it for a moment before lighting it. "Well," he said at last, "there's nothing you can do about it. You didn't move the body from the premises, and you don't know who did. Maybe it'll turn up again and maybe it won't. In the meantime, go home to bed and stop worrying."

"Pleasant dreams to you too," Helene said acidly. "But just out of idle curiosity, I wonder who did take it away?"

"I don't know. Maybe the murderer. Maybe some other person."

"How did this unknown person—whether he was the murderer or not—know the body was in the fiddle case? After all, the case was locked."

The little lawyer glared at her. "Obviously, he had X-ray eyes." He ignored the face she made at him.

Jake drew a long breath. "Malone's right. The best thing for us to do is go home to bed." He scowled. "Tomorrow's bound to be a bad day, whatever happens."

Malone nodded. "Whether the body turns up or not, there's going to be excitement when the midget is missing. Where did he live, anyway?"

"In our hotel," Jake said. "Had a very fancy suite there, I've been told. I've never seen it myself."

"Well," Malone told him, "maybe you'll be informed that he's disappeared. Maybe you'll be informed that he's been found up an alley somewhere. Whatever happens, just remember you don't know a thing about it."

Jake said, "Don't worry about that. Do you think I'm a dope?"

"Yes," Helene said suddenly. Her face had turned very white. "I think we're all three of us dopes."

The two men stared at her.

"That bottle," she said, in a voice that threatened to develop a quaver. "The bottle of Scotch. Malone thought it was poisoned. And being three dopes, we went off and left it here."

Jake frowned. "Well damn it," he said, "we could hardly have carried it out and set it on our table."

"And besides," Malone began. He paused and said, "Between hiding the midget's body and your announcement about the stockings, the bottle just slipped our minds."

"In the meantime," Helene said, "someone's come in and drunk half of it."

Malone wheeled around, picked up the bottle, stared at it, and set it down again.

"Someone," Helene said, "is going around with half a bottle of poisoned liquor in his insides."

Jake felt for the chair, found it, and sat down hard.

"And," she finished, *we don't know who it is!*"

For a good thirty seconds, the silence could have been cut with a knife.

"Look here," Jake said weakly. "Malone could have been mistaken. That Scotch may not be poisoned at all."

"Do you want to drink it and find out?" she asked.

"No," he confessed.

Malone unscrewed the cap of the bottle and sniffed. "Smells all right. But there's still some of that whitish stuff along the edge." He pointed to the neck of the bottle. "When the liquor was poured out, it washed the powder off one side of the rim, but not the other." He picked up the cap, held it to the light, and ran a finger inside it. The finger came away with its tip covered with white powder. He sniffed at it thoughtfully.

"Don't taste it," Jake said. "I'll take your word for it. It's poisoned."

"I've got a friend who's a chemist," Malone said. "Tomorrow morning I can have him analyze this and find out what it is."

"Damn it," Jake said. "What's the difference what kind of poison it is, I want to know who got it. Anybody could have wandered in here, seen the room empty and a bottle of expensive Scotch sitting on the dressing table, and helped himself."

"It could have been the murderer," Helene said.

"Not if the murderer put the poison in the bottle," Jake pointed out scornfully.

"Then if the person who carried away the fiddle case wasn't the murderer, it could have been the person who carried away the fiddle case," Helene said.

"Your wonderful reasoning powers," Jake said. "That's what I really love you for."

"Or," she said, "it could have been one of the orchestra men, or one of the waiters, or one of the chorus girls, or—anybody."

"For the love of Mike," Malone said suddenly. "Jake, have you any liquor around this place that isn't poisoned? Because if you have, I need it bad. After all, this is supposed to be a saloon."

"Don't call it a saloon," Jake said, "and all the liquor is locked up for the night. That's the last thing the head bartender does before he goes home."

"A fine thing," Helene said. "Own your own night club, and you can't get a drink. Wait a minute." She was out the door and down the hall before either man could stop her. In two minutes she was back again with three paper cups and a nearly full bottle of rye. "It's Angela Doll's," she explained, "but she won't mind."

Malone poured three drinks, said gloomily, "I wonder if this is poisoned too," and drank his. "We've got to do something fast, but I don't know just what."

"We could call up all the people who might have come in here tonight, and ask them how they feel," Helene suggested.

"Wonderful!" Jake said nastily. "And the one who doesn't answer the phone is It."

"It couldn't have been a quick-acting poison," Malone said very slowly, "or the person who got it wouldn't have lived long enough to leave the Casino. So, that person may still be alive now."

"And could still be saved, if we found him in time," Jake added.

"*If* we knew who it was," Helene said.

"Maybe Helene was right," Malone said. "Maybe the thing to do is call up everybody who might possibly have come in here tonight and give out a warning. It looks like the only thing to do."

Jake said, "And thereby advertise the fact that we knew there had been a bottle of poisoned liquor in the midget's dressing room the night of his disappearance—or murder, if his body turns up. We're trying to keep out of trouble, not get into it." He paused. "Still, we can't let some perfectly innocent person die, just to keep out of trouble."

"Oh, but Jake," Helene said with a little gasp,

"there's forty or fifty people who might have come in here. And by the time we got to the right person on the list—"

"Besides," Jake said gloomily, "we don't have all their telephone numbers, either. Heaven only knows where Ramon Arriba's boys hang out."

Helene lit a cigarette very slowly and deliberately, and poured herself a drink of rye. "Well, we can eliminate Angela Doll. She left the Casino before the midget finished his last performance. And all of Al Omega's band. They were on the bandstand all the time between when we were first here and when we came back. We can eliminate the girls in the chorus because I gave a party for them and none of them will touch Scotch. They all stick to rye or gin."

"Good bright girls," Jake said admiringly. "So do I."

There was a momentary pause. Malone strolled over to the dressing table, picked up the bottle, and looked at it again.

"That's a hell of a lot of liquor for just one person to drink in that short a time," he observed thoughtfully, "unless he or she had the capacity of a tank car."

Helene dropped her paper cup on the floor. "Of course!" she exclaimed. While the two men stared at her, open-mouthed, she jumped to her feet, pulled her wrap over her shoulders and began fastening it. "Ruth Rawlson!"

Jake had only started to say, "But look here—" when she put her hand over his mouth.

"Ruth was telling us about having a nice chat with Angela Doll, when we knew Angela had gone home. I thought she'd been chinning with the chorus girls, but now when I think about it, I know they'd all have gone home by that time. They don't lose any time getting out of here after their last show. There's only one other place where she could have been: here, all by herself, in the midget's dressing room."

Jake jerked his head away and said, "Not necessarily—" That was as far as he got.

"Listen to me!" Her eyes were like blue fire. "She was wandering around back here looking for someone who'd buy her a drink. She stuck her head in here and saw that the room was empty and that a bottle of Scotch was sitting on the dressing table." Helene paused long enough to draw a quick breath and went on, "Malone just said whoever drank that much liquor in that short a time must have the capacity of a tank car. That's a thumbnail description of Ruth. And you said yourself—when you put her in the taxi she was practically paralyzed. That wasn't from the liquor—it was from what was in it!"

"She's right," Malone said.

Helene stamped her foot impatiently. "Come *on*, then. This isn't any time to stand around talking about it." She wheeled around and started for the door. "I know where she lives, and my car's parked right outside. And Malone, stick that bottle of rye in your pocket. We might need it to bring her to."

"If anything would bring her to," Jake prophesied, "that will."

Snow—a light, damp, April snow—was falling as they went outside. Malone shivered, growled something about the spring weather, and looked ominously at the streets. He'd ridden with Helene before when she was in a hurry.

It was nine blocks from the Casino to the dreary Walton street rooming house where Ruth Rawlson lived. Jake and Malone preferred to forget how short a time it took for Helene to make the trip in the blue convertible.

She slid the car neatly up to the curb directly in front of the doorway and said, "Ruth's light is on. That's her place—the English basement."

Jake grabbed her elbow as she started up the walk. "Wait a minute. Suppose you're right about this, how are you going to explain it to her?"

Helene shook her arm free indignantly. "When somebody's been poisoned, you pump the poison out first and explain things afterward." As an afterthought she added, "If she asks any questions, I'll tell her you put the poison there for me."

At the steps Jake paused. "But if you aren't right —if she didn't get the poison—then how do we explain this three-o'clock-in-the-morning visit?"

Malone growled, "Tell her I couldn't wait till tomorrow to see her again. Besides," he added, "she may not be here."

"I told the cab driver to see that she got here," Jake said.

Helene peeked through the window into the basement room. "She's here all right. I can just see one foot through the window, but I'd know those slippers anywhere."

Jake rang the bell. Fifteen seconds later he rang it again. The third time, he simply pushed one finger against it and left it there. Malone went into the hallway, found the right door and pounded on it, long and loud.

There was no answer. After one final try of ringing and knocking, Helene took another look through the window. Ruth Rawlson hadn't moved.

Chapter Five

"THIS IS NO TIME to rouse the landlady," Jake said, "but obviously we've got to get in." He looked reflectively at the window. "Lucky there's no grating. I think I can pry it open, if you two will keep an eye peeled for people coming down the street."

Malone gazed down the street through the veil of snow. Snow in spring, he thought. He remembered the snow ballet in one of those long-ago revues, with Ruth Rawlson as the snow queen, her red-gold hair rippling over her white arms. He'd been pushing a hack in those days to pay for the last months at night law school, but he'd managed to go to the theater twice a week during the show's entire run. Fabulous Ruth Rawlson, who never wore any fur save white fur (he hadn't known about press agents in those days, Malone reflected) nor any jewels save pearls. The little lawyer glanced through the dingy window

at that dangling foot with its still unfastened slipper,
and shuddered.

"Come, come, Malone," Helene said sternly. "She
couldn't have been that beautiful."

He glared at her. "If she's dead," he muttered, "it's
my fault. I should have had sense enough to put that
bottle out of anyone's reach."

"Its just as much Jake's fault, and mine," she told
him.

Malone shook his head. "You aren't expected to
have that much sense."

The sound of the window sliding open choked off
whatever Helene had been about to say.

"Go on down into the hall," Jake said. "I'll slip
in and unlock her door from the inside." He disappeared through the window, closing it behind him. A
moment later he opened the door for them.

It was a large, disordered, and dingy room, obviously improvised into a housekeeping apartment by
the addition of a cupboard and a gas plate supposedly
concealed behind a faded cretonne curtain. The walls
had once been calcimined a muddy green, now they
were a discolored, mottled grey. Most of the collection of autographed theatrical photographs hung
slightly askew, and the threadbare rug was rumpled
at one end. There was a dun-colored flannel bathrobe
on one of the sagging overstuffed chairs, a pair of
slippers and a polo coat on the other. A pile of newspapers, five empty bottles—one milk, one gingerale,
two beer, and one gin—a corset, and three overflow-

ing ash trays occupied the single table. And on the studio couch was sprawled Ruth Rawlson, motionless and deathly white, but breathing.

"We're in time," Malone said. He made it sound as though the marines had landed. While Jake and Helene looked on anxiously, he made a quick examination of the unconscious woman.

"She hasn't been poisoned," he announced at last. "She's been drugged."

He reached for a cigar, lit it, picked up one of the ash trays and emptied it into the wastebasket, and sat down beside Ruth Rawlson.

"How do you know?" Helene demanded. "Because in case you're wrong—this is no time for guessing games."

"I can tell by the way she's sleeping and the way her eyeballs look," Malone said. "I've seen knockout drops work before. That's what was in that whiskey," he added. "Dope." He withdrew the bottle from his overcoat pocket and looked at it thoughtfully. "I hardly even need to have this analyzed now, but I might as well, just for the record. If we'd used our heads, of course, we'd have known it all the time."

Helene sniffed. "If we'd gazed into a little crystal ball, you mean."

"No," Jake said, "Malone's right. If the idea had been to poison the midget, the murderer wouldn't have bothered to come back and hang him. Instead, he doped him, and then when he was out, came back and arranged his little noose."

"The murderer could have poisoned him and then tried to make it look like a suicide," Helene objected.

Malone shook his head. "Even a murderer of very slow intelligence would have made a better job of it."

"All right," Helene said. "I won't argue." She looked closely at the sleeping woman. "What shall we do about her, Malone?"

"Tuck her in bed and leave her in peace," the lawyer growled. "She's good for twelve to twenty-four hours. We'll drop back from time to time and make sure she's all right, and try to be around when she wakes up, because she'll probably feel like hell. But that's all we can do."

Helene dropped her wrap on the back of a chair. "To bed she goes, then."

While Helene busied herself with the unconscious woman, Malone prowled restlessly around the room. It was, he reflected, a horrible-looking place in which to wake up with a double hangover. He knew, because he'd occasionally waked up in places that looked about as bad. Suddenly he peeled off his coat, rolled up his sleeves, and went to work.

From a cupboard shelf he took the last clean pillow case, and put it on the pillow Jake was preparing to tuck under Ruth Rawlson's head. Then he emptied ash trays, wiped them clean, and put them back in convenient locations. He hung up clothes, put away slippers and stockings, dusted the table, and plumped up cushions. He emptied the coffeepot, washed it out, and put it away ready for use. Then he tiptoed down the hall with the wastebasket, emptied it into the container by the back door, returned it, and straightened the pictures.

By that time, Ruth Rawlson was sleeping peacefully in her bed, and Helene was donning her wrap again. For just a moment Malone stood looking down at her; then he brushed a wisp of hair from her forehead. For all her tousled grey hair and haggard face, she looked at this moment like a dreaming child.

"Sleep well," Malone whispered. He reached into his pocket, drew out the bottle of rye Helene had filched from Angela Doll's dressing room, and put it on the table beside the bed.

"The supreme sacrifice," Helene said coldly, under her breath.

Malone glared at her. "Let's get the hell out of this place," he said fiercely, "and head for the nearest cup of coffee you can find."

He carefully slipped the key of Ruth Rawlson's apartment into his pocket.

Fifteen minutes later, they settled down around a table in an all night drugstore.

"She's going to be all right, isn't she?" Helene asked anxiously.

Malone nodded. "Outside of the way she'll probably feel when she wakes up, and I don't even want to think about that." He sighed and stirred his coffee. "Besides being the famous midget entertainer," he said, "who was Jay Otto?"

Jake frowned. "No one seems to know," he said.

"All the life stories in his press book seem to start with his being about twenty-one years old. There's none of the usual stuff about being born in a small town in Indiana, or a village in the Bavarian Alps."

"Just strayed into this world, full grown," Helene murmured, "from that other world where everybody is a midget. He probably was bright blue all over when he landed, but that faded out little by little."

Jake made a rude face at her and went on. "He never seems to have been in any of the regular midget shows. He was always a solo act. Turned up first on some fifth-rate vaudeville circuit, and was an immediate hit. If you ever read the entertainment pages, you know the rest of his history."

"I don't," Malone said, "but I'll be satisfied to guess at it."

"Wasn't he mixed up in some kind of scandal a few years ago?" Helene asked.

Jake nodded. "He had a very gorgeous secretary who toured with him for a few years. She jumped out of a New York hotel window, and there was quite a stink about it. He came out of it all right, though."

"And he has all kinds of money," Helene said. "He can't have been saving his salary all these years, because he spends it like so much hay, and from all I hear about him, he always has. But in spite of the size of the salary he gouged out of Jake, he lived as though he had about four times as much."

"The rumors I've heard about his personal life," Jake said, "shocked even me. But you know how people talk about anybody who isn't exactly like everyone else. And he was such an unpleasant little guy."

Malone yawned. "I don't know why the hell I should be asking all this, at this hour in the morning."

"Somebody's got to ask," Helene said reasonably. "Just the way somebody's got to find out who murdered him." She hummed briefly, "And it might as well be you."

The lawyer yawned again, long and luxuriously. "I don't think I'll need to, now. If the midget's body had been found in the Casino, then Jake would have been on the spot, and I'd have had to get to work. But now—the body is probably at the bottom of the Chicago river, by this time. There will be a flurry of excitement because of the midget's disappearance, and the Casino will get a lot of publicity, and that'll be the end of it."

"You think so," Jake said.

"I hope so," Malone told him.

"But," Helene insisted, "what makes you think it's at the bottom of the river?"

The little lawyer leaned his elbows on the white-top table and looked at her wearily. "Because," he said patiently, "the only reason anyone would have had for taking the body out of the dressing room was to dispose of it."

"But how," Helene demanded, "did he know the body was in the fiddle case?"

Malone sighed heavily and looked at Jake. "Why did you ever marry her, anyway?"

"I couldn't help it," Jake said. "She kidnaped me. I really wanted to marry the girl who makes the doughnuts in the window on Madison street, but Helene forced me into her car and— Ouch! Stop pinching me!"

"All right, Malone," Helene said calmly. "Now. How did he know? And don't give me that Superman stuff again, or I'll pinch you too."

"It's like this," Malone said. "For some reason the murderer came back to get the body and dispose of it. We don't know what that reason was, but we'll assume there must have been one. All right. He came into the dressing room, and the body was gone. There hadn't been any excitement around the Casino, so he knew whoever had taken down the body had hidden it. Do you follow me so far?"

"A very pretty line of reasoning," Helene said, "and credible, too. Go on."

"The first thing our murderer would do would be to look around the premises, and the only place where the body might have been hidden was the closet. So, he looked in the closet. And what did he find there?"

"I know," Helene said coyly, "but you tell me. You fascinate me."

"He found the fiddle," Malone said. "And he knew the fiddle case was in the dressing room. So probably he picked up the fiddle case, discovered that it was heavy, reasoned that the body was in it, and carried it away. Simple, isn't it?"

"Too simple," Helene said. "I like the first theory better, that he had X-ray eyes."

"All right," Malone said, "then we'll strike the whole thing off the record, and leave it that he had X-ray eyes. What do you care, anyway? Whatever way it happened, the body won't be found on the premises, and Jake won't be in a jam."

"That's right," she agreed. "All our problems are solved, except one. Finding Allswell McJackson a job. Come on, let's go home so we can get an early start on it."

They drove Malone to the Loop hotel where he had lived for fifteen years, said good night to him at the door, and started home. Helene settled down comfortably in the driver's seat, turned into Michigan avenue, and drove slowly northward through the softly falling snow. Jake moved an inch or two closer, and rested one cheek gently against the smooth fur of her wrap.

"Jake, why did you marry me, really?"

"For your money," he said promptly. "I've told you so a hundred times, and you keep on asking and asking—"

"No Jake, *really*."

He sighed. "Because you're so beautiful, and so smart, and so reasonable, and such a wonderful cook, and don't bother me with a lot of damn fool questions."

Three blocks later. "Jake, I'm glad everything turned out as it did. I was afraid for a while we were in for a lot of trouble."

"So was I. We seem to attract it. Would you have minded?"

"What do you think?"

"I think you'd probably have loved it."

"So would you, and don't try to tell me different."

"If I didn't love trouble," Jake said, "I wouldn't have gotten mixed up with you in the first place—Stop, you'll drive us into a tree!"

At the canopied entrance to the immense apartment hotel just off the drive, Helene turned her car over to the doorman and hurried across the sidewalk, Jake close at her heels.

"Just the same," she whispered as they crossed the lobby, "I'm glad things turned out as they did. After all that happened last summer, and after all the excitement of opening the Casino, we need a little peace and quiet for a while."

"Don't mention peace and quiet," Jake begged. "Because every time you do—"

"I know," she said. "But this time it's going to be different."

They rode up to their floor, said good night to the elevator boy, walked down the corridor to the corner that led to their door, and stopped dead in their tracks.

Right beside their door, leaning against the wall, was the missing bull fiddle case.

Chapter Six

Without a word, Jake unlocked and opened the door with one hand, grabbed the fiddle case with the other, and shoved it into the apartment. Then, with the door closed safely behind him, he stood staring at the case.

"I'm a patient man," he said under his breath, "but this is too damned much. How in the hell did that thing get here?"

"Somebody brought it," Helene said.

"Marvelous deduction, Hawkshaw," Jake said reverently. "Now tell me why."

"Because he liked us and wanted to give us a nice present," she said between her teeth. "Don't just stand there and goggle at it. What are we going to do?"

Jake didn't answer. For the next thirty seconds he discussed the habits, inclinations, parentage, and probable future of the person who had deposited the fiddle case beside their door. Suddenly his voice trailed off in the middle of a word.

"Helene, when I picked it up—" He paused, picked up the case, set it down again, and looked at it, his grey eyes wide.

"It's light," he said. "Helene, it's—empty."

"Nonsense! It can't be empty."

"Lift it yourself. See?" He ran one hand over his forehead. "Wait a minute." He knelt beside the case and tried the catch. "And it's still locked. The key's in my pocket and it's been there ever since I locked it."

"Oh no," Helene gasped. "Things like that just don't happen. Bodies don't get out of locked fiddle cases—even bodies of midgets!"

"Even midgets," Jake repeated in a whisper. For a moment he felt as though he'd unexpectedly stepped into an ice-cold shower. He found himself remembering all the shuddery stories he'd heard as a boy, about malicious small beings who couldn't be killed, and who couldn't be confined in any space, no matter how securely locked and fastened.

"Even if what you're thinking is true," Helene said very calmly, "that midget was certainly dead when we found him in the dressing room. And anyway he couldn't have carried that big bull fiddle case all the way over here by himself."

Jake relaxed. "You looked a little pale yourself, and don't tell me otherwise."

"I feel pale," Helene told him. "And I'd much

rather have it *be* magic. Because leaving the magic out of it—just how did the midget's body get out of there?"

"Somebody took it out," Jake said slowly, "God knows how, and decided to stick us with the fiddle case, God knows why."

He took the key from his pocket, knelt down, and unlocked the case. The eleven silk stockings were still there, wadded up in the narrow end. He took them out and tossed them on a chair. Then he relocked the case, slipped the key back in his pocket, stood up, and began buttoning his coat.

"Jake, what are you going to do?"

"Wait a minute," he said. "I'm thinking." He stood there for a moment, scowling, then walked across the room and picked up the telephone.

"Hello, the desk? This is Mr. Justus. Did anyone deliver a parcel or anything to me sometime during the night? Would you mind checking with the elevator boys and see if anything was brought up for me?" He stood waiting, one hand drumming on the table-top. "There wasn't, eh? Thanks very much." He hung up the phone.

"It must have been brought up the back way," Helene said.

"And it's going out the back way," Jake said grimly. "Give me the keys to the car, Helene."

"What are you going to do with it?" she asked, handing over the keys.

"I'm going to take it back to the Casino, put the fiddle back in it, and leave it right there in the midget's dressing room. From that point on, as far as we're concerned, we never even heard of a fiddle case."

"I want to go too."

"You're not invited. Stay here and guard the premises."

"What for?"

"In case anyone decides to deliver the midget to us too." He kissed her warmly, said, "I'll be back in fifteen minutes," picked up the fiddle case, and slipped out into the hall.

The first pale-grey light of a stormy April morning was shining through the windows when he came back into the apartment. Helene had changed into a gleaming ice-blue house-coat, and for a moment he stood just inside the door admiring her, oblivious of his weariness and of the cold wet snow that had accumulated at the back of his collar and around his ankles. Her corn-silk-color hair was smooth and shining, her pale, delicate face looked as though she had just risen from a good night's sleep.

"Is it all right?" she whispered.

He nodded. "Very much all right. I don't know what I've ever done to deserve it."

Her eyes widened. "You didn't leave your mind over there along with the fiddle case?"

"No. I might have married a girl who wasn't beautiful, or who wasn't smart, or who couldn't cook, but instead I married you and everything is very much all right."

"Idiot! I'm talking about the fiddle case."

"Oh. Every now and then when I look at you I forget everything else. Yes, the fiddle is back in its case and the whole works is there in the dressing room. Nobody saw me leaving here or going into the Casino."

He sighed wearily, took off his overcoat, and sank down into a chair. "It's too late to go to bed and too early to stay up." He looked up at her wistfully. "And besides, I'm hungry."

"Now isn't that an amazing coincidence?" Helene said. "I got hungry myself while you were out, and so the coffee's all made, and the omelet is practically done, and the ham is all broiled and—stop it, you're breaking my ribs!"

The last morsel of omelet was gone and the last cup of coffee was poured before Helene said, "And now Jake, about our murder—"

"Look here," Jake said sternly. "We don't have a murder. We don't even know anything about a murder. If the star performer from the Casino has disappeared overnight, we'll be very sorry and we'll do our best to help find him, but that's all."

Helene sighed. "I was afraid you were going to be stubborn about it."

"Stubborn hell," Jake said. "I'm being sensible. If the police learn that we discovered a murder and not only didn't call them right away, but proceeded to hide the body with an eye to removing it from the Casino, and did everything possible to destroy or conceal evidence, they aren't going to like it one bit."

"The police," Helene said gravely, "take a very narrow-minded view of things."

"So do I, as far as this particular affair is concerned," Jake said. "Let the police find out what happened. It's their worry, not ours."

"You're perfectly right," Helene agreed, just a shade too meekly. She lit a cigarette, leaned on the table, and said, "Aren't you even the least bit curious?"

"No," Jake said firmly. "Not the faintest bit curious. I'm not even interested."

"Well," Helene said, "let's forget it then."

"It's a funny thing, though," Jake murmured a few minutes later, "about those stockings."

She perked up fast. "You mean their all being different sizes?"

"No. I mean there only being eleven of them. If those stockings were used to hang the midget because the Casino chorus was someway involved, why weren't there twelve stockings? There's twelve girls in the chorus."

"I thought of that too. I wonder which girl of the twelve wasn't included."

"So do I. Wonder if it would be possible to find out. Not that I think it has any bearing on the murder, but—" He caught Helene's eye across the table and reddened faintly. "I was just talking. Didn't mean a thing."

Before she could say a word, the telephone rang. Jake looked at his watch, scowled, and went into the other room to answer it. When he returned, his scowl had deepened.

"That was Betty Royal. She wants to see us. I told her to come up. She says it's very important."

"At six-thirty in the morning," Helene said, "it must be." She rose and started making a fresh pot of coffee. "Maybe she murdered the midget and wants us to recommend a good lawyer."

"I hope that's it," Jake said. "Malone needs the money. But I'm afraid it isn't. What would she want to murder the midget for? She didn't even know him."

"Maybe she didn't like his act," Helene commented. "A severe form of criticism, but effective."

A moment later there was a knock on the door. Jake opened it to admit the young debutante, still in evening dress, and a pale, dark-haired young man.

"Hello," Betty Royal said. "I'm so glad you weren't asleep. I'm so glad you let me come up. Helene and Jake, this is Pen. Pendleton Reddick." She spoke breathlessly, and as though she were thinking of something else.

Jake murmured something, and looked curiously at the young man. Pen Reddick had been a joy to the newspapers since he had inherited one of the nation's larger fortunes at the age of five. He appeared to be a serious, indeed almost glowering young man, totally unlike the gay and debonair character Jake—and the columnists—had imagined. The dark eyes below his thick, heavy eyebrows seemed to contain a smoldering fire; his square jaw was set in a firm, hard line. Not a person to fool with, Jake decided.

"Helene and I went to the same school," Betty Royal was saying in the same disturbed voice.

"Except that she went to it years later than I did," Helene murmured. "Sit down. I'll get you a cup of coffee."

"Thanks," the girl said. "I could use one."

Did that school turn out nothing but beauties? Jake wondered, looking at Helene, and then at the seventeen-year-old Betty Royal. The girl's chestnut-brown hair, that reached just below her shoulders, had been softly tumbled by the wind. The unusual pallor of her skin was sharp against the shining russet satin of her dress. Her face wasn't beautiful, strictly speaking, Jake realized. The brilliant mouth was too wide and full, and the little chin too sharply pointed. Yet somehow she gave the impression of beauty. Yes, even now, worried as she was.

She took the coffee Helene offered her almost absentmindedly, stirred it, sipped it once, set it down, and forgot about it.

"It was terrible of me, barging in on you at an hour like this," she said. "For all I knew you might have been sound asleep. But I was so frightfully worried. And I didn't know anyone else to go to. Certainly I couldn't let any of the family know. In fact, that's the whole trouble." She paused for breath.

"What on earth's the matter?" Helene asked.

"It's her brother," Pen Reddick said. "Ned Royal. We're afraid he's eloped with a chorus girl."

"We know he has," Betty Royal said, her voice shaking a little.

Jake stared at her for a minute. "For the love of Mike!" he said weakly. "Is that all?"

"Isn't that enough?" Betty Royal demanded. "Don't you know my family?"

"I know of your family," Jake said slowly. "And I guess I see what you mean."

"It's *awful*," she said. "Simply *awful*."

Pen Reddick added, "She's right, you know, Mr. Justus."

Jake sat down and lit a cigarette before he spoke again. "I understand. But don't you think you might be taking it a little hard? Chorus girls can be pretty nice people, you know. If they're really in love with each other, it might turn out to be a very happy marriage."

"I wish it was like that," Betty Royal said, "but I know it isn't." She drew a long, sighing breath. "I may be only seventeen, but I'm nobody's fool. Ned only met this girl yesterday, and when I ran into him at the Casino last night, he was drunk as a goat. And he had some perfectly frightful-looking man with him, who was stone cold sober."

"Oh," Jake said. "One of those things."

"I was afraid he was getting into some kind of trouble again," the girl went on, "so Pen and I started out to find him when we left the Casino, and finally we learned he and this girl had gone off to Crown Point to get married, and the man Ned was with was driving the car." She paused. "Now do you see what I mean?"

Jake nodded. "Yes. I see."

"Jake," Helene said. "Call Malone."

"Oh yes," Betty Royal said. "I know about him. He could do something. I know he could."

Helene said, "Call him right away. If he could get hold of the girl as soon as they got back from Crown Point—and arrange for everything to be kept quiet—"

Jake turned to Betty Royal. "How much cash money could you and your brother raise, in a hurry?"

She shook her head helplessly. "Not much. The family has money, but we just have our allowances, and they aren't too big."

"Well," Jake told her, "don't worry. There's other ways of handling these things." He looked at the phone, said, "Malone is going to love being called at this hour of the morning. Lawyers really aren't supposed to be called out for emergencies in the middle of the night. They aren't like doctors."

"This lawyer is," Helene said firmly.

Jake carried the phone into the kitchenette, shut the door, and was gone a long time. When he returned, he was scowling heavily.

"Malone is out."

Helene stared at him. "Out! Why we just took him home a little while ago!"

"I know it," Jake said crossly, "and there was a message there for him to call somebody, and he called her from the lobby and told her he'd be right over, and went out."

Helene opened her mouth to speak, shut it again, caught her breath, and said, "Did the clerk tell you who left the message for him?"

Jake nodded grimly. "One of the girls in the Casino chorus. Annette Ginnis. I suppose I can reach him there—"

Betty Royal had leaped to her feet, her face dead white. "Oh no! Annette Ginnis! No, it can't be her! Because that's the girl Ned went to Crown Point to marry!"

Chapter Seven

"WELL," Jake said very quietly, "either you were mistaken, or else they didn't lose much time sending for a lawyer. Maybe they thought a preacher wasn't legal enough."

Betty Royal sank back into her chair. "I don't understand it. Where's Ned?"

"He may be there," Jake said, "and if he is, he's in good hands. Or—wait a minute."

He went back to the phone, looked up the number of the Edward R. Royal town apartment and called it. A sleepy-voiced manservant answered.

"Is Mr. Royal Junior in?" Jake asked.

"Yes, sir. But I'm afraid he can't be disturbed. He's sleeping, sir."

"You don't know what time he got in, do you?"

"No, sir. I have no idea. Is there any message?"

"Just tell him George Washington called," Jake said, and hung up. He returned to the living room and said, "Well, your brother's home and sleeping too soundly to be disturbed."

The girl gasped. "But why did he go home?"

"I don't know," Jake said. "Maybe he thought the cooking was better." He wondered if it would be polite to add, "Why don't you go home too?"

"You see?" Helene said consolingly. "You really haven't anything to worry about. The whole thing may have been a mistake."

"It couldn't have been," the girl insisted.

"Well, if it wasn't," Jake told her, "it's on the road to being straightened out right now."

"You'd better let me take you home, Betty," Pen Reddick said. "There isn't anything you can do now in any case, and you need sleep."

She nodded absentmindedly, her brows still knit.

"Don't worry about it," Helene said. "Everything's all right."

Betty Royal managed a faint smile. "I hope so. I'm sorry I bothered you about all this."

"It's perfectly all right. It wasn't any bother," Jake lied. "Just any time at all. It's part of our regular service to the Casino's guests."

The smile widened a little at that. "I'm crazy about the Casino. And the show is wonderful."

"That midget!" Pen Reddick said. "He's absolutely tops. I'm coming back to see him tonight."

"Do!" Helene said warmly.

"And good morning," Jake said cordially, opening the door.

He closed it after them and stood for a minute clinging to the knob.

"I wish to heaven I'd never heard of the midget. What am I going to do about tonight's show?"

"Nothing," Helene said. "If the midget's disappearance—or murder—is in the papers today, you'll draw a crowd from curiosity. And if it isn't in the papers, you'll have a crowd anyway, of people who've come back to see the midget. And you'll have to tell them he's vanished. It's tomorrow night's show you need to worry about."

"That's right," Jake said wearily. He slumped down in a big easy chair and ran one hand through his red hair. "Annette Ginnis. What do you know about her—as a person, I mean?"

Helene frowned. "She isn't the kind of girl who would rush a rich young man off to Crown Point when he was plastered and marry him before he knew what had hit him, if that's what you want to know."

"That's what I thought about her, too," Jake said. "Of course, we could be mistaken."

"I doubt it. She's a gentle, sort of wishy-washy little thing. It takes a certain amount of cool nerve to pull off that sort of business, and Annette certainly doesn't have it."

"Still," Jake said, "those kitteny, soft-looking little brown-eyed blondes can be crafty as hell. I remember once in Detroit—" He paused and added, "That was a long time before I met you."

Helene sniffed indignantly. "Stop trying to look as

if you knew anything about women, outside of what you learned from me."

"The fact remains," Jake said, scowling, "that it looks as though Annette Ginnis and Ned Royal at least started for Crown Point. And I don't think she called up Malone at five o'clock in the morning because she admires his handsome face."

"It's possible you're right," Helene said, starting to clear up the coffee cups. "At least, Ned Royal is the sort of young man you'd expect that sort of thing to happen to, sooner or later."

"I've seen ideas expressed more clearly," Jake said, "but you've been without sleep all night, and anyway I know what you mean. What is the sort of young man Ned Royal is?"

She made a face at him, carried the cups into the kitchenette, and returned. "He's the kind of rich young man that makes everybody hate rich young men. Not bad, or vicious or anything like that. Just a kind of combination of limp and vague. Always getting drunk and noisy in night clubs and having to be tossed out."

"And marrying chorus girls who promptly send him on home and telephone for a lawyer," Jake added.

Helene yawned and stretched. "Well, it's none of our business. And you said yourself Malone needed a few clients."

Jake looked at his watch. "It's seven-thirty. Do you think it's bedtime?"

She looked at him. His lean, pleasant face was pale

and drawn, his red hair was rumpled. "I don't know whether you should be put to bed, or just buried the way you are. Wait right there, and I'll get your slippers for you."

He lit one last cigarette, leaned back comfortably in his chair, and looked at the familiar room around him. He knew every inch of it, yet he still loved to gaze around him and pretend it was for the first time. The soft blue-grey of its walls, the immense windows on the south wall that looked over Chicago's roofs toward the spires of the Loop, the big, comfortable chairs and sofas, the painting of Helene in a pale gold dress which hung over the mantelpiece. For a moment he almost purred.

If the remodeled and reopened Casino didn't succeed, and Max Hook took it over—no, he wouldn't think about that now. Not this morning.

Helene came back with the slippers. "Put them on, and then go tuck yourself in bed, and sleep for hours and hours and hours."

"I don't want to go to sleep," he said, in the tone of a fractious small boy. "I just want to stay right here forever and look at you. All I want in the world is just to be alone with you, here, like this."

The phone rang.

Helene sprang to answer it, waving to Jake to stay where he was.

"Yes, he's in," she said, "but I don't like to disturb him right now. Are you sure it's important? Oh. Oh yes, I'll call him."

She handed the phone to Jake and said, "It's the hotel manager. He says it's very important."

Jake's side of the phone conversation consisted almost entirely of "Yes" and "I see," and ended with, "I'll be right down." Then he put down the phone, turned to Helene and said, "Put the slippers away."

"Jake, what is it?"

"The manager is very worried. It seems that Mr. Jay Otto left a very important call for seven-thirty this morning. Now it develops that they aren't able to rouse him. The manager is afraid Mr. Otto may have been taken ill or something, and wants me to come down and be present when they break in."

"When they break in," Helene repeated, "and find that he isn't there." She started unfastening the clip at the neck of her housecoat. "Wait a minute, Jake."

"What for?"

"I'm not going down there in a housecoat. And I'm not staying behind, either. And you aren't going down there in a wrinkled tux."

Jake looked down at his clothes. "I guess you're right. I'd better change."

She picked a dress out of the closet, laid it on the bed, and unzipped the housecoat. Then suddenly she paused.

"Jake, send for Malone."

He dropped one shoe on the floor and stared at her. "What for?"

"They're going to discover Jay Otto has disappeared. There will probably be a fuss about it."

"Nonsense," Jake said, taking off the other shoe. "They'll just think he stayed out all night."

"Allswell McJackson will tell them he never stayed out all night. Allswell will insist on sending for the police. You'd better have Malone there to do the talking."

Jake sighed. "All right. Do we have Annette Ginnis's phone number?"

"It's in the little book right by the telephone. She lives on Oak street, and he ought to be able to hop a cab and get here in five minutes." She slid an almond-green wool dress over her shoulders and began fastening it.

Jake returned from his call and reported, "He'll be right over. And you can imagine for yourself what he said on the subject of coming here at this hour."

"We haven't had any sleep either," Helene reminded him.

"Stop rubbing it in," Jake growled under his breath.

They were dressed and ready to go downstairs when Malone pounded on the door.

"A hell of a thing," he said by way of greeting. "Eight o'clock in the morning. I hope the reason is worth it. What is it?"

Jake told him.

"Well," Malone said, "it was bound to happen

sometime today. Too bad it had to be so early. Why in blazes did he have to leave a seven-thirty call, anyway?"

"To make life hard for us," Jake said bitterly.

"Malone," Helene said suddenly. "What about Annette Ginnis?"

"She'll be all right," the little lawyer said. "I got one of her girl friends to come in and stay with her, and she'll probably be able to get some sleep."

"Wait a minute," Jake said. "What is this? What's happened to her?"

"I forgot you didn't know anything about it," Malone snapped. "There's no time to talk about it now, though. Wait till we get back up here."

"She hasn't been hurt or anything, has she?" Helene asked anxiously.

"No," Malone said. "She's just scared. I said I'd tell you about it when we get through breaking into the midget's apartment."

Jake set his jaw hard. "I hope it's nothing serious," he said. "Because one more thing right now would be one more thing than I can stand." He picked up the phone and informed the manager that he'd meet him by Jay Otto's door.

The manager, an apprehensive, jittery little man with highly polished hair, was waiting for them at the door when they arrived. He looked anxiously at Helene and Malone.

"We were all having breakfast together," Jake said, "and my wife and Mr. Malone thought they'd better come along, in case Mr. Otto was ill or anything."

The manager looked relieved. "I would have sent for Mr. McJackson," he twittered, "but I didn't know where to reach him. I do hope there's nothing wrong. But Mr. Otto is so punctual in his habits, and he called after he got in last night so the clerk knew it must be very important, and when he didn't answer his phone this morning I felt very disturbed, and that was why I called you."

"He called after he came in?" Jake said, lifting an eyebrow.

The manager nodded. "It was quite late. Yes, it must have been after four, because Briggs took the call, and he took over the board at four. Mr. Otto couldn't have expected to get much sleep, if he got in at that hour and wanted to be called at seven-thirty. Of course, he might not need as much sleep as"—he coughed—"ordinary people. It's most unusual for Mr. Otto to get in as late as that. Almost invariably he's back here right after his last performance—"

"Something may have detained him," Jake said. "Well, let's go in and see what's the matter with him." He wondered if his voice sounded hoarse. "Do you have a passkey?"

"Right here," the manager said. "I wonder if you'd be so kind—seeing that—"

"Yes, of course," Jake said tersely. He put the key in the lock, turned it, stood there holding it for a split second, and flung open the door.

The other three came into the room right behind him.

"Well, he's here all right," the manager said. Then he gave a startled little squeak.

"Yes, he's here," Malone said grimly.

The tiny form of Jay Otto lay in the exact center of his enormous, specially made bed, clad in gaudy silk pajamas, his head resting on his elaborately embroidered pillow. The marks of the noose that had strangled him still showed, dark and ugly, on his throat.

Chapter Eight

"I CERTAINLY AM NOT GOING to go back upstairs while we wait for the police," Helene said firmly. "This is the first chance I've had to see this room. And besides, I'm sure it wouldn't be legal for me to leave before they get here."

"Strong-minded woman, isn't she?" Jake said to the manager.

The manager tittered nervously, then remembered where he was, and said, "Oh dear!"

"It's all right," Jake said. "You can stay, as long as you're careful not to look at any of the pictures on the walls."

The manager glanced around, turned faintly pink, coughed, and finally said, "Mr. Otto was very broad-minded, wasn't he?"

Malone said, "Broad-minded is one word for it."

It was an immense room, the largest in the building. The pictures on the walls, a rather remarkable collection of books on the shelves, and an enormous Chinese vase on the table by the window were the only additions the midget had made to the hotel furniture. But in the bedroom beyond—a room almost as large—he had installed his own bed, wider and longer than any bed Malone had seen before, and covered with a magnificent brocade spread. There was an equally outsize dressing table covered with elaborate perfume bottles, and the walls were adorned with a collection of Oriental prints which, if anything, outdid the bright-colored pictures in the living room.

"You should see his car," the manager said, trying to change the subject.

"I have seen it," Jake said. "Half a block long, and purple." Suddenly he thought of something. "Where's the car now? Did he come home in it last night?"

The manager looked surprised. "I don't know. Wait, I'll phone the garage." He called, asked a few questions, and said, "That man who worked for him, Mr. McJackson, brought the car in about two o'clock."

"That was just after he left the club," Helene said. She caught a warning look from Jake and went on quickly, "Mr. McJackson stopped and spoke to us when he left."

"He wasn't taking Mr. Otto with him, though," Jake said. "Evidently he thought Mr. Otto had gone on home by himself."

"But he hadn't," the manager said, frowning. "Mr. Otto didn't get home until after four."

Malone opened his mouth and closed it again, and Jake said fast, "I wonder where he could have been all that time."

A couple of cops came in. One of them said, "Don't touch anything." They glanced at the bed and the tiny corpse, and the other one said, "Don't nobody leave until Captain von Flanagan gets here."

Helene turned a high-voltage smile on them and said, "We wouldn't dream of trying to leave."

They smiled back at her instinctively, took a closer look at the remains of Jay Otto, the Biggest Little Midget in the world, agreed that he was dead all right, and started prowling around the suite, surreptitiously calling each other's attention to its decorations.

"It's going to be so nice to see von Flanagan again," Helene murmured reminiscently.

That was the moment when he arrived. From his first appearance in the doorway, it was obvious that he was in a bad frame of mind.

Captain Daniel von Flanagan of the homicide squad had never wanted to be a cop. When circumstances had landed him in the police department, he'd promptly gone to court and had the "von" added to his name, because Dan Flanagan sounded too much like the name of a cop. He hadn't wanted to be promoted, either, particularly to the homicide division.

Von Flanagan didn't like murders, they always caused him too much trouble. Nor did he like murderers, looking on them as malicious persons who went around killing people just to make life hard for Captain von Flanagan of the homicide squad. Especially, he didn't like murders and murderers that necessitated his dashing across town in a hurry (the sound of sirens always gave him a headache) at eight o'clock in the morning.

Even more than that, he didn't like murders in which Jake and Helene and Malone were even remotely involved, because he'd learned from experience that these affairs were invariably complicated and difficult. The fact that he was deeply fond of the trio, especially Helene, and that their association had always turned out well for him in the past didn't temper his feeling in the least.

He paused just inside the door, put his hands in the pockets of his jacket, and glared at them, while his big round face turned slowly pink, then cerise, then crimson, and finally purple.

"I might have known it!" he said. He drew a long breath and held it till Jake feared he might explode. "As if it isn't bad enough to have to get up here at eight o'clock in the morning, after being at my brother-in-law's birthday party last night. Now I have to find you mixed up in it." He took another step forward and said, "Wherever you are, there's trouble."

Malone said smoothly, "Oh, Jake attracts trouble" —he paused—"like a magnet attracts flies."

"You mean," Helene said sternly, "like a honey attracts eyes."

"This really isn't any of my affair," Jake said to the big police officer. "The guy just happened to be appearing at my night club, that's all. When they couldn't rouse him this morning the manager called me, we broke in, and I called the police."

Captain von Flanagan snorted suspiciously. "You're probably lying to me, but I'll never find out the truth from you, so what's the difference. What happened to the guy anyhow, or don't you know?"

"I didn't look very close," Jake said, "but I think he was strangled."

The red-faced police officer stepped to the bedroom door, looked, and said, "He sure was a little one, wasn't he?" He shook his head and added, "Imagine anybody having to murder a guy that size! Swell layout he had here." He glanced around at the walls, caught his breath, and said, "Great Jumping Joshua!"

He was followed into the room by a tall, thin, apologetic-looking man whom Jake recognized as Dr. Wickett, an assistant medical examiner, and by the experts from von Flanagan's department. "The scientists," von Flanagan called them scornfully. The men from the morgue brought in their big wicker basket and rested it just inside the hall door.

Malone glanced at it and said, "For the love of Mike, didn't you have a smaller one?"

"Standard size," one of the men said. "We can't help it if the guy was a midget." He glanced toward the bedroom and said, "Jeepers, you could carry him out in a fiddle case."

Jake felt one of the muscles in his cheek twitch. Helene said delicately, "What a horrible idea!"

The "scientists" and Dr. Wickett were getting to work. Von Flanagan prowled unhappily around the bedroom for a few minutes, then came back to the living room and tactfully closed the door.

"I suppose you knew more about him than anybody else around town," he said to Jake. "Who killed him, and what was the idea?"

' Hell, I didn't know anything about him," Jake said in an injured tone. "He just happened to be appearing at the Casino. Started last night"—he paused —"and finished last night. I know he was a midget, I know he was an entertainer, and I've read his life story from his press book, but you know what publicity stories are. And that's all I know." He paused, frowned, and said reflectively, "except one thing."

Von Flanagan said eagerly, "What?"

Jake said, "He's dead."

"Damn it," von Flanagan moaned, "nobody ever has any consideration for me." He wheeled furiously on the manager, who jumped slightly. "You said you broke in. I suppose that means the door was locked."

The manager nodded, scared speechless.

"Who had keys to the door?"

"T-two. Mr. Otto had one and his assistant Mr.

McJackson had the other. There was a passkey of course."

Von Flanagan growled something about people who got themselves strangled in locked rooms just to make it tough for the police department of the city of Chicago. "Where's this McJackson guy?"

Nobody seemed to know.

He turned to Jake. "When did you see the midget last?"

"At the Casino," Jake said promptly. "He did his last performance there about midnight." He took out a cigarette and tapped it on his thumbnail. "We went back to see him about one o'clock, because I wanted Malone to iron out a clause in his contract, but when we got there"—he paused to light the cigarette—"he was gone."

"And he didn't get here until four," the manager said helpfully. Von Flanagan looked at him questioningly and he went on in a rush, "I know, because he called downstairs then and left a call for seven-thirty this morning."

Malone and von Flanagan both started to speak at at once. Finally von Flanagan got out, "That don't mean he couldn't have been here for a couple of hours before he left the call. How do you know he didn't get here until four?"

The manager looked puzzled and unhappy. "I don't know. The clerk downstairs said he didn't get here until then."

Von Flanagan muttered something about damned

inefficiency, got the clerk on the telephone, and barked questions at him.

"The clerk doesn't know when the hell he got in," he said, banging down the phone, "except that he had a coupla calls around three and didn't answer the phone, and at four he called and asked to be waked up at seven-thirty. One of the elevator boys must remember what time he was brought up."

After a number of calls, it developed that none of the elevator boys remembered having seen Mr. Otto coming home the night before.

"He might have walked up the stairs," the manager said faintly.

"Or he might have come in the window in a glider," von Flanagan roared, "only I don't think he did. This is the eighth floor and a heluva long climb, especially for a little guy." He paused, baffled, and began slowly turning scarlet again.

There was the sound of a key in the lock. Everyone turned to watch the door as it opened. Von Flanagan looked as though he were ready to spring.

It was Allswell McJackson who came in. He looked at the people in the room, at the wicker basket, and turned pale.

"What are you doing here?" he asked in what was almost a whisper. "Mr. Otto won't like it. He won't like it a little bit."

"Allswell," Helene began, "Mr. Otto—"

Von Flanagan waved her to silence. "And who might you be?" He added, icily, "Professor."

"This is Allswell McJackson," Jake volunteered, "Mr. Otto's assistant." He turned to the big man. "This is Captain von Flanagan. He—"

"Don't talk so loud," Allswell McJackson implored. "You'll disturb Mr. Otto."

"Oh no we won't," von Flanagan said. "We won't disturb him a bit." He looked at the newcomer as though he were preparing to pounce." So this is Mr. McJackson. Well now, perhaps you can tell us when Mr. Otto came home last night."

"I don't know," McJackson said in a troubled voice. "I didn't bring him home. I don't know how he got home. I took Miss Doll home right after I got off stage, and when I got back, Mr. Otto was gone. I don't know why he went home by himself. He'd never done such a thing before. And"—he paused and frowned unhappily—"he didn't come straight home, either."

"How do you know?" von Flanagan roared.

McJackson said, "Sssh!" and looked apprehensively toward the closed door. "I brought his car back to the garage and went home myself. Then I got to worrying and so I came back here to see if he was very angry with me, and he wasn't here. I don't know where he was."

Captain von Flanagan's eyes began to gleam. "Ah. And what time was that?"

"It was almost four o'clock," McJackson said. "I stopped in the drugstore for a malted milk on my way home and it was ten after four then." He looked as though he might wring his hands any minute. "I'm afraid Mr. Otto is furious. I don't know what he'll say to me."

"He won't say a word," von Flanagan said almost pleasantly. "I promise." He turned to Jake. "Then he couldn't have got here before about four o'clock. He went someplace and got home and called the desk at four and left a call for seven-thirty. And then—"

"Please," Allswell McJackson said. "Is anything wrong? Because—"

"Just one little thing's wrong, professor," von Flanagan said.

"Please," the big man said again. "I'm not a professor."

"What the hell do you talk like one for then?" von Flanagan demanded. Not waiting for an answer, he went on, "The only thing wrong—"

The bedroom door opened at that moment and Dr. Wickett came out, buttoning his cuffs.

"You can carry him out now, boys," he said to the men with the basket.

Allswell McJackson took one horrified look through the open door. "Mr. Otto!" he squealed.

"Strangled, all right," Dr. Wickett said, putting on his overcoat.

Allswell McJackson gave a horrified little moan and slid into a chair.

"Strangled!" von Flanagan growled. "I could've told that myself. What I want to know is what he was strangled with, and when it was done, and who did it. What do we pay medical examiners for?"

"*You* worry about who did it," Dr. Wickett snapped. "What do we pay a bunch of dumb cops for? I don't know what he was strangled with. There's nothing in the place that looks as if it could have been used for it."

Jake's and Helene's eyes met, and silently asked each other if those silk stockings should have been planted up in the midget's room.

"But WHEN?" von Flanagan howled.

"Hell, I don't know," Dr. Wickett said. "Can't give you more'n a vague idea now. Maybe I can tell more when we look in his stomach at the autopsy, but I won't promise you anything."

The police officer scowled at him. "A lot of use you are! All we know now is he was killed some time before seven-thirty, and some time after four."

"Four?" Dr. Wickett paused in the buttoning of his overcoat. "I can tell you this much: He was dead a long time before four o'clock. It couldn't have been later than two, and probably it was earlier than that."

Von Flanagan's eyes grew round and bright as marbles. "But he made a telephone call at four o'clock."

"He came to life long enough to do it, then," the doctor said calmly. "Because he sure was dead at four o'clock this morning." He opened the door, said, "See you at the morgue," and went out.

"He was a midget," von Flanagan said suddenly, in an odd, tight voice. He too had listened to all his grandmother's tales. "No! I don't believe it!" He wheeled on Allswell McJackson, who turned a shade whiter. "All those medical examiners are crazy anyway. He had to be alive at four this morning. What's more, you're the only guy who could've got in here, because you had a key. I believe you done it yourself, and I'm gonna take you right down to headquarters and make sure of it—hey!"

Helene moved quickly to the side of the big man who had slid quietly down to the floor. After a moment she looked up at von Flanagan.

"Now look what you've done," she said reproachfully.

Allswell McJackson had fainted.

Chapter Nine

"WHAT D'YA MEAN, he didn't do it?" von Flanagan roared. "He worked for him, didn't he? And it stands to reason a big guy like this would hate to work for a little guy like that. And he was the only person who could've got in here, on account of he had the other key. And nobody knows where he was last night when the midget was being killed."

"But nobody knows what time Mr. Otto was killed," the hotel manager said unhappily. "Nobody even knows how he got home. Nobody saw him get home."

The big policeman glared at him for a moment, then suddenly sat down, hard.

"That's a hundred percent correct," he said slowly. "None of your elevator boys saw him come up in the elevator. He couldn't've walked up all that way. So somebody must have took him up. And Doc Wickett couldn't find what he was strangled with." He looked triumphantly at Malone, who was trying unsuccessfully to appear unconcerned. "I guess I can use deduction as good as anybody. That little guy was killed someplace else, and then he was brought here."

"Brilliant," Malone murmured.

"But," Helene objected, "that doesn't mean that Allswell did it."

Von Flanagan growled at her, "If he didn't do it, who did?"

"Little elves," Jake said gloomily.

"Listen here," von Flanagan told him, "you stick to hiring comedians, not trying to impersonate 'em." He turned to Malone. "Are you this professor's lawyer?"

Malone said, "No," in the same instant that Helene said, "Yes," and just as loudly. They scowled at each other for a moment before Malone declared, "I'm having nothing whatever to do with the case," and Helene followed him briskly with, "That's perfect nonsense. Of course you are."

"Why don't you toss for it?" von Flanagan said.

Allswell McJackson had finally found his voice, and it was a feeble, plaintive one. "But what makes you think I need a lawyer? I haven't done anything wrong."

"Shut up," Malone said, "and let me do the talking."

"There!" Helene said triumphantly. "I told you so."

"And I protest your taking him to jail on insufficient evidence," Malone went on, ignoring her. "And if you do take him, I'll be down there in a hurry to get him out."

Von Flanagan beamed, and laid one hand on his prisoner's arm. "Come along, professor. We'll be seeing you, Malone." He turned to the two policemen who had preceded him. "Keep everybody out of here, including"—he grinned maliciously at Jake and Helene—"all these sightseers."

Allswell McJackson opened his mouth for another protest, and closed it again when the little lawyer waved at him. "Don't worry," Malone told him reassuringly. "I'll fix it up. I never lost a client yet."

He was ominously silent, however, all the way back to Jake and Helene's apartment. Once there, he shed his hat and coat, lit a cigar, and stood for a minute looking at them both indignantly.

"A hundred and forty million people in the United States," he began, "and you always get me stuck with a client who doesn't have any dough."

"If you'll just be patient," Helene said, "we'll find you one with lots of it. And you couldn't desert poor Allswell in a spot like that." She lit a cigarette. "Did Annette Ginnis marry that young man? And why was she sending for you at five o'clock in the morning?"

Jake frowned at her. "Never mind about that. We've got other things to worry about first. The Royals' family scandal can wait, and this can't. Malone, what do you think? Is von Flanagan right?"

"Every now and then," the lawyer said. "It stands to reason a man can't be wrong all the time." He went out into the kitchen and turned on the coffeepot.

"I mean is he right about Allswell murdering the midget?" Jake asked.

"Could be," Malone said laconically.

"Damn you," Helene said. "He's your client. Do you think he's guilty or not?"

"If he has me for a lawyer," Malone said, "who cares?" He watched the coffee for a few minutes, finally poured himself a cup, returned with it to the living room and sat down. "As a matter of fact, though, he can't be. He left the Casino before Jay Otto finished his act, to get Angela Doll out of the way before that impersonation of her went on. Of course, he could be lying about that."

"He could," Helene said. "But it would be easy enough to find out."

"Assuming that he's telling the truth," Malone went on, "and that he didn't get back to the Casino until we saw him come in, then he couldn't have murdered Jay Otto—because we went backstage and found Jay Otto dead before then."

"But," Helene pointed out, "we can't tell von Flanagan that." She frowned. "If the police decide on a time when the midget must have been murdered, and if Allswell has an alibi for that time—" She paused, and added, "Or if we find someone who did murder the midget—"

"If we do, I hope it's someone with money," Malone said gloomily, "who wants me for a lawyer."

"What I don't understand," Jake said, "is who took the midget out of the dressing room, carried him home and put him carefully to bed in his own pajamas, and then brought the fiddle case up here and left it leaning against my door." He briefly told the morning's events to Malone, and finished, "Was it the murderer or was it someone else? And in either case what was the idea?"

"What was the idea of murdering the midget in the first place?" Helene asked. "We don't even know that yet."

"Nine o'clock in the morning," Malone moaned, "and she puts problems to me. Who murdered the midget? Why? What was the idea of using eleven silk stockings, all different sizes, to hang him with? Who carried him out of the Casino and put him to bed in his own bed and left the fiddle case here by Jake's door, and why? And how am I going to spring Allswell McJackson from the jug, and will I ever get paid for it if I do?" He stared indignantly at them both. "Do you realize I haven't had any sleep?"

"What do you think I've been doing since we left you this morning?" Jake snapped. "Knitting sweaters?"

The little lawyer didn't appear to have heard him. "The midget was dead," he whispered. "He couldn't have gotten out of that locked fiddle case, with the

key in Jake's pocket all the time, and propped the
case against Jake's door from pure maliciousness, and
put himself to bed. He couldn't. I don't believe it."
He looked appealingly at Helene. "Is there any more
coffee in the house?"

"There is," she told him, "but you'd better have a
drink. And the midget was dead, and he didn't get
out of that fiddle case by himself." She swung open
the hinged bookcase that concealed a built-in bar
and poured him a healthy swallow of straight rye.
"Besides, Malone——"

He took the glass and stared at it for a moment.
"That whiskey. It wasn't poisoned. It was doped. I
forgot to tell you. I got my chemist friend out of bed
and he tested it."

"Well," Helene said, "that drink you're looking at
suspiciously isn't poisoned either. It isn't even doped.
I'm sorry, but the service around here is terrible. I've
complained again and again to the management about
our whiskey not being poisoned, but——"

"Ruth Rawlson," Malone said in a hoarse voice.
"She'll be waking up before long, feeling like a zom-
bie. And then there's Annette Ginnis. I promised to
get back there as soon as I could." He looked around
the room desperately, gulped down the drink, and
half choked on it.

"And now," he finished, as soon as he could get
his breath, "this! Allswell McJackson. He not only
hasn't money enough to hire a swell, expensive lawyer like me, but I don't even like the guy. Why

couldn't he have murdered the midget? Hell, we've got to have somebody who murdered the midget." He took down the last drops in his glass, relit his cigar, and growled, "I wish I'd never known either of you."

"Think of all the fun you'd have missed," Helene said soothingly. "Now, what's all this business about Annette Ginnis? Did she elope or didn't she? And in either case, why is she shouting for a lawyer?"

"She did," Malone said, "and she didn't." He drew a long breath. "It's like this." Jake and Helene both leaned forward expectantly. "Annette Ginnis called me up this morning and asked me—"

The telephone rang.

The *Times* reporter down in the lobby asked Jake if he had any comments on the murder of Jay Otto, and what he was going to do about the floor show at the Casino that night.

Jake told him politely, if a shade profanely, that he had no comments to make, and that the floor show was going to be a big surprise.

"To me," he said gloomily as he hung up, "the surprise will be if there *is* any floor show. Helene, what did you do with those stockings?"

She blinked. "Stockings? All this couldn't have unsettled your mind, could it? Oh." A different look came into her eyes. "You mean *those* stockings."

"I'd say the shock had unsettled both your minds," Malone growled. "Or have I forgotten something?"

"The stockings that strangled the midget," Jake

told him. "Eleven of them. Remember now?" He turned to Helene. "What did you do with them?"

"I hid them," she said promptly, "while you were out taking the fiddle case back to the Casino. I didn't know what might happen next, and I didn't want to take any chances, so I hid them."

"Good girl," Jake said admiringly. "Only why didn't you play a hundred percent safe and destroy them?"

She stared at him in horror. "They're evidence."

"We've destroyed enough evidence already," Malone said, "that we shouldn't draw the line at eleven silk stockings."

"I've a hunch we're going to need them," Helene said firmly. "Besides, did you ever try to destroy eleven stockings in a kitchenette apartment with no incinerator?" She drew a long breath. "You're a lawyer. How would this scene look in court, when the midget's murderer is being tried? 'What did you find in the fireplace of Mr. Justus' apartment, Officer So-and-so?' 'I found the charred remains of eleven silk stockings, which—'"

"Oh all right," Jake said crossly. "You couldn't destroy them. Where the hell did you hide them?"

"You'd never guess," she said proudly, "but it's a good, safe place."

"*Where?*"

"In fact," she went on, "you could search this place for a million years and never find them. I'd just like to make you a bet—"

"For the love of Mike!" Jake exploded. "This is no time to play hide-the-thimble. Or hide-the-stockings. Where are they?"

"All neatly rolled up in pairs," she told him, "with the extra one tucked into one of the rolls. And they're all in my stocking drawer, mixed up with my own stockings. The last place in the world anybody would look for them."

"If anybody wanted to look for them," Malone said. "Hell, nobody knows they were used to strangle the midget, except us. Us, and the murderer." He scowled. "Eleven extra-long silk stockings. All different sizes. All belonging to girls in the Casino chorus. Why?"

"That's what's been puzzling me," Jake said. "Why go to all the bother of stealing eleven silk stockings from the chorus girls' dressing room and making them into a rope? Why not just use a rope, and be done with it?"

Malone shook his head. "No, that's not what I meant at all. Why the devil weren't there twelve stockings?" He rubbed out his cigar in the nearest ash tray. "Maybe it was just an oversight. But I don't think so. I think there was some very definite and deadly reason for leaving out that twelfth stocking. The question is—what was it?"

"And another question," Helene said: "Which one was omitted, and how are we ever going to find out?"

"And my question," Jake said, "is, what's going to

happen to the Casino?" He kicked a small and entirely inoffensive footstool.

Helene glanced at him. "That's right," she said very quietly. "After all, we're not in business to find out who murdered Jay Otto. We're running a night club, and there's tonight's show to worry about, and—a lot of other things." She paused to light a cigarette. "There's Ruth Rawlson, and Betty Royal's brother, and Allswell McJackson, and Annette Ginnis." She looked up expectantly at Malone.

The little lawyer drew a long breath. "She called me up," he began.

There was a knock at the door. Jake and Helene looked at each other for a moment before Jake murmured, "We might as well open it. As soon as we get a minute we'll go look for a monastery."

Helene said, "I don't want to be selfish, darling. Let's settle for a convent."

He opened the door, said, "Well—," caught his breath and added, "I'll be damned. Come in, Artie."

Helen said, in what sounded to Malone like a faintly quavering voice, "Why, hello, Artie." It seemed to the lawyer that she had paled.

"This is Artie Clute," Jake said to Malone. "Mr. Malone, Artie."

Malone nodded, and wondered if he should know who Artie Clute was, without further explanation. He saw a short, chubby man with a round, almost cherubic, and—at the moment—extremely worried face, plentifully sprinkled with freckles, below a halo of curly, yellow hair. The little man's blue eyes were wide and without guile. Indeed, his whole appearance —save for the anxiety that wrinkled his forehead— was a mixture of childlike innocence and good will toward all the world.

He stood for a moment spinning a blue pork-pie hat on one forefinger, nodding to Malone, and sending a feeble smile in the direction of Helene. At last he drew a breath, gulped, and finally managed to speak to Jake.

"I'm sorry to bother you at this time of the morning," he said apologetically, "especially knowing you must have a lot on your mind right now, and if it wasn't so important to me I wouldn't do it, but it is important to me, and so I didn't think you'd mind." He paused.

"Of course," Jake said heartily. Almost too heartily. "Anything I can do for you, Artie, anytime at all—"

"Well," Artie said, "it's like this." He drew another breath, this time almost strangling on it. "Mr. Justus, now that the midget's been murdered—can I have my bass fiddle back?"

Chapter Ten

THE REASON he loved Jake and Helene so dearly, Malone reflected, was the perfect aplomb they displayed under almost any circumstances. He was, he hoped, keeping back any faint flicker of excitement that might have showed on his own countenance, as he watched Helene lighting a cigarette with a hand that hardly trembled at all, and Jake picking up a match folder from the floor in the most carefree manner imaginable.

"How's that again?" Jake said, stowing the match folder in his vest pocket. "And would you mind saying it a little slower?"

"My bull fiddle," Artie Clute said, beginning to blush a little. "He is dead, and it is important because Al told me to let him know right away."

"Artie is the bass fiddle player with Al Omega's orchestra," Jake said to Malone, as though that explained everything. "I mean, he *was*."

"Al was perfectly right in firing me, too," the musician said. "But now I've promised him I'll never do it again and he told me he'd hire me back today, and if you ask me it was a dirty trick of that midget to hang on to my fiddle when the only way I could pay him back anyway was to go back to work for Al."

Malone wondered what the moon-faced young man could possibly have done that would have merited his being fired from Al Omega's band. He said, "Let me get this straight. The midget kept your bull fiddle because you owed him some money when you got fired from the band, and now you can go back to work in the band if you have the fiddle, only the midget wouldn't give it back to you, but now he's dead. Is that right?" It occurred to him that only a few moments' association with Artie Clute was affecting his own speech.

"That's it," Artie said. He beamed admiration at Malone and added, "You lawyer fellas make everything sound so easy."

"You've got it wrong," Helene said, shaking her head at him. "They go to school for years, just learning how to make the simplest things sound hard."

That was a little too involved for Artie Clute. He giggled appreciatively, said, "Yeah, I guess that's it a'right," and looked blank. "About this fiddle," he began hopefully, looking at Jake.

Jake managed to look stern and said, "Yes?"

"I didn't owe him so very much in the first place," the musician said, talking fast. "Just what I lost one night at the Hook's joint, and not having enough with me to pay off, they told me—the guys at the Hook's joint, I mean—why didn't I borrow it from the midget, hell, he had all kinds of dough, so I called him up and he said it was okay, but then Al fired me, not that he wasn't perfectly right in doing so, and first thing you know the midget is wanting his dough back and I don't have it, so he takes the fiddle, and"—he paused for breath—"now he's dead, so can I have it back?"

"This is where we came in," Helene said under her breath.

Jake said, "Well—" dragging it out into two syllables.

"It isn't as if the fiddle would do him any good now that he's dead," Artie Clute said urgently. "Not that it ever would have when he was alive. And look at all the good it would do me right now. Besides"— he looked appealingly at Malone—"nobody else wants it. He don't have anybody to inherit it. How could a midget have any heirs?"

Malone coughed discreetly and said, "He might have a father and mother."

Artie Clute looked skeptical, and said nothing.

"Besides," the little lawyer went on, "from all that I've heard—"

Jake said quickly, "I imagine if any heirs do turn up, they'd be satisfied with the money instead of the fiddle, and if Artie has his job back"— He turned to the unhappy musician. "Funny Al didn't tell me he was going to hire you again."

"It was only last night," Artie Clute said. "He wouldn't have hired me back if it hadn't been that I was buying a pint at the liquor store over on Clark street and I didn't have enough dough to pay for it, so I looked up at the clock and figured the band boys were out in the intermission. So then the guy in the liquor store said his delivery boy would walk over to the Casino with me and the pint, and I went in to borrow the eight cents from one of the boys and the delivery boy went in with me, carrying the pint, and there was Al, and he said, 'For Crissakes, Artie, if you can get your bull fiddle away from that damn midget, you can have your job back starting tomorrow night,' and Mac lent me the eight cents and the delivery boy gave me the pint and beat it back to the liquor store, and now you see, Mr. Justus, all I need is to get my fiddle and I'm all set."

"That's all," Malone said cheerfully. "Only whatever happened to the pint?"

Artie Clute looked hurt. "That's gone a'ready." His face brightened suddenly. "But if you feel like a drink, Mr. Malone, I got two dollars I borrowed from the chambermaid, and I can send out for some gin."

"Never mind," Malone said hastily. He turned to Jake. "About this bull fiddle. I don't see why not—"

"Sure," Jake said. He looked thoughtfully at a spot on the wall just over the musician's head. "Do you know where it is?"

Artie Clute blinked and said, "The liquor store? It's on the corner of Clark and—"

"No, no, no," Jake said. "The fiddle."

"Oh, the fiddle," Artie said. His round, pleasantly childlike face began to lose its color. "You mean, do I know where the fiddle is? No, I don't know where it is. And if I don't know where it is, then I don't suppose I can get it back, and—"

"Never mind," Helene said, "I know where it is." She lit a cigarette, blew out the match and dropped it in the ash tray at her elbow. "It's in the midget's dressing room. I saw it there myself."

"That's right," Jake said brightly. "I saw it there too." He looked at his watch. "Joe must be there by now looking after the cleaning. I'll call him up and have him check on it."

He phoned the Casino, asked if a bull fiddle and case were in the midget's dressing room, waited five minutes and was answered in the affirmative, and arranged for both articles to be delivered by messenger to their original owner.

"Isn't he wonderful?" Artie Clute said admiringly. "Now I never would have thought of that." He took one of Helene's cigarettes, lit it, and said, "Have you got a drink around here, Mr. Justus? You have? Thanks." And while Jake went into the kitchenette, "This is swell. Here Al's hired me again, and I'm going to have my fiddle back again, and everything's okay." He downed the drink Jake had poured for him, went to the door, opened it, paused, and said,

"Oh, and another thing, Mr. Justus. Now I've got my job with the band again, and seeing as how you've lived here a long time, would you mind telling the manager here that it's okay if I don't pay my share of the rent on our joint until a week from Saturday?"

"Nothing would give me greater pleasure," Jake said. He closed the door.

Malone blew a smoke ring, gazed at it with one eye closed, and said, "I still don't see why I wanted to be a lawyer, when I could have been a bull fiddle player."

"That's von Flanagan's line," Helene chided him. "He never wanted to be a policeman, he wanted to raise mink."

"Not mink," Jake corrected her. "He wanted to retire with a Georgia pecan grove."

Malone said, "The last I remember, he wanted to buy a weekly newspaper and"—he coughed—"become a journalist. But as long as he doesn't want to be a bull fiddle player, I don't care. If he did, he'd probably want us to come and listen to him practice."

"Just leave it that he never wanted to be a policeman," Helene said, "or that you never wanted to be a lawyer. Stick to the script, Malone. Jake's in a jam, and what are you going to do about it? And how about Annette Ginnis? And there's another thing I want to know—"

A thunderous knock at the door interrupted her. Jake opened the door and Artie Clute stuck in his head and shoulders.

"I had to come back," Artie said, "because I just

wanted to say thank you very much, Mr. Justus, and I appreciate all you've done for me." He started to close the door.

"Wait a minute," Jake said suddenly. He half-dragged the musician into the room. "You said you lost your dough at the Hook's place. How come you boys in the band go down there, when you must know it's crooked?"

Artie Clute looked surprised and hurt. "Well, you know how it is, Mr. Justus. A guy sits around with the band all night, and nothing to do but look at the floor show and watch the pretty girls on the dance floor, and golly, he's got to have some relaxation. Just because a guy plays a bull fiddle, it don't mean he's no slave."

"I don't give a good red damn what you do in your spare time," Jake said pleasantly. "All I want to know is why you hang out at the Hook's, with all the places there are to go to in Chicago."

"Oh," Artie Clute said, blinking. "Oh, that's like this, Mr. Justus. Most of us owed him a little dough. Not much, maybe, but a little. And then he had something on a couple of the other guys. So when he said we should go to the Hook's instead of maybe some other joint, there wasn't nowhere else none of us could go."

The angry indrawn breath between Jake's teeth sounded like escaping steam. "You're talking about the Hook? You mean he said that?"

"Oh no," Artie Clute told him. His blue eyes were like saucers. "Not the Hook."

"Then *who*?" Jake shouted at him.

"Why the midget, of course," Artie Clute said. "Who else?" In the silence that followed, he half-closed the door, opened it again, repeated, "Thank you Mr. Justus, for everything," and was gone down the hall before anyone moved.

"Once upon a time," Malone said, several minutes later, "I sat in the Drake bar near a nice middle-aged lady who was knitting a sock. She'd had eight Martinis, and she'd dropped four stitches, and when I watched her she was trying to pick up those stitches and figure out where all the threads came from and where they were supposed to belong."

"A heartbreaking picture," Jake snapped. "I hope she finished the sock satisfactorily. But what does that have to do with any of this?"

"Just," Malone said, "that I know exactly how she felt." He relit his cigar. "I feel as if I had a lot of threads in my hands, and they all come from the same pattern, but I'm damned and double-damned if I know where they all fit in."

"And I still haven't had an answer to the question in my mind," Helene said. "In fact, I haven't had a chance to ask it yet." As the two men stared at her, she went on, "How did Artie Clute know that the midget is dead?"

Jake opened his mouth, closed it again, stared at her, choked, and finally said, "The newspapers—"

"The newspapers aren't out yet," she told him, looking at her watch. "Of course he may be a clairvoyant—"

He wheeled around and flung open the door, muttering, "I'll find out—" He stopped dead-still in the doorway, one hand gripping the jamb.

"Well, *Mister* Justus," Angela Doll said, in a voice that oozed acid. "You son of a bitch!" She kicked the door shut with one gold-heeled sandal and stood leaning against it, looking like a petite, enameled angel, the delicate brown curls that framed her face escaping from the hood of her evening cape. Before anyone could say a word, she went, fast, into her next line. "You told me," she said, "you told me"—Suddenly she crossed the six-foot distance between herself and Jake in two bounds, slapped him sharply across the face, and leaped away again. "You told me," she screamed, "if I came to work this God-damned flea circus you call a night club, I'd get every consideration. And what happens?"

Jake hadn't been a press agent for nothing. He lit a cigarette, straightened his tie, and looked calm. "All right, pet," he said, "you tell me. What happens?"

"He asks me what happens!" Angela Doll exclaimed to the lighting fixture in the center of the ceiling. "All right, I'll tell you what happens." She pinned a buttonholing eye on Jake. "I'm a young girl. I want to be an actress. When I was six years old I was playing Little Eva. Nine years old, and I'm playing Little Lord Fauntleroy. Then I'm ten years old—"

"And you're playing Juliet," Jake said coldly, "or was it Lady Chatterly? I forget. You can skip the next ten years of the routine, because I wrote it. Now you were saying—"

"I was only ten years old," Angela Doll said automatically. She stopped, stared at him, and her face hardened. "Look here, you dope. I spent years working up my act. We won't talk about my act now. I know how good it is. You don't have to tell me. Look what it did in Detroit." She caught her breath. "Look here, Mr. Justus. My act is my livelihood. My old father's in a sanitarium. My brother George has been out of work for five months. And do you know how much I have to pay my maid? Mrs. Justus, you listen to me"—she turned to Helene—"I work. I kill myself, I tell you. You're a woman. You'll understand. I go through my act three times every night. I tell you, every time I go through my act it takes twenty-five years off my life. Three times a night, seven nights a week." She held her exquisite little hands over her face, and tears began to stream between her fingers. "I'm dying. I'm dying right here in front of your feet. My act, it's all I've got. When I was six"— She stopped herself, skipped the repetition, and began again, "I've worked, I've slaved, I've killed myself, and now"— Suddenly she ripped her evening cloak and the dress underneath it from her right shoulder, and her voice rose hysterically. "Seven hundred and fifty dollars I spent just having a birthmark taken off, and that—that *midget* goes and makes a parody of *my act!*" For a moment she stood there in the center of the room, the torn dress hanging dramatically from one shoulder, peeking out between her fingers. Then suddenly she dropped her hands and glared at Malone. "What the hell are *you* pacing up and down the room for?"

"Don't ask," Malone said calmly. "You're not a lawyer. You wouldn't understand about nerves."

She glared at him for a moment; then unexpectedly laughed, lit a cigarette, and relaxed.

"Now," Jake began, "you listen to me."

She waved at him. "Oh, I know," she said amiably. "There's nobody I can sue. Hell, I don't want to get mixed up in lawsuits anyway. But just the same"— her eyes began to blaze—"even if the little bastard is dead, I still say it was a lousy trick to play, and"—her voice began to reach for high C—"if he were alive, by God, I'd—I'd kill him, that's what I'd do."

"You'd better not go around saying that," Helene told her, "or people might get the idea that it was retroactive."

Malone said gently, "She means that maybe you had that idea *before* he was dead."

Angela Doll's rosebud mouth opened wide, and shut again like a trap. She sat down in the nearest chair.

Jake handed her an ash tray, smiled at her agreeably, and said, "Yes, and while we're about it, how did you know he was dead?"

"Because"—she stared up at him helplessly—"Ruth

Rawlson told me. When she called up to tell me about—what he'd done to my act. Ruth's a friend of mine. She was a friend of my mother. They were in the Follies together. Poor old girl, I feel so sorry for her."

"That," Jake said, "has nothing to do with the midget's being murdered. Just for the record, and strictly between the four of us"— He sat down opposite her and spoke in a soft, confiding voice. "Allswell McJackson took you home from the Casino last night, didn't he?"

She nodded silently.

"What time did you get here? What time did he leave?"

"We got here about one o'clock, I guess. And what business is it of yours if he did stay for a couple of hours? I like Allswell."

"So do we," Helene said, "and we'd like to see him get out of jail. But the cops seem to think he murdered the midget."

"Oh no!" Angela Doll said. "No, he wouldn't do a thing like that. Why, he's as gentle as a child. You mean a bunch of dumb cops have gone and tossed him in the can? I'll fix them!"

Malone said, "Keep your shirt on." He reflected that was hardly the phrase to use to a strip tease artist, paused, looked at her thoughtfully, and went on, "And speaking of shirts. Am I behind the times, or is that ensemble you're wearing the latest thing in morning clothes?"

"Oh, this," Angela Doll said casually, glancing down at the lamé evening dress and pulling a corner of the evening cloak over her shoulder. "I slept in it. It does look a little odd at this time of day, doesn't it? I just couldn't be bothered to undress and go to bed after Allswell left last night. As a matter of fact"— she looked up at Jake, her eyes suddenly sharp and bright—"I don't know what time it was when he left, because I was asleep. I know it was a couple of hours he was there, but I don't know exactly when he left." She looked anxiously at Malone. "You're a lawyer. You get him out of this."

"I expect to," Malone said sourly. "And all I expect to get for it is gratitude. Meantime"—he frowned at her—"don't you talk to anybody except us."

"Oh, I won't," she promised. "Not even reporters."

"Especially not reporters," Jake said.

She sighed. "It's all right about photographers, though, isn't it?" she asked. "I mean, if they insist?"

"If any photographers insist on getting a picture of you," Jake said with a grim smile, "don't struggle."

Angela Doll smiled back at him understandingly. "I guess I'd better go and get my clothes changed, in that case," she reflected. "I should have changed them before I came down here, but you know how it is. I woke up, and right away I got to thinking about that dirty trick the midget pulled last night, and I got so mad I just came right down here to see you, without bothering about a thing. That little—" She began to blaze with anger again, suddenly caught herself and burst into a laugh. "Just the same, I wish I'd seen it. He was one of the meanest little bastards I ever knew in my life, but he was a hell of a good entertainer. That take-off on my strip must have been a riot."

"I didn't think so," Malone said. "I thought he should have been ashamed of himself for even thinking of it."

Angela Doll frowned at him coldly. "The trouble with you lawyers," she told him, "is that you don't understand art." She rose, moved gracefully over to the door and stood posed there, looking like a small china angel. "Oh, Mr. Justus," she said, in tones that should have been accompanied on a harp, "what I really came down to ask you about"—she put her head on one side and smiled at him—"you know I really should have been featured on the bill at the Casino all the time. And now that the midget's dead—"

Jake shook his head. "I'm sorry, dear," he said gently. "But I'm getting another act to replace the midget. For a class night club—"

Angela Doll turned an electric green with rage, and in a shrill scream went through the entire routine beginning with Little Eva at the age of six and ending with the seven hundred and fifty dollars it had cost to have the birthmark removed. She ended by shrieking, "Class night club! I've seen more class in the gents' room of a grind house," diving into the hall, and slamming the door.

She left a vacuum-like silence in the room. It was

a good two minutes before Malone said, "I wish I'd seen her as Little Eva."

Helene rose slowly, stretched, picked up a cigarette, and lit it deliberately. "Maybe I have a one-track mind," she said thoughtfully, "but I keep getting back to the same thing. Malone, would you guess that Ruth Rawlson could be awake and stirring by this time?"

The little lawyer shook his head. "She might be awake," he said, "but I'll bet the last hair on my head she isn't stirring."

"That's what I thought," Helen said. "In that case"— She regarded the end of her cigarette as though it were a crystal ball. "Yes, I do have a one-track mind. Artie Clute knew the midget was dead. How? If Ruth Rawlson did tell Angela the midget was dead, she must have done it before she passed out last night. In that case, how did Ruth Rawlson know about it? And if Ruth Rawlson didn't tell Angela, then—how does Angela know?"

The two men stared at her helplessly.

"I see what you meant about the dropped stitches," she said to Malone. "And I don't blame you for looking right now as though you might start unraveling any minute."

"Damn it!" Jake it. "All I'm trying to do is to run a night club. And all Malone's trying to do is get his client out of being jailed for a murder he didn't do. And all you're doing is—"

"All I'm doing," Helene interrupted him, "is trying to find out about Annette Ginnis. Malone—"

Someone knocked at the door. Helene moved between it and the two men.

"I don't care who it is," she declared. "This time I'm going to have my question answered. Malone, did she get married or didn't she?"

"No," Malone said. "No, she didn't."

"All right," Helene snapped. "Now, the second question. What's happened to her? What's the matter, that she's sending for you at four o'clock in the morning?"

"For the love of Mike!" Jake exploded. "All this hasn't anything to do with the midget."

The knock at the door was repeated, a little more thunderously.

"But it does," Malone said suddenly. "It has everything to do with the midget. Because the trouble with Annette is that she's been scared right up to the point of a nervous breakdown."

"But what's scared her?" Helene demanded.

"The midget," Malone said in a hoarse, almost screaming voice.

Helene caught her breath. "Then why don't you tell her he's dead?"

"She knows he's dead," Malone said. His face had turned a sickly white.

A third knock at the door set all the ornaments in the room to trembling.

"She knows he's dead," Malone repeated. "That's it. Now she's more afraid of him than ever."

Chapter Eleven

THE MAN who had been knocking at the door turned out to be Pendleton Reddick.

His impeccably tailored dinner jacket had been changed to a faultlessly draped set of tweeds, and his scarf-tie was knotted with exactly the right degree of carelessness. But there was the beginning of a growth of beard blue against the pale skin of his square jaw, and his dark, deep-set eyes were burning with fatigue.

"Where is she?" he demanded hoarsely, skipping the formality of a greeting.

Jake blinked. "If you mean Angela Doll," he began, "she just—"

"Betty," Pen Reddick said. "Betty Royal. She isn't here, is she? Then where has she gone?"

"The answer to the first," Helene said calmly, "is, obviously not. The answer to the second is, we don't know. Sit down and have a cigarette, and don't look so alarmed."

Pen Reddick obeyed, substituting looking puzzled for alarmed. "But where else would she go?" he asked helplessly.

"For the love of Mike," Jake said. "Chicago is full of places where she might have gone. The beauty parlor, or a milliner's, or—"

"No," Pen Reddick said. "It isn't anything simple like that. Because she was terribly upset over this business last night. More than you'd expect her to be over just—her brother's elopement. And when I left her at her door, she asked me to come back for her at ten this morning. I did, but she'd gone out hours before, and she'd left a note for me saying just that she'd found out something." He rubbed a hand over his forehead. "I thought she must have come here. But now I don't know what to think."

Malone frowned. "I seem to have missed something here. What's all this about Betty Royal being upset about her brother's elopement? And who did he elope with?"

"According to you, he didn't elope with anybody," Helene said. "Because he was going to elope with Annette Ginnis."

"This is where I came in," the lawyer groaned.

"This is where you're going to come in," Helene said firmly. "Because this was no ordinary elopement. Tell him the whole story, Pen."

Pen Reddick did. When he reached a description of the man Ned Royal had been seen with throughout the evening, Malone stopped him with a scowl.

"That sounds like one of the Hook's boys. But Annette said—" He paused.

"Go on. Malone," Helene urged.

Malone shook his head. "Later. What's the rest of it, Mr. Reddick?"

"That's about all," Pen Reddick said. "Except that apparently the elopement didn't come off, because when I went back to the Royal house this morning at ten, I found out Ned had arrived home, with no wife. So I don't see—" He looked up anxiously. "Maybe I'm imagining things. But it seems to me there's something behind all this that's—that's not nice."

"You're damned right," Malone said, chewing savagely at his cigar. "If that *was* one of the Hook's boys with young Royal last night, then I admit I don't know what the angle is. Because while I couldn't get much out of Annette Ginnis this morning, all I did get out of her was, 'The midget, the midget, the midget'."

"Oh God!" Pen Reddick said, burying his face in his hands. "He seems to have been mixed up with everything." He looked up at Jake. "Look. There's something else. Do you know where the midget would have kept his private papers?"

Jake stared at him for a moment, puzzled. "I'm not sure. He had a box, a leather-covered metal strong box—"

"That's it," Pen Reddick said excitedly. "Where is it?"

"In the safe at the Casino," Jake said slowly. "I suppose the police will be coming after it as soon as I get there to open the safe."

"No!" the young man exclaimed. "That would be terrible! Listen, Mr. Justus. The police—nobody—must get that box. Nobody! Do you understand?"

"For Pete's sake!" Jake said mildly. "What's in it?"

"I—" Pen Reddick looked at him imploringly. "You'll have to trust me, Mr. Justus. Let me go with you, and we'll get that box out of the safe. We'll open it together, and—I'll let you examine the contents. I'll—have to trust you too. If you don't agree with me that—whatever is in it should be destroyed, I'll let you do whatever you want to with it—"

"Come now," Malone said. "If it's something the midget's been blackmailing you with, then the chances are you murdered him."

The young man managed a wan smile. "If I had," he said, "don't you think I would have told you?"

Malone thought it over for a minute. "Come to think of it," he said pleasantly, "I guess you would. You wouldn't have confided it to anybody else, but you're smart enough to know a good lawyer when you see one." He turned to Jake. "I think you ought to take up the young man's proposition. Especially as there may be other things too in that box—things you ought to know about."

Jake nodded slowly. "All right. I'll do it. But—damn it," he sighed, "there's so confounded many things to do, and all of them need to be done at once."

Helene tried to look like an executive. "They'll all get done. Malone, you've got to go and see if your patient has waked up yet."

"Oh Lord yes," Malone said. "I should have been there hours ago."

"I'll go with Pen," Jake said, "and Malone can go there, and you can get a few hours' nap."

Helene shook her head. "I'm going to see Annette. She knows me and she likes me and she trusts me, and I bet I can get things out of her that neither of you ever could."

"It's not a bad idea," Malone said. "If you could find out the connection between the midget and Max Hook, and why she was so deathly afraid of the midget—"

"Leave it to me." Helene said confidently. She found an almond-green scarf that matched the soft wool of her dress, and knotted it skillfully over her gleaming pale hair. "And meantime, if any of us happen to stumble on who murdered the midget, romp right down and get poor Allswell out of jail, because I have a hunch he doesn't like it down there."

"Hell," Malone growled. "With everything else on my mind, I have to have that too."

"Don't complain," Helene said. "He's your client." She slid into her fur coat and picked up her gloves. "I'll meet you all back here at twelve o'clock."

They rode down the elevator together, parting at the front door of the hotel. Front-page headlines of the papers for sale in the lobby had complained about unseasonable weather. Now, out on the sidewalk, Jake looked at the grass in the parkway, already turning green, at the trees that were beginning to bud, and at the snow which insisted on falling, incongruously, on them.

"Ah, April!" Malone declaimed.

"Careful of the walks, Mr. Justus," the doorman said. "It's bad underfoot."

"It's worse overhead," Jake observed. "Oh well, it's only a little way. We'll walk."

He stood for a moment watching Helene and Malone, headed down toward Oak Street, and wondering if any girl in the world had legs as beautiful as Helene's. Indeed he would have stood there, imagining her, long after she had vanished, if Pendleton Reddick hadn't muttered something about the need for hurry. Then with a long sigh, he started up the street in the direction of the Casino, the young man swinging along at his side.

Pen Reddick glanced at him. Jake's lean, pleasantly homely face was pale and set in grim, hard lines.

"I don't think you'll regret this, Mr. Justus," he said, "once you know what it's all about."

Jake shrugged his shoulders. "I have a hunch I'm going to regret everything connected with this business," he said gloomily, "before I'm through with it. And this blasted box is the least of my worries right now."

"It's not the least of mine," Pen Reddick said

"So it seems," Jake said. "I thought you were so all-fired worried about finding Betty Royal."

"I am," Pen Reddick told him. "It just happens this has to come first."

Jake walked half a block in silence before he spoke again. "I suppose the midget was managing a little quiet blackmail, as a sideline. I wondered where all that extra dough of his came from."

Pen Reddick shook his head. "No, it wasn't blackmail."

"But this business of the box"— Jake frowned. "And he certainly was spending more money than he made as an entertainer."

"It wasn't blackmail," Pen Reddick repeated grimly. "It was something more damnable—something deadlier."

Jake lifted his eyebrows, said nothing.

"You'll have to wait till you see what's in that box," Pen Reddick told him. He drew a long breath.

Jake waited a moment or so before he tried again. "Have you known the midget long?"

Pen Reddick smiled with one side of his face. "A surprisingly long time. And yet I've never spoken to him in my life."

Jake decided to save any more questions until the box had been located and opened. He did steal a look at the young man out of the corner of his eye. Pendleton Reddick III, heir to *the* Reddick fortune and family name, the one as considerable as the other. He thought of Pendleton Reddick II—this one's father—who had inherited the fortune made in Civil War days and added to it, who had been an Ambassador to England, and who had accumulated one of the most notable collections of Oriental art in the world. He thought of Pendleton Reddick's mother, a famous Virginia belle, of whose two sisters one had become a leader of New York society, and the other a Duchess in England. Now, Pendleton Reddick III—an orphan, handsome, intelligent, gifted, and rich. What in the name of heaven could be the connection between him and Jay Otto, the Big Midget?

"I have the damnedest feeling," Pen Reddick said suddenly, under his breath, "that we're not taking this little stroll unaccompanied." He walked on steadily, his face a mask.

Jake glanced around, saw no one.

"Someone in a green overcoat," the young man said in the same casual tone. "He was across the street when we left the hotel. As a matter of fact, I think he followed me there. He just popped into the cigar store on the corner, and I suspect that when we turn into the next street, he'll come right along."

"It could be the police," Jake suggested.

Pen Reddick nodded. "I thought of that. And in that case"— He paused.

"If he is tailing you, instead of me," Jake said, "maybe you'd better not come along when I open the safe."

"That's what I was wondering," Pen Reddick said.

Jake thought for a minute. "Look here," he said suddenly. "At this next corner we'll say goodbye, and you go straight back to my hotel and wait for me in the lobby. I'll make sure that no one's watching me when I go in the Casino, and if there isn't I'll just open the safe, get the box, stick it in a briefcase, grab a cab, and beat it back to the hotel. Then we can go up to our apartment and open up the box."

Pen Reddick nodded. "Good idea." He walked on to the corner, paused there, shook hands with Jake and wished him goodbye as though not expecting to see him again for a month, turned sharply and strode back in the direction of Goethe street.

Jake waved a farewell to him, and turned into the last half-block that led to the Casino.

He unlocked the side door of the Casino, let himself in, and turned on the light. It was a dismal, shivery place at that hour of the day. The cleaners had finished their work and gone home, and he was alone. For the first time he wished that it wasn't so big.

Not so long before, he'd carried the empty bass fiddle case down this corridor to the midget's dressing room. And not so terribly long before, someone—but who?—had carried the fiddle case, with the midget's body, through this same corridor and out of the Casino. Carried the midget's body back to its own hotel room and put it to bed there, dressed in gaudy silk pajamas. But why the devil would anyone bother to do that? Would they ever know who it was, and why?

He opened the door to his office, turned on the light, and stood for a moment, listening. It seemed to him that he'd heard a sound, somewhere in the Casino.

Nonsense, he told himself. He knew the place was empty. Nerves and lack of sleep, that was all that was the matter with him.

Still, there was something about the office—something he couldn't define or explain—just a feeling that someone had been there before him.

The office chair he'd left where it usually belonged, between the safe and his desk, had been moved aside.

Hell, the cleaning woman had done it. He lit a cigarette, took a long, slow drag, knelt down, and began opening the safe.

There was the box. He took it out and examined it, a long, narrow, metal box, covered with black leather, not large, but substantial. Looked as though it would take an axe to open it. Well, he'd worry about that when he got back to the hotel.

He laid it on the floor and began closing the safe. Suddenly he paused, listening, sitting back on his heels. Was that a sound in the corridor, or was his imagination playing a game with him?

It was a sound. A footfall.

Jake started to wheel around. In exactly the same instant, the office lights went out. He leaped to his feet, blinded by the sudden darkness.

There was one brilliant flash of light in the darkness, it seemed as though the ceiling had dropped on his head, and that was all Jake remembered.

Chapter Twelve

"NO MURDER has any business being as mixed up as this one," Malone complained as they turned down Rush street. "Especially when it happens to me."

"This murder really happened to the midget," Helene observed.

The little lawyer sniffed indignantly. "He should worry! All he has to do is appear at the inquest, and even that's arranged for him. I've got everything in the world on my hands now, including"—he cast a sidelong glance at her—"you and Jake."

"Malone, he's worried. He doesn't act it, but he is."

"I would be too, if I wanted to keep on owning the Casino, and I'd borrowed dough to remodel it from Max Hook. What the hell made Jake do that, anyway?"

Helene shrugged her shoulders, sending two little avalanches of snow sliding down her fur coat. "Nobody else would lend it to him, except me, and he wouldn't borrow it from me. It must be hell to have a rich wife."

"It must be worse to be a rich wife," Malone said softly.

She smiled at him. "Don't ever tell Jake that. Malone, what do you suppose is in that precious box?"

"A clue to the murder of Jay Otto, the Big Midget, I hope," Malone said. "Though as I said before, I don't care. I'm not even curious. If I didn't have Allswell McJackson on my shoulders"— He raised his eyes accusingly to Heaven. "Damn it, I've got everything on my shoulders. I'm like Jupiter."

"You mean Atlas," Helene said. "He had the world on his shoulders."

Malone shook his head. "Can't fool me. Atlas is the guy who says that 'You Too can be a New Man.' Not a bad idea, either, the way I feel right now. I'd like to be a couple of new men, and neither of 'em John J. Malone."

"It's too bad about you," Helene said unfeelingly. "I wonder how Ruth Rawlson is feeling now?"

"I don't know," Malone said, frowning. "The knockout drops in that whiskey were funny stuff. The guy who analyzed it for me gave me some dope to give Ruth Rawlson when she wakes up. Because she may wake up feeling perfectly okay and not knowing anything hit her, and then after a while just pass out again and stay passed out for hours. The dope he gave me is an antidote."

"Even if she woke up feeling wonderful," Helene objected, "I should think she'd know she'd been drugged. She'd remember the way she felt before it laid her out."

"Not with this stuff," Malone said. "She wouldn't remember going out. She wouldn't even remember she was a little dizzy first."

"Well," Helene said, "you revive Ruth Rawlson and find out anything you can from her, and Jake can get the midget's precious little box, and I'll see what Annette Ginnis will confide in me. Maybe when we meet again at the hotel we'll know something."

"I doubt it," the lawyer said sourly. "We'll probably know less than when we started out. That's the way things always happen to me."

"If I had time," Helene said, "I'd burst into tears. This is where we part, and I'll see you at noon."

She turned up Oak street toward the lake, walking more slowly. The soft April snow falling against her face was cool and pleasantly caressing, like a snow facial. At the entrance to the tall apartment building where Annette Ginnis lived she paused a moment, letting the snow revive her spirits. During the short walk since she'd left Malone, she'd felt suddenly like a very small girl, frightened and helpless.

"Look here, my good woman," she told herself sternly. "This isn't like you at all. You've been in worse spots than this and enjoyed them. And gotten out of them. What's bothering you, anyway?"

The midget.

Even now that he was dead, he seemed to have left some mark on the world, dark, frightening, and curiously evil.

Helene shivered ever so little, said to the doorman, "It's damned cold for April," and went on into the apartment building.

In the lobby, sitting in a big leather chair beside an ash tray piled high with cigarette stubs, twisting the finger of a glove, was Betty Royal.

Helene stared at her for a moment before she crossed the lobby.

"Well, well," she said, as though she'd been at an alumnae tea. "How nice to run into you."

"Oh!" Betty Royal said. It was more than half gasp. "Thank goodness! I've been sitting here for an hour, trying to get up nerve enough to go up and see her."

"If you mean Annette," Helene said, sitting down on a couch beside her, "why do you want to see her in the first place? And why are you afraid to in the second place?"

"I don't know what to say to her," Betty Royal said. "I thought I did when I came here, but now I don't. And yet I've got to do something."

"You left a message for Pen Reddick saying you'd found out something," Helene said firmly, hoping Betty Royal wouldn't ask how she knew. "What did you find out, and why did it bring you here to see Annette?"

"She'd been married before," Betty Royal half-sobbed.

Helene said, "For the love of Mike. That's nothing to get excited about." She lit a cigarette and thrust it between the girl's fingers.

"You don't understand," Betty Royal said. She took a drag on the cigarette that wore it down half an inch. "It was the same sort of thing. After Pen took me home I couldn't sleep, and I got to worrying. And I remembered a boy friend of mine, Jack Norris, who got into exactly the same kind of a jam about six months ago, and he got out of it all right. So I called him up, and he told me about it, how he went out on a tear one night with some friend he'd picked up, and next morning he woke up married to this awful chorus girl. And his mother had heart trouble and Lord only knows what would have happened if any-one had heard about it. And then this same friend he'd picked up got him a lawyer, and the lawyer man-aged a quiet annulment so that nobody ever heard about it, only he had to pay this girl some terrific sum."

"I see," Helene said quietly. She was beginning to feel uncomfortably cold, in spite of her furs and the warmth of the lobby.

"And the girl," Betty Royal said between tight lips, "was Annette Ginnis."

Helene was silent for a minute. "It must be true," she said slowly, at last, "but it's damned hard to believe. Because Annette Ginnis—I can't imagine her thinking of such a racket, or lending herself to it if anyone else thought of it. And besides, she certainly doesn't seem to have much money." She lit a cigarette for herself and sat frowning at it. "Then you decided to come over here and confront her?"

"Not then." Betty Royal shook her head. "I just sat and worried and almost went completely mad. You know the family. We went all over that before." She drew a long, sighing breath. "Finally I decided I had to find Ned, and find her, and tell him the whole thing, and—well, maybe scare her into not asking him for money, at least. But I didn't know where she lived. So I went into Ned's room, thinking he'd have her address, and there was Ned."

"Not married at all," Helene said.

"No. I was frantic, honest. I went through his pockets and found her address. and then I shook him and tried to wake him up, but he was passed out. I shook him and shook him, and finally he blinked a little and said, 'The midget's dead!' and laughed and passed out again."

Helene said, "Oh," and took one quick nibble at her lower lip. The uncomfortable cold seemed to be reaching the center of her bones now.

"What did he mean by that, Helene?" Betty Royal begged.

"He meant the midget," Helene said. "*The* midget. And *the* midget is dead."

The chalky pallor crept slowly over Betty Royal's

face, so slowly that Helene could almost watch its progress. Suddenly Helene reached out and caught the girl's hand.

"Listen, Betty. This is important. Do you have any idea where your brother went last night, or what time he was anywhere, or when he came home?"

"I—" Betty Royal's eyes grew wide. She shook her head slowly. "No," she whispered. "No, I don't." Her face was dead-white now. "What shall I do? Oh, what shall I do?"

Helene thought fast. "Go home," she said quickly. "Go straight home and get some sleep, and don't talk to anybody. Except your brother, and try to talk to him before anybody else does. Don't say anything about this to him—I mean about Annette—or about the midget, but ask him where he was last night, and when, and if he remembers"— She paused and frowned. "Look. No matter what he says, don't let him talk to anybody—*anybody,* understand?—except us, or—Malone."

Betty Royal nodded dumbly. She rose, all at once looking about ten years old, wet-eyed, and dead for sleep.

"Now beat it," Helene snapped, getting to her feet, "and—don't worry."

Betty Royal's lips formed the words, "I won't," but no sound came, and the smile that passed quickly over her face was more than half ghost. Then she turned and dived through the revolving doors, waving to a taxi as she reached the sidewalk.

Helene toyed for a moment with the thought of getting in touch with Pen Reddick and letting him know Betty was safe and on her way home, and then gave it up. It wouldn't be long before she'd meet him, back at the hotel. She went on into the elevator, said "Twelve, please," let her shoulders rest against the elevator wall, and regarded herself in the mirror opposite her.

For someone who hasn't had any sleep, she reflected, and who has a murder on her mind, to say nothing of a possible scandal, a frightened debutante, a worried husband, and now a probably hysterical chorus girl, you're doing very well, Helene my girl. The tall, ash-blonde young woman who stared back at her from the glass was bright-eyed; her pale skin still glowed faintly from the April snow.

"Twelve," the elevator operator said, looking at her admiringly.

At the door to 1267, Helene paused, listening. It occurred to her suddenly that Annette Ginnis had had a bad night, that she'd been hysterical when Malone had been here earlier, and that she might just possibly have fallen asleep at last. And yet—Helene hardened her heart, and tapped lightly on the door.

"Go away," said a voice sounding, even at that distance, thick with weeping. From behind the door Helene heard a slow, terrible sobbing.

"Open the door," she called softly, knocking again, "or I'll have to tear it down with my bare hands, and I just got a manicure yesterday, and—"

The sobbing broke off suddenly, in a gasp. The voice said, "Wait a minute." There were a few quick motions inside the room, and then the door opened. Annette Ginnis said, "It's you! Come in, quick!" and shut the door so rapidly after Helene that the breeze blew a little gust of ashes from one of the trays.

"A fine thing," Helene said cheerfully, peeling off her gloves, "to come visiting at an hour like this, and then be left standing out in the hall. Is there any coffee in this rat-hole, or do I have to make it for myself?"

"Yes. Yes, there is," Annette Ginnis said. She smiled automatically, still breathing fast. "I just need to heat it up. I'll heat it up. Sit down and take off your coat. There's cigarettes on the table." She seemed to be talking in a trance.

"Thanks," Helene said. She sat down, let her furs slip off, and, while Annette Ginnis was in the kitchenette, looked around her.

It was a small room, typical of those buildings which offer a smart address, an elaborate lobby, and "tasteful decorations," and not enough space to swing so much as a kitten. Everything in it, from the white-framed flower prints on the sage-green walls to the rose rep cover on the disguised bed, showed the touch of a mass production interior decorator, everything, that is, save the little touches that were definitely Annette Ginnis. The double photograph, in an embossed leather frame—Ma and Pa, Helene decided. The autographed glossy print of Angela Doll. The

Chinese cigarette boxes, and the sweet-grass basket full of undarned stockings.

Through the half-open doors of the kitchenette, Helene could see Annette Ginnis carefully filling two coffee cups and setting them on a tray, pouring condensed milk into a glass pitcher with a not too steady hand, finding the sugar box in the cupboard and filling the sugar bowl. She was looking intently at a last week's newspaper left on the coffee table when the chorus girl carried the tray into the living room.

"Cream? Sugar?" Annette Ginnis asked.

"Neither, thanks," Helene said. She noticed that the girl took hers black too, and that she spilled a little of it as she carried the cup across the room.

"Cold for April, isn't it?" Annette Ginnis said. She put her coffee cup down on the end table beside her chair, and lit a cigarette.

"Unusually cold," Helene said.

She stirred her coffee slowly, watching Annette Ginnis through her eyelashes. What was the phrase Jake had used? "Those kitteny, soft-looking, little brown-eyed blondes." He knew what he was talking about, Helene decided.

Annette Ginnis was a small girl, with a heart-shaped face and an underdeveloped, trembling chin. At least, it was trembling now. She wasn't pretty. Her nose was too short, her melting brown eyes were too large, and her painted lower lip was too full. Her hair looked soft and fine, like baby hair, corn-silk hair that had never grown up. Her thin pale hands played with it continually, twisting it, curling it around one finger, pushing up the waves at the back of her neck, fluffing out the bangs that hung over her forehead. Suddenly Helene found herself remembering a kitten the gardener had given her when she was nine years old, a tiny, half-trembling, half-playful thing that had licked its paws and chased its tail, and snuggled close to her for affection, and that had suddenly had a fit and died, beating its own little brain out against the fireplace wall.

Helene put down her coffee cup, crushed out her cigarette, and said, "Mind if I use your bathroom? Thanks. I can find it."

When she returned five minutes later, Annette Ginnis was powdering a freshly dampened face, her cup of coffee still cooling, untouched, on the end table.

"Just between us girls," Helene said, reaching for the lipstick in her purse, "what do you do with all the money?"

Fifteen seconds later Annette Ginnis gasped, "Money?" as though she'd never heard of it before.

"Sure," Helene said, finishing with the lipstick and putting it away. "You certainly aren't spending it on yourself. What are you doing with it?"

This time the chorus girl waited thirty seconds and then said, "What money?"

"Come on now," Helene said. "You can't be working this multiple-marriage racket for sheer childish willfulness, even at your tender age." She hated to do it. It was like giving that medicine the veterinary had prescribed to the kitten. And the kitten hadn't survived. She caught her breath and went on, fast. "Tender age is right. How old are you, anyway? Twenty?"

"Twenty-one," Annette Ginnis said.

"That's pretty young for so many unhappy marriages," Helene said, shaking her head sadly. "Where did you marry Jack Norris, anyway?"

"In South Bend," Annette Ginnis whispered.

"And who was this guy you married in Crown Point a few weeks ago?"

"His name was Harold Williamson." Suddenly the girl jumped to her feet, her face chalk-white. "What do you mean? What are you asking all these questions for?"

Helene pretended not to have heard. "It's been a hard life," she said with mock sympathy. "Often married, but never a bride. Or am I wrong about that?"

"It wasn't really marriage," Annette Ginnis said between tight lips. She sank back into her chair. "I mean, I never—you know what I mean. I'm not even sure if it was legal or not."

"Oh, it was probably legal all right," Helene said, shooting into the dark. "And it must have been pretty damned easy. A young guy, not too smart, susceptible, and full of liquor—a grafting justice of the peace—a bright lawyer—and a quick annulment. A nice racket! Look, I don't give a hoot, you understand. It's none of my business. I'm just being inde-

cently curious. What did you do with the money?"
She paused, lit another cigarette, and smiled across
the room at Annette as though to say, "It's your play."

"I never got any money," Annette Ginnis said, in
that strained little voice.

"Nonsense," Helene said, almost crossly. "Don't
try to tell me it was all a whim. Plenty of money was
paid for those annulments."

"*He* got it all," Annette said.

Helene didn't even ask who *he* was. She said
quickly, "How did he make you go through with it?"

"I was afraid of him," Annette whispered. "I'm
still afraid of him." She didn't seem to be talking to
Helene now, nor to anyone—just talking. "I'm more
afraid of him now than I ever was."

"Good grief!" Helene exploded. "Afraid of him!
A little guy like that? He was only a midget!"

"I know that," the chorus girl said. "I could have
picked him up with one hand, and wrung his neck,
any day, if it had only been a matter of—size and
strength. But he'd look at a person. And smile." Now
she'd completely forgotten Helene was in the room.
"If he hadn't looked so terribly human—but he did.
It wasn't like—regular midgets. I worked once on the
same bill with a midget act. They were such swell
little people. One of them was a girl, about my age.
We used to go out to the drugstore for sodas between
the shows, and I'd lift her up on the soda-fountain
stool. But *he* wasn't like that. He looked exactly like
any other person, only tiny. And he hated everybody.

He hated everybody so much that the hate seemed to ooze out of him, like sweat." She reached for her coffee cup, spilled a little coffee into the saucer, and set the cup down again without drinking from it.

"There are things people don't talk about," she said calmly—too calmly—"things they don't even think about, not if they're decent people. But he—"

Helene held her breath and counted to ten before she said, very quietly, "I still don't know what hold he had over you."

Annette Ginnis stared at her, reached out toward the coffee cup, drew her hand back again, fumbled for a moment with the pin at her throat, and finally said hoarsely, "I was his wife."

Chapter Thirteen

"WELL," Helene said, as soon as she felt reasonably sure her voice wouldn't tremble. "Now you're his widow. I bet you'll inherit a comfortable piece of change."

"Oh no," Annette Ginnis moaned. "No, no, no."

"That's the first time I ever heard anyone say 'no no no' to inheriting money," Helene told her.

"You don't understand," the girl said. "Even if I would inherit his money—I couldn't come forward and claim it. Because if they knew I'd been his wife, they'd put me in jail."

"For the love of Mike," Helene said. "There aren't any laws against marrying midgets."

"No," Annette whispered, "but there's a law against bigamy." She bit her lip. "I've told you this much. I'd better tell you the rest of it."

"You're damned right," Helene said, "and this time, try beginning at the beginning."

"I went out with him—with the midget—one night," Annette began, in a low voice. "He asked me, and I thought it might be rather fun. I didn't think there'd be any harm in—such a little guy. It was sort of scary, though. I mean, it wasn't like being out with a full-sized person. But it was sort of fun at the same time. You know. Heck, I'd been going out with boys in the band and unemployed actors, and here was a midget spending all kinds of dough to show me a good time, taking me to swell joints and buying me that drink that's half brandy and half champagne." She looked up appealingly at Helene. "I really don't drink very much, you know. It raises hell with my complexion. But that stuff must have had an awful wallop."

"And you got plastered," Helene said amiably, nodding her head.

"I passed out," Annette said. "And when I came to, I was in that elegant hangout the midget fixed up for himself, and it was eleven o'clock in the morning. He was sitting in a great big easy chair, in fancy striped silk pajamas, smoking a cigar and grinning at me, and I guess I passed out again because the next thing I knew it was one o'clock. And he'd gone out somewhere. So I dressed quick and beat it home. I felt sort of silly about saying anything about it to anyone. You know. A midget! So I kept my trap shut. And he never said anything to me, and he never paid any more attention to me. And then some of the girls began talking about him, kids that had gone out with

him. You know how girls will talk. It was—well, he
never—did anything. You know what I mean. But
he'd get them to come up to his hangout, and he'd
get into his pretty pajamas and sit smoking cigars,
and—" She looked up at Helene, her cheeks faintly
pink, and said, "Oh hell, use your imagination."

"All this is interesting as all get-out," Helene said.
"But let's skip the details and get to the most important points, like"—she looked at her watch—"this
bigamy gag."

"I'm getting to it," Annette said. "That's part of
it. After hearing some of the things the girls said, I
especially didn't want anyone to know I'd ever been
out with him, because I felt sort of silly about it, and
because I didn't want anyone to think I'd done—any
of the same things. And besides I was sort of crazy
about this other guy. So I sort of tried to forget about
this whole thing, and one night after the last show I
went out with this other guy and we decided to get
married. Only we were going to keep it a secret because he was afraid he might lose his job. But somehow the midget found out about it. And the next
night he met me after the show and made me come
into his dressing room, and he told me I was a big-
amist, because the night I'd gone out with him we'd
gotten married, only I'd been plastered and hadn't
known it." She paused and blew her nose.

"He could have been lying, you know," Helene
said.

Annette shook her head. "He had the certificate

and everything. And he told me how long they'd send me to jail."

"I don't suppose you thought of seeing a lawyer," Helene said.

"He warned me not to," Annette whispered. "He said that if I did, he'd not only tell the police, but he'd tell—the other guy. He said—if I'd be a—good girl, and do just as he said—he wouldn't tell a soul." She looked up helplessly. "You know, even without something like that to back him up, he could make a person do pretty much what he wanted. Because he —he *scared* people."

Helene said, "Yes, yes, I know. Go on."

"So—" Annette Ginnis drew a long, sighing breath. "The first thing I had to do was leave this guy, without telling him why, and to refuse to talk to him. Then—this—racket of his."

Helene began to feel a cold, murderous rage rising in her brain, a rage directed against a tiny man who was already dead. She lit a cigarette very slowly and deliberately, and watched a curl of smoke rise toward the ceiling before she spoke again.

"I can't understand what he wanted to bother with it for," she said at last. "He certainly didn't need money."

"Lord no," Annette said. "He didn't need money. He had plenty of it. Lots more than he ever made as an entertainer, too."

"I wonder where he got it," Helene said, hoping

Annette knew. To her disappointment, the chorus girl shook her head.

"I haven't any idea. I just know he had it."

"Blackmail?" Helene suggested.

Annette shook her head a second time. "No. I got my nerve up once and called him a blackmailer. He laughed that funny little laugh of his and said he'd never blackmailed anybody, ever. Funny, but I believed him. He said he was just spending his life getting back what had been taken away from him through no fault of his own."

"What the devil," Helene said, her brows contracting. She was silent a minute, frowning. The midget. Where had he come from? What was his origin? Why was he so full of hate that—as Annette had said—it seemed to ooze out of him like sweat?

Helene sighed, and put out her cigarette. "So you were just his tool in this marriage-and-annulment game, and you never got any of the dough."

"No," Annette told her. "No, never. He just told me what to do, and what would happen to me if I didn't do it, and that was all there was to it."

"It wasn't a bad racket," Helene said thoughtfully. "Pick some rich young dope of terribly good family —making sure it would raise absolute hell with him if the news got out he'd married a chorus girl while on a bender. Soften him up with liquor, date him up with the girl, drag him around to a few bars with her, then probably give him enough knockout drops to make him stop thinking, while he was still able to move around and to say 'I do' "— She paused. "It must have been knockout drops."

Annette nodded. "Yes. I don't know what. Some special stuff *he* knew about."

"And then," Helene went on, in the same meditative tone, "an obliging county clerk and justice of the peace. And the young man wakes up in the morning with a headache—*two* headaches." She grinned at the girl. "Pardon me."

Annette Ginnis managed to grin back. "That's all right. The real headache was that marriage certificate and wedding ring, and a good reliable witness." She looked down at the tips of her embroidered mules. "All I had to do," she added, "was to be there when he woke up. You understand."

"That," Helene murmured, "and to offer to call a lawyer because you might have both made a big mistake. Am I right about that?"

"You're right." The girl pushed back a strand of soft, babyish hair. "Then I just beat it, and the lawyer did the rest."

"A quick, quiet annulment," Helene said, "and a big settlement. Which the midget got." She scowled. "But he couldn't have worked this all by himself— and yourself. He must have had help." She went on thinking fast.

"He did," Annette said.

"And another thing," Helene continued. "Malone wasn't the lawyer in this annulment racket. So why did you call for him at the crack of dawn this morning?"

Annette looked up, her face white. "It was because the midget was murdered. And because I was afraid of what they might do to me. And I'd been out once with Mr. Malone and he was so nice, and he gave me a present of a lovely cigarette case, and I knew he was a good lawyer, so I sent for him."

There was a knock at the door. Annette gasped.

"I'll go," Helene said. "If it's anybody you don't want to see, I'll tell 'em to scram." She opened the door a tiny crack. "Oh, Mrs. Goldsmith."

Mildred, Mrs. Lou Goldsmith, who'd kept her job in the Casino chorus even after marrying the slot-machine king. Even at this hour of the day she glittered, yellow hair that caught every reflection of the light, blue-violet eyes that were much too bright, diamond earrings that were downright dazzling, and fingernails that might have been bloody mirrors.

There was a little gasp from Annette as she said, "Tell her to come in."

"Of course," Helene said pleasantly. She closed the door after her.

"Annette sent for me," Mildred Goldsmith said, unfastening the silver fox. "She told me she wasn't feeling well, poor little girl."

"I think she's feeling much better now," Helene said. "We've just been sitting here gossiping."

Mildred Goldsmith took off her tiny feathered hat and folded the veil carefully as she laid it down, tucked her gloves into the pocket of her coat before she hung it over a chair back, and took her cigarette case out of her purse. "But I'm sure she's too tired to gossip any more now," she said. "Aren't you, dear?"

Annette Ginnis nodded dumbly.

"I thought you were," the woman went on. "But you'll feel much better after you've rested a bit."

Annette Ginnis looked at the new visitor for a moment, then turned to Helene. "It was kind of you to drop in. Do come and see me again. I hope you don't mind—I do think Mildred is right. I need a rest."

"Sure I don't mind," Helene said cheerfully. "I'm always getting tossed out of places." She fastened her furs and began pulling on her gloves. "So nice of you to come look after Annette, Mrs. Goldsmith."

"We all feel responsible for our little Annette," Mrs. Goldsmith purred.

"Well," Helene said. She wished she could say, "Don't worry about anything," to Annette. But no, not with this woman present. Better not give away that Annette had told her a thing. She tried to flash the "Don't worry" with her eyes. "Well, I'll see you both later." She wondered if it sounded as lame to them as it did to her.

Halfway through the lobby she paused, thinking. Mildred Goldsmith. She fitted into this somewhere. But where? Annette Ginnis had sent for her. Or had she? Hardly the sort of woman one would send for in

an emergency, for comfort. There was something un-
pleasantly snakelike about her.

For a moment Helene considered going back, and
simply refusing to leave. It would be pretty hard to
do, though. Annette had practically asked her to go
and leave them alone together. Besides, she'd be
meeting Jake and Malone in a few minutes.

After that moment of indecision, she went on out
into the street, still frowning.

The thing that really puzzled and worried her was
the way Annette Ginnis had looked at the newcomer.
Not as though Mildred Goldsmith was a friend who'd
been sent for in a time of trouble. No, the little
chorus girl had been afraid of her. Almost as much
afraid as she'd been of the Big Midget.

Chapter Fourteen

"You'll be all right," Malone said comfortingly. "Just as soon as you can keep some of this stuff down for a few minutes, you'll feel fine."

He mixed a little more of the antidote his chemist friend had given him, and poured it between Ruth Rawlson's grey and unprotesting lips. She moaned something indistinct about being poisoned, and lay still again.

"I could stand being poisoned myself, right now," Malone muttered to himself. He looked reflectively at the bottle of antidote and wondered about its alcoholic content. Looked pretty deadly, though. Suddenly his eye lighted on the bottle of rye he'd left beside Ruth Rawlson's bed. It hadn't been touched since he'd put it there the night before.

"Indian giver," he accused himself as he unscrewed the cap. He took down a good quarter of the remaining contents, patted himself on the chest, murmured, "Indian giver two times," and took one more drink before putting the bottle back on the table.

He'd stood outdoors in the April snow for at least fifteen minutes before going in, fingering the key he'd kept the night before, and staring at the wisp of greyish window curtain that hung limply over Ruth Rawlson's window. Not that he was worried about his reception. That was something he knew how to handle. Rather—well, he was—wishing.

Wishing that he was knocking at the door of that swanky apartment, using the famous ivory knocker carved with Ruth Rawlson's more famous figure, carrying a spray of white orchids—Ruth Rawlson never wore any but white flowers—waiting to take her out to dinner, to supper, anywhere. He could do it, now. He was no longer the West-side hackie working his way through law school. He was John Joseph Malone, the great criminal lawyer. Of course, right now—today, for instance—he'd have to borrow the price of the orchids from one of his City Hall pals, but he could do it.

He could, but now— This wasn't the door with the famous ivory knocker: this was the basement of a cheap Walton street rooming house, and he had the key in his pocket.

At last he'd knocked and, hearing no answer, gone in timidly, to find Ruth Rawlson just waking up, looking very white and disheveled, and feeling terrible.

The little lawyer sighed, looked at the remaining rye in the bottle, finally finished it off, and said apologetically to the motionless form on the bed, "I'll buy you another one, honest I will."

Fifteen minutes later Ruth Rawlson moaned again gently and opened her eyes.

"How do you feel?" Malone asked anxiously.

"Wait a minute," she said, "and I'll tell you." She lifted her head experimentally, sat up very slowly. "I feel fine." She blinked, rubbed one hand over her face, and pushed the hair back from her forehead. Then suddenly, "Why, Mr. Malone! I don't remember you bringing me home."

Malone opened his mouth to speak, but before he could get a word out, she went on, coyly,

"Oh dear. I'm afraid I had just a drop too much last night, didn't I? You know I don't drink, usually —that is, not very much. A cocktail or two now and then. And you know how it is with a person like that. Just one too many—" she sighed. "I know you'll forgive me, won't you? I do hope I didn't do anything" —she giggled—"*too* terrible."

"You didn't have one too many," Malone said cheerfully. "You were doped."

"*Mister* Malone!" Her eyes were wide. "How could you do such a thing!" Her voice wasn't accusing, just surprised.

"I didn't," the lawyer began indignantly.

She was paying no attention. "Oh, Mr. Malone. Is

there just one teensy-weensy little drinkie left in that bottle over there?"

"No," Malone said, feeling like a Judas.

"Oh." It was a sigh. "Still, we can always send out for some, can't we?"

"We can," Malone said gallantly, "and we will. In fact, if I just run up to the corner—"

By the time he'd returned from the corner, Ruth Rawlson had donned a faded rose negligee, straightened her hair, powdered her nose, and climbed back into bed. He poured her a drink, lighted her a cigarette, and sat down beside her.

She beamed at him.

"And now, my dear man," she said sweetly, "do tell me why you doped me."

"It wasn't me," Malone said. "It—" He paused abruptly. It hadn't occurred to him before, but this was going to be a damned awkward thing to explain to Ruth Rawlson, without giving anything away.

"Oh my gracious!" Ruth Rawlson said. "Gangsters. They're trying to kidnap me."

"No, no," the lawyer said. "It was—well, like this. Someone there at the Casino was trying to play a silly joke on the midget, and put dope in the bottle of whiskey on his dressing table. Luckily we found out about it in time. But not before someone—and we found out it was you—had gotten some of it." He mopped his brow with a damp, wrinkled handkerchief, lit a cigar, and hoped he'd never have to explain that story in a courtroom.

"For heaven's sake!" she said. "Can you imagine anyone doing such a thing!" She paused briefly, then gave him her still winsome smile. "Do you suppose that he knew it had been doped when he gave it to me?"

"When who gave it to you?" Malone asked. He felt a little confused.

"Why, the midget, of course. Dear boy. So wonderful to be able to rise as he did, in spite of such a handicap! Don't you think it was wonderful?"

"Indeed I do," Malone said. He mopped his face again.

"I think the greatest thing in the world is to be able to rise above handicaps. That's been my most wonderful fortune, to always be able to rise above mine." She suppressed the very tiniest ghost of a hiccup.

Malone said, "I'm sure of it. Now, you say the midget—"

"Simply incredible, the way he's been able to turn such a terrible handicap to his own advantage! That's really the thing to do, you know, to turn your handicaps into golden treasures. There was the most marvelous girl in a show with me once, who always used to say that. Of course she meant spiritual treasures, you know, Mr. Malone."

"Naturally," Malone said. He tried another approach. "Do you think the midget could have known the bottle of whiskey was doped when he offered you a drink from it?"

Ruth Rawlson pouted. "Oh, I don't—think—so. No, really not. I just dropped in—you know how it is. I know so many dear people backstage at the Casino, and I love to drop in and chat with them. It really seems like old times, you know. Let's see—where was I?"

"You'd just dropped in on the midget," Malone prompted.

"Oh yes, yes, yes. Such a charming little fellow. I thought I'd just stop by and have a word with him, if he wasn't busy, and he wasn't. I didn't stay long, you know. Just sat down for a few minutes and chatted, and he poured me a few drinks from the bottle on his dresser, and then I just popped along home. Dear me, I'm sure he didn't know he was giving me anything like—that." Suddenly her eyes filled with tears and she clasped Malone's hands. "You wonderful, wonderful man!" she breathed. "Why, you saved my life."

"Oh no," Malone said modestly. He had an uncomfortable suspicion that he was blushing. "No, really, it wasn't anything like that."

"But you did, you did!" She caught her breath. "I don't know what you think of me, living in this—terrible place. And I must look simply frightful. I know I do."

"You look beautiful," Malone said, from the bottom of his heart.

The damn thing was, he thought, she did look beautiful. Not like the Ruth Rawlson with the red-

gold hair rippling to her knees. But right now, leaning back against the dusty and wrinkled pillow, the
haggard lines momentarily erased from her face, she
had beauty.

It was a beauty, though, that needed a hell of a lot
of fixing up.

"Look here," he said suddenly. "I've a hunch you
aren't really a drunkard, you just drink too much."

"Why, my dear Mr. Malone!" She sat bolt upright.
"Who ever told you I was a—a drunkard! I can't
imagine anyone doing such a wicked thing!"

"Come now," Malone said. "We're pals. Besides, I
just said you weren't a drunkard."

"You said I drink too much." She pouted at him
prettily and appealingly.

"It's not the same thing. I mean you don't *have* to
drink. You just do it. I don't know why."

"There just isn't anything else to do," Ruth Rawlson said. It was the first time he'd heard a deep, unhappy note in her carefully managed voice.

Yes, that was it. He glanced around the room again.
The kind of tiny pension Ruth Rawlson got wouldn't
pay for more than the barest necessities of life. He
remembered the shabby black satin evening dress,
and the way her hair had looked the night before.
Suddenly he leaned forward and took her hand.

"Listen," he said. "I want a date with you."

A sudden vision flashed before his eyeballs: Ruth
Rawlson, twenty years later, but still Ruth Rawlson,

the still rippling hair red-gold again, the still well
modelled face carefully made up.

"Tonight!" he said. "We'll meet at—at the Casino."

"I'd love to!" He saw her face fall, and knew she
was thinking of the old black satin dress.

"And wait a minute. I want you to make yourself
beautiful for me." He reached into his coat pocket.
"Just a little loan, until—you have your next engagement."

"You dear man! You know, I really shouldn't—
but—it has been a long time that I've been between
shows, and—I'm going to sign a new contract any day
now."

"Of course," Malone said hastily. He looked into
his wallet, saw a crumpled dollar bill and a torn
newspaper clipping. "Yes, of course you are." He
wondered how much his checking account was over-
drawn. Suddenly he remembered that cute little
beauty parlor owner who used to work at the Chez
Paree. "I'll tell you, my dear. You go to this place—"
He scribbled a name and address on a slip of paper.
"It's right around the corner. I'll call them up and
make an appointment, and I have a charge account
there. Have anything done that you want. And then
I've a charge account at Saks." He remembered the
last time someone had used it, groaned inwardly, and
hoped for the best. "I'll let them know you're coming. Pick out just what you need. But"—he smiled at
her—"a *white* evening dress."

"You marvelous, marvelous man!" Ruth Rawlson breathed. "You remembered!"

"Could anyone forget?" Malone said.

Halfway out the door, he paused, remembering one more thing he wanted to know. "By the way, Angela Doll says you told her that the midget was dead. It's none of my business really, but how did you know?"

She stared at him for a moment before answering, "Oh, that. Why, I heard it on the radio. The news broadcast. One program that I really never miss. I don't care for much else in the daytime programs, but I always listen to the news. I think a person really owes it to herself to keep up with things."

Well, that answered that, Malone told himself. He went on out to the street, where the unseasonable April snow had fallen off to a few white flakes that drifted down now and then.

Out on the sidewalk, Malone looked up at the overcast sky and talked to Heaven about the number of different kinds of fool a man could be, including the kinds he'd been in the past and would be in the future.

Still, it was worth it.

He strolled on to the corner of Rush street, and turned north, thinking happily of the mistakes he had made. Yes, and with reasonable luck his life should be long enough to crowd in a few more mistakes. Quite a few more.

He paused for a moment at the corner of Rush

and Division streets. He was going to have to dig up some dough somewhere. Would it be better to try and borrow it, or to collect from some of the clients who owed him money? As soon as he got to the office, he decided, he'd try both.

Oh well, who cared about being broke? Make it, spend it. What was a better use for money than to spend it on women and liquor?

He stopped dead-still in his tracks, his eyes wide. Women and liquor.

That bottle of whiskey in the midget's dressing room. The midget couldn't have given a few drinks to Ruth Rawlson. Because the whiskey had been poured out of the bottle after the midget was dead.

His mind ran quickly back over all she'd said.

Yes, another thing. She couldn't have heard about the midget's death on the radio, because, by the time it was generally known and could have been in a news broadcast, she was passed out cold.

Malone wheeled around, tore down the street, and arrived, breathless, at the basement door. There he pounded, fruitlessly, for a good five minutes before giving up.

It was no use. Ruth Rawlson had gone.

Chapter Fifteen

PENDLETON REDDICK was sitting on a pale-green and
mauve striped davenport in the lobby when Helene arrived back at the apartment house, her cheeks
softly pink from the April snow. He looked as though
he'd been waiting a long time.

The young socialite's handkerchief, dangling from
one hand, gave all the evidence of having been
twisted, knotted, braided, and finally shredded. The
ash tray at his elbow was overflowing with cigarettes that had been lighted, puffed at once, and
thrown away. And as Helene came in the door, he
ran his hand through his hair for what must have
been the hundredth time.

"Thank God!" he said by way of greeting. "I've
been looking at that door for hours. Looking, and
waiting."

"If I didn't know what you were waiting for," He-

lene said, plumping down beside him on the davenport, "I'd be flattered."

Pen Reddick groaned. "This isn't any time to make
jokes. Did you ever sit and watch for someone to come
through a door? But only strangers come, and finally
you start making resolutions like you won't look at
your watch again until the elevator behind you goes
up and down ten times, or you'll wait until twelve
more people have come through the door and then—"

"Did you ever try making a resolution," Helene
said sternly, "to keep calm?" She lit a cigarette, and
wished that her stomach would stop pretending it
was a bouncing tennis ball. "I saw Betty Royal, and
she's all right, and nothing's worrying her now, and
she's gone to get some sleep. So if you'll please stop
tearing your hair—" She broke off suddenly and
stared at him. *"Where's Jake?"*

"That's what I want to know," Pen Reddick said
miserably. "Where is he?"

"But—!" Helene gasped, dropped her cigarette,
and caught it just before it set the rug on fire. "You
were going somewhere together, and now here *you*
are, and he isn't here—"

"We decided to separate at the corner near the Casino," Pen Reddick said hastily, "because there was a
man in a green overcoat."

The cigarette, twisted double between Helene's
fingers, finally fell into the ash tray. "As long as it
wasn't a little man in a bright green suit," she said,
"with a pointed green cap on his head, I don't care.

Pardon that twanging sound you heard: it was just my last nerve snapping off."

He smiled with pale, tense lips. "I'm sorry. Jake is all right. It was just that—" He told her what had happened.

"Oh," Helene said. "I was beginning to think you'd garroted him and dropped his limp, motionless form down a drain." She lit a new cigarette, and the color began to come back into her cheeks. "A perfectly natural conclusion to leap to, all things considered." She looked at her watch. It said twelve-fifteen. "Then he ought to be along any minute. Jake is seldom more than fifteen minutes late." She began watching the revolving doors.

"It's that damned box," Pen Reddick said. "I can't tell you how important it is. If he'd only come in here, with it under his arm—"

"He will," Helene said consolingly, "any minute now." A heavy-set woman in a mink coat came through the revolving doors; then a motion-picture star in Chicago on a personal appearance tour; then two chattering debs meeting a luncheon date in the lobby; then a dignified, white-moustached man in a derby hat; then a professional model accompanied by a newspaper photographer. "Any minute," she repeated. Automatically she began counting. When ten more people had come through that revolving door, none of them Jake—

The ninth person who came through the door was Malone.

The little lawyer was pale, out of breath, and looked as though he were hunting for nails to bite. His forehead was like a freshly plowed field, one damp lock of black hair had escaped from under his hat brim, and even the gaudy necktie which had crept up to his left shoulder registered a badly suppressed fury.

He strode up to the davenport as though he were about to destroy it with his bare hands, met Helene's coolly quizzical gaze, and said indignantly, "None of your double-damned business! Besides," he added, attempting unsuccessfully to straighten his tie, "she's still a very beautiful woman."

"I'm sure of that," Helene said. "And as long as you didn't believe anything she may have confided in you—"

"I didn't," Malone told her, his face reddening. He took off his hat, made an ineffectual stab at pushing the hair back from his forehead, pulled up a chair and sat down. "Well, now that we're all here—" His voice broke off suddenly. He stared first at Helene, and then at Pen Reddick. "Jake! Where the hell is he?"

Helene said, "He'll be along any minute now." She directed one more hopeful glance at the revolving door, then looked at her watch. It was twelve-twenty-five.

Pen Reddick repeated his story of the man in the green overcoat, and why Jake had gone to the Casino alone.

Malone lit a cigar, glared at it as though it were responsible for all his misfortunes, and said, "Oh well, in that case, he'll be here pretty soon."

"Yes, of course," Helene said, not looking the least bit worried.

For five minutes nobody said anything. Finally Helene tore her gaze away from the door and said brightly, "It never occurred to any of us that he might have called the hotel and left a message. Just a minute, and I'll ask at the desk." Before either man could offer to run the errand for her, she was up on her feet and halfway across the lobby.

Pen Reddick leaned forward and said in a hoarse, low-pitched voice, "It would have been my fault. I could never forgive myself. You don't imagine anything's happened to him, do you?"

"Hell, no," Malone said with a hollow-sounding cheerfulness, knocking a half inch of ash off his cigar. "Nothing ever happens to Jake." At least, he reminded himself, nothing had up to now.

Helene came back from the desk, her cheeks very pale, her eyes bright. "He's an inconsiderate so-and-so! At least he might have telephoned to tell us he'd be late." She sat down and lit another cigarette.

Malone pretended there was still more ash on his cigar, avoiding her eyes. "Oh well," he managed at last. "You know there's bound to be a lot of things Jake had to tend to today: tonight's show, publicity, the reporters, everything. There may have been people waiting for him at the Casino, and he might not have had a chance to let us know he'd be delayed."

"That's probably it," Helene said, much too calmly.

It was Malone's turn to watch the revolving doors. The next person who came through them might be Jake. The next person was not Jake, nor the next, nor the next, nor the next. Perhaps Jake would telephone. A bellhop was going through the lobby now calling someone. The bellhop came nearer and apparently was calling a Mr. Snazzlefassle. Nothing could have happened to Jake; nothing ever happened to Jake. The doors remained motionless for a terribly long time.

Malone tried to blow a perfect and nonchalant smoke ring. It came out as a pale-blue blur. He wouldn't have been surprised if it had turned out as a double ring, an eight, eight for eight-ball. That look on Helene's face! He'd seen it before, half terror and half determination, and a hundred percent good manners. And this guy, Pen Reddick, tearing his hair out one wisp at a time. What the hell was in the midget's damn box anyway? What could be worth anything like this?

As soon as seven more people had come in through that revolving door, Malone resolved, he'd get up and telephone the Casino.

The seventh person who came through the door was a tiny, bewildered old lady in sealskins who turned out to have come to the wrong address.

Malone rose, said, "Pardon me, gotta make a phone call," and strolled across the lobby to the Outside Telephones, repressing an urge to break into a gallop.

He dialed the Casino number, listened to the repeated buzzes, told himself, "If there's no answer after they ring it ten times, I'll hang up," and finally hung up just after he lost count.

"Was there any answer?" Helene asked as he came back, looking up with that terribly bright smile.

"No," the little lawyer said. "He must be on his way here now."

He sat down again, concentrating on keeping his eyes away from the door. By shifting his arm a little, he discovered, he could look at his watch without Helene seeing it.

It was twelve-thirty-six.

"I wonder if I ought to go and look for him," Pen Reddick said helpfully.

"Oh no," Helene said. "He'll be here in a few minutes."

Twelve-forty. Malone wondered if he could count to sixty before the second hand went all the way around, discovered that he couldn't, and decided the watch was wrong.

"Jake could take care of himself anywhere," Helene said.

"I should imagine so," Pen Reddick said.

Malone wondered if he could count to sixty before the second hand went all the way around, if he were looking the other way. He beat the second hand by twenty.

It was twelve-fifty-five.

"Even if anybody—" Helene paused, and then said, "After all, nobody knew he was going there except us."

"That's right," Pen Reddick said. His handkerchief by now appeared to be nothing but lint, and he dropped it in the ash tray. "There's nothing to worry about."

"Of course not," Malone said. If the next person who came through that door—make it the third one —no, if the fifth person who came through the revolving door wasn't Jake, he'd call the police.

By the time the third person had come through the door—a tall woman in black, with an extravagant bright-green veil—the little lawyer was laying a completely ruined cigar to rest in the ash tray. At the fourth person's arrival—a thin, cross-looking man wearing a derby hat—Malone was on his feet.

"Just one more!" he told himself.

The door remained motionless for what seemed like a century or so, then spun around to vomit out a pleasant-faced, middle-aged woman in a Persian lamb coat, carrying an armful of rental library books under her arm.

"If you'll excuse me for a minute," Malone said. He paused for a breath, wondering if he ought to wait for, well, say, five more people. The watch said one-three. No, he was damned if he'd wait another minute. "I've got to make another phone call," he finished.

Helene smiled wanly. "Tell the police he's five-foot eleven, weighs—"

"Oh no," Pen Reddick interrupted her. "Not the *police*. We can't—"

"That's right," Helene said. "After all, Malone—" She rose to her feet, pulled the furs around her pale little face. "Come on, let's all go to the Casino and find the body."

The lawyer started to speak, but the breath died in his throat. He lifted the last inch of fur over Helene's shoulder, buttoned his own coat, pulled out another cigar, stuck it in his mouth without lighting it, and said, "Okay, Mr. Reddick. Let's go."

The three walked slowly across the lobby. Pen Reddick said, "I'm sure there's nothing to worry about," and Malone murmured, "Of course not, but—"

Helene stepped into the first compartment of the revolving door, Malone followed her, and then Pen Reddick. Suddenly, before she could put a foot on the sidewalk, something spun the door around as though it had been struck by a flying projectile. She grabbed the handle and felt herself flung around, as on a merry-go-round gone mad. The sidewalk whirred by and then the lobby and then the sidewalk again, before she was flung out, grasping desperately at the empty air for support, just as Malone was catapulted into the lobby beside her, and as Pen Reddick seemed to rise from his feet and then, with one small, strange sound, like a strangled balloon, fall flat on his face on the thick mauve carpet.

In the same instant a voice muttered, "You son of a bitch!"

One lock of Pen Reddick's hair tumbled over the toe of Helene's beige suède sandals. A thin line of blood appeared on his mouth at the exact point where the blow had landed. A large, freckled, white-knuckled fist hung over him, threateningly.

"*Jake!*" Helene gasped.

There was a violet-grey bruise on one of Jake's sickly pale cheeks. His red hair was a volcanic mess. His clothes were covered with dust, and his eyes were blazing blue fire.

"This is fine," Malone said between his teeth, looking down at Pen Reddick. "Now we can *all* go to jail."

The hotel manager, who had been somewhere near the elevators, bawling out one of their operators, scooted across the lobby like a small streak of scared lightning. He braked himself to a sudden stop by digging his rubber heels into the carpet, said, "Why Mister Justus!" looked down at the socially prominent young man who had just been knocked out by one of the hotel's most important guests, realized the position he was in, and turned the color of a newly laundered napkin.

"Please, Mr. Justus," he squeaked. "I—don't know what to do."

"Call a cop," Jake said, biting out the words, "and

tell him to stand by and be a witness while I kill this wall-eyed bastard."

Instinctively the manager said, "Yes, Mr. Justus," and started toward the desk. Then he stopped himself. "What did you say?"

"Nothing," Helene said quickly. She added in a low voice, "Just one of Mr. Justus's practical jokes. You know how he is. Try to keep people away, and we'll take Mr. Reddick upstairs."

The hotel manager caught the wink she gave him, saw an out for himself, and said, "Yes, Mrs. Justus. Just a little joke, of course. Do you think Mr. Justus and your friend can carry Mr. Reddick upstairs, or shall I call a bellboy?"

"I can carry him myself," Jake said hoarsely, "with one hand, and by the throat."

"Isn't he a clown?" Helene said to the hotel manager, who tittered nervously.

Malone had been down on one knee, giving Pen Reddick a quick once-over. Now he rose. "We can make it upstairs without any help," he announced cheerfully. "Come on, Pen old man." He got Pen Reddick up on his knees, pulled out a handkerchief and wiped away a few drops of blood. At the far end of the lobby a woman gave a terrified little yelp and dived into the bar. " 'At's the boy, Pen. Just grab Jake's arm, there."

Jake automatically caught the limp elbow.

"Shanks, Zhake," Pen Reddick mouthed around his cut lip.

" 'At's right, 'at's right," Malone said. "Now, right over toward the elevator."

"Practical jokes can be so stupid," Helene said with a little laugh. "I'm sure Jake didn't mean to hurt him, did you, Jake?"

"Not at all," Jake said. "I just meant to break his God-damned neck."

The hotel manager darted away to reassure a frightened woman guest with the explanation that—"a little accident in the revolving door"—

The elevator operator took one quick look, and didn't offer to lend a hand. Not a word was said in the elevator, nor in the corridor, nor, indeed, for a good five minutes after Jake and Malone had deposited Pen Reddick on the couch and Helene had bathed his face with warm water. During the five minutes Jake stood leaning against the window frame, a cigarette burning itself to nothing between his fingers.

At last Pen Reddick sat up, groaned, put one limp hand against his jaw, and stared bewilderedly around the room.

"Are you feeling all right now?" Helene asked sympathetically.

Pen Reddick nodded and mumbled something that sounded like, "Shink sho."

"The dirty crook," Jake said. "He might have killed me."

Malone glanced up at him. "First time I ever heard

of anybody being nearly killed by having someone else run into his fist."

"Listen," Jake said, "I didn't—" He broke off suddenly, strode across the room, grabbed Pen Reddick by the shirt front and dragged him half-upright. "I hope you're able to talk now."

Pen Reddick waggled his head and said, "Shure." He put one hand to his mouth and murmured, "Vront tooche."

"If you have a loose front tooth," Jake said. "I'll be delighted to pull it out for you. Now, what was the idea of luring me up to the Casino, carefully arranging to separate from me half a block away from it, and then sneaking in after me, conking me on the bean, and running off with your blast-to-blazes box?"

"Jake!" Helene gasped. "Jake, you're all right?"

"I'm all right," he told her, "except that my head hurts a lot more right now than his—'vront tooche'." He leaned angrily over Pen Reddick. "Would you like me to knock out another one and make it a pair?"

Pen Reddick took the hand away from his mouth and said, "I didn't do a tzhing to you."

"I'm just a visitor in this madhouse," Malone said calmly, "but if I'm not asking too much—" He signaled to Helene to keep her mouth shut, poked Jake in the chest with a friendly forefinger until he shoved him into a chair, and then said, "*Well?*"

"*He* talked me into going up to the Casino to get this buried treasure of his," Jake said, glowering at

Pen Reddick. "Then halfway there he went into this routine about little green men—well, damn it, men in green overcoats, it's the same thing—and made it look like it was a good idea for us to split forces. So I went on to the Casino alone, while he ran around the block and came in a window or something, and hit me over the head with a blackjack." He went on to tell in detail about the sounds, the footsteps, the lights that went out, and the blow.

"I woke up on the floor of the Casino office," Jake went on, "feeling as if the top of my skull had been shoved halfway down my spine, with this damn box of his gone—and not a soul in the place. So I lay there dying on the floor until I realized that he'd blackjacked me, the dirty louse, and then I pulled myself up on my two hind legs and came back here to murder him, the double-crossing son of a blue-faced ape." He caught his breath, caught Helene's eye, and added, "I'm sorry, my darling. But this so-and-so tried to blackjack me."

"I did nosshing"—Pen Reddick waggled a loosened tooth with his thumb and forefinger, and finally got his speaking apparatus organized—"nothing of the sort. I left you at the corner and I came right straight back here, and I've been waiting for you ever since."

"Prove it," Jake said.

"All right, I will. When I came into the lobby, I went to the cigar stand and got a package of cigarettes. And while I was waiting for you people, I went back there a couple of times and kidded with the cigarette girl. She'll remember. Call her up and ask her."

Jake said, "My God, you might be telling the truth!"

"Call her up," Pen Reddick said. "Prove it."

"No," Jake said. His voice was strained. "I'll believe you." The breath seemed to explode in his throat. "I'm sorry as hell. But you can understand why I figured things out that way. How's your tooth?"

"Fine," Pen Reddick said. "Nothing a good dentist can't fix. People are always knocking that same tooth out, and I'm always having to have it put back." He smiled bloodily and impartially at everyone present.

"In time," Malone said, "you'll learn to duck."

"And in time," Jake said, "I'll learn to keep my temper. Only I probably won't live that long. But you can guess how I felt, waking up there on the floor of the Casino office, with skyrockets shooting off inside my skull, and that damned box gone—" He paused suddenly.

"Oh my God!" Pen Reddick said. "The box!" What little color had come into his cheeks faded out again. He stared at Jake for a moment, then groaned, and buried his face in his hands. Jake started toward him, and then stopped himself.

"No, Jake," Helene said quickly. "You don't think he—"

"I don't," Jake said tersely. His face was grey. "But —if he didn't sneak into the Casino office and knock me out and run off with that box—who did?"

Chapter Sixteen

"As a matter of fact," Malone said, looking into the dregs of a cup of coffee, "Pen Reddick hasn't enough alibi to tuck into his lost front tooth."

"But the cigarette girl," Helene objected.

"The cigarette girl is probably telling the truth," Malone told her. "But if he was really trying to pull a fast one, he could have come here, bought a package of cigarettes, beat it to the Casino in time to knock out Jake, grabbed this damn box and hidden it somewhere, and gotten back in time to do a little high-powered chatting with the girl." He put the coffee cup back on the table and waved for a refill. "After all, he was pretty anxious to get that box, and even more anxious to keep its contents secret."

"He could have done it," Jake said slowly, "and God knows he did want that box." He paused and snapped out his cigarette against the edge of the restaurant table. "Oh, the hell with you two. You're just talking, trying to make me stop feeling like a fool."

The three were sitting in a little restaurant around the corner from the hotel. Pen Reddick had been quieted down and coaxed into going to visit his dentist. Jake had combed and dusted himself, Malone had retied his necktie and wiped a spot off his vest, and Helene had changed into an early spring suit of pale-violet wool, lavish with caramel-colored fur.

Now she pulled her wide-brimmed violet felt hat a little nearer to her left eyebrow, and said, "I'm not so much concerned with your feeling like a fool as I am with your acting like one. And I'm talking to both of you."

Malone said, "What the hell?" and Jake said, "Now look here, darling—"

She ignored both of them. "This isn't any time to sit around looking like the principal attraction at a post mortem," she went on. "I'm not half so interested in what might have or even what did happen, as I am in what's going to happen."

"Buy her a crystal ball," Malone growled into his coffee cup, "and a book on astrology, and maybe she'll shut up and leave us in peace."

"Damn you, Malone," Helene said amiably. "That box. If Pen Reddick didn't conk Jake on the head and walk off with the box, someone else did. But that isn't the point either. It's— We'd jolly well better get it back—and fast."

As the two men stared at her, she continued, "Because there might very well be something in that box that would lead us to whoever murdered the midget, and get us out of what might be a nasty mess. And don't say we aren't in a nasty mess, because we are. Any hour now, von Flanagan may stumble on the fact that we tried to move the midget's body last night to conceal the fact that he'd been murdered in the Casino."

"Helene," Jake said desperately, "if we all just sit tight and say nothing——"

"Von Flanagan already knows the midget wasn't murdered after four o'clock, and suspects he wasn't murdered there in the hotel. Whoever did move his body and parked the empty fiddle case outside our door might decide to get conversational with the cops. And what with tonight's show at the Casino and one thing and another, Jake has enough on his mind without having to worry about how to saw through those steel bars of the Cook County jail." She lit a cigarette and stared at them through its smoke.

"Besides," she finished, "Malone has a client: Allswell McJackson."

"Helene's right," Jake said hoarsely, after a long silence. "That's the trouble with women, they're always right. And that box——"

"Someone wanted it badly enough to follow you to the Casino and blackjack you," Helene said, "and might have wanted it badly enough to murder the midget."

Jake opened his mouth, shut it again, finally said, "Pen Reddick must have known something about what was in that box. He might have known enough about it to tell us who else wanted it."

"If he felt like telling us anything right now," Helene reminded him. "Besides, he's in a dentist chair at this moment and couldn't talk if he wanted to." She added, "It's a good thing that was a peg tooth and not a real one, or on top of everything else, he'd probably be starting a lawsuit."

"Good old reliable Jake," Malone said bitterly. "Whenever we're already in a jam, you can always count on him to lose his temper and sock somebody."

"I don't lose my temper very often," Jake said. The gleam in his eyes warned that he might lose it again, any minute now.

"No," Helene agreed. "But you do it at the damnedest times."

"And," Malone added, "to the damnedest people. When you pick out somebody to sock—"

Jake drew a quick breath. "For the love of Mike. I don't—"

A dreamy look came into Helene's eyes. "Remember Hyme Mendel?" * she said meditatively. "And John St. John? † And Leonard Marchmont ‡ and that Blake County cop § and Harry Foote, the deputy sheriff in Jackson, Wisconsin?" ‖

"Hells bells!" Jake exploded. "I had plenty of

* *Eight Faces at Three*
† *The Corpse Steps Out*
‡ *The Wrong Murder*
§ *The Right Murder*
‖ *Trial by Fury*

provocation, and I had plenty of it this time. You'd have done the same thing, in my place."

"No doubt," Malone said gently, remembering the swing he'd taken at the substitute bartender in Joe the Angel's City Hall Bar a few nights ago, over some unflattering remark about Robert Emmet. "But as Helene pointed out, this is no time for post mortems. Where do we stand, and what are we going to do now?" He turned to her. "We know what happened to Jake in the past couple of hours. But what about you? How is Annette Ginnis? And what did you learn?"

Helene sighed, flung off the wide-brimmed violet hat, and ran two pale, slender hands over her ash-blond hair.

"Under twenty-five," she said, "suffers from hang-overs, has trouble sleeping well, needs to have a tooth pulled, was in New York about five months ago, South Bend Indiana about two months ago, and Crown Point a few weeks ago. She has a mother in Keokuk who suffers from stomach trouble and who is inter-ested in her daughter's welfare, and she uses one toothbrush at night and one in the morning. And she has a very tender skin, and really ought to wear glasses."

"She certainly must have gotten confidential with you," Malone said.

Helene shrugged her shoulders. "Oh, I knew all that before she'd told me one single thing."

Jake waited until his jaw had stopped dropping

before he said to Malone, "Maybe she doesn't need that crystal ball and the book on astrology."

"Nonsense," Helene said. "It was all in her bathroom cabinet." She put out her cigarette, lighted a fresh one, and smiled at the two men. "Any girl can tell you that you can find out more about a person, or even a whole family, by peeking into the bathroom medicine cabinet than you can by asking questions for twenty-four hours at a stretch. In this case I found out enough to let me make a couple of rough guesses, and the rest was pure pie."

"That's all very fine," Malone began, "but—" A look from Jake silenced him.

"She washes her own hair," Helene said. "There was a half-used bottle of shampoo in the cabinet. But no hair rinse, and after the age of twenty-four or twenty-five, that kind of hair needs a rinse. There were two bottles of hangover cures, and boxes of three different kinds of sleeping pills. One of them was a doctor's prescription, made up in New York in November last year, and another was made up in South Bend last February. There was a box of aspirin bought in a Crown Point drugstore, about half empty —just about a normal two weeks' supply. There was a box of pills made up in Keokuk for Mrs. Myrtle Ginnis labeled, 'Take one or two for distress after meals' and written on it in a different handwriting was, 'Try these, they've done wonders for me', signed 'Ma'. There were two toothbrushes, exactly alike, hanging beside each other, one damp and the other dry. And there were two bottles of skin lotion, and a whole collection of remedies for eyestrain." She knocked the ashes off her cigarette and said, "Anything else you gentlemen would like to know?"

Malone blew a smoke ring, closed one eye, and stared through it. "A rather young girl," he said slowly and reflectively, "from an Iowa town. A fragile girl, nearsighted, and with a baby-like skin. Carefully brought up, and taught to brush her teeth properly. And with enough hell breaking loose in her life that she needs sleeping pills, and gets hangovers. But," he fixed a stern eye on Helene, "what was the hell that broke loose?"

"I'll tell you that, too," Helene said. She gave them Annette Ginnis's story, up to the point where the visitor had arrived.

"Mildred Goldsmith," Malone repeated thoughtfully. "Where in blazes does she fit into this? In fact—" He paused and scowled. "Lou has enough dough to buy fur coats and jewelry for nineteen wives if he wanted them. And he's crazy enough about Mildred to give her anything she asked for. But she's kept right on working in the chorus."

"She's a career woman," Jake said.

Helene's scornful sniff told him what she thought of that.

"And Annette seemed afraid of her," Malone went on. "She is a mean-looking babe at that. Lord only knows what Lou Goldsmith sees in her, but every man to his taste." He wondered how Ruth Rawlson was getting along at the beauty salon. "But maybe that helps to answer a question. The midget must have had assistance in this racket of his. One of Max Hook's boys provided part of it. We know that, because he was with young Royal last night. And there's some tie-up between the midget and Max Hook. The rest of the assistance very likely came from Mildred Goldsmith."

"That's just a guess," Jake said.

"Sure it is," Malone told him. "Care to make a better one?"

"One of them murdered the midget," Helene hazarded. "Max Hook's boy, or Mildred Goldsmith."

"Why?" Malone asked, looking at the end of his cigar.

"In order to work the racket themselves, without having to give most of the profits to the midget."

"But with the midget dead," Jake pointed out, "they wouldn't have had any hold over Annette Ginnis."

"You think not?" she said coldly. "You should have seen Annette's face when Mrs. Goldsmith came in. And you should have seen her worrying for fear someone would find out that she's the midget's widow."

"All right," Jake said. "I won't argue. Suppose one of them did murder the midget. Then what?"

"Then," Malone said suddenly, "what was the idea of using eleven silk stockings, all different sizes, to do it with, and of taking the midget home and putting him carefully in his own bed? And how did anyone find out the midget was in the bass fiddle case?"

Helene glared at him. "All right, since we're asking questions—what did you find out from Ruth Rawlson?"

"That she's feeling better," Malone said. He felt a slow flush creeping into his cheeks.

"That's wonderful," Helene said. "I hope she continues to feel better. I hope she feels swell. How was she able to tell Angela Doll the midget was dead, and how did she happen to take a drink from that bottle of doped liquor?"

"I don't know," Malone said miserably.

Helene dropped her cigarette, and picked it up again quick. "You mean you didn't ask her?"

"Sure I asked her," Malone said. "And she told me. Only—" He reminded himself that Jake and Helene were his friends, and that there was no reason for feeling embarrassed. "Only, she told me the damnedest things." He repeated his conversation with Ruth Rawlson, omitting any mention of the date he had with her, of the beauty salon, and of the white evening dress she was going to buy at Saks'.

Jake scowled. "But she—the midget couldn't have offered her a drink from that bottle, because—"

In the same moment Helene said, "But she couldn't have heard about the midget's murder on the radio, because—"

"I know," Malone said in a small, unhappy voice. "I figured that out myself." He failed to add that he'd figured it out after he left Ruth Rawlson's apartment.

Jake half-rose to his feet. "Well, damn it!" he roared, "If you knew she wasn't telling you the truth, why didn't you—"

"She had an appointment at a beauty parlor," the stricken lawyer said.

"Holy conundrum!" Jake roared. "You let a dame tell you a phony story like that, and then don't raise enough hell with her to find out the truth just because she has to go out and have her hair combed!" He sank back into his seat, ran a distraught hand through his red hair, and muttered, "Damn it, I'll get another lawyer."

"*Get* another lawyer!" Malone shouted back at him. "Get ten other lawyers. The way things are going, you'll need them."

"Now never mind," Helene said gently and understandingly. In the silence that followed she picked up her hat, brushed an infinitesimal speck of cigarette ash from the brim, and performed the miracle of putting it on without a mirror. "For two bits I'd lost my temper, too. Anybody here got two bits?" She surveyed her already perfect face in her compact mirror. "All right, make it fifteen cents. I'll lose my temper for fifteen cents. Anybody make it a dime? No? Okay, I'll lose my temper for free." She brushed a fleck or so of powder on her exquisite nose, snapped the compact shut and dropped it in her purse.

Jake said, "Helene, please—"

"Is anybody else here going to get mad?" she asked,

ignoring him. "No? Fine. And while we're sitting here wringing each other's hands, poor Allswell is beating against the bars of the jailhouse. Let's do something about him, before we get really down to calling each other names."

"Now look," Malone began.

"It's our fault he was arrested," Helene went on, "because we hid the midget's body. If we hadn't, he'd have had a perfect alibi. But since we did—"

"He still has an alibi," Malone muttered. "Angela Doll."

"Go tell von Flanagan," Helene told him, "and get Allswell out of jail. After all, he's your client. In fact," she added, "let's *all* go tell von Flanagan." She rose and pulled her furs around her throat.

"Now wait a minute," Jake said, getting to his feet. "What are you trying to do? What are you trying to prove?"

"It may take all three of us," she said, "to get von Flanagan to let Allswell go. And that's the first thing to be done." She began pulling on her gloves. "Because Allswell was closer to the midget than anyone else, and he might be able to tell us who would have wanted to murder him, and who would have wanted that box, and what was in the box." She picked up her purse and said, "Well?"

"Helene's right," Malone said. "We've got to get Allswell McJackson out of jail." He laid an inch of dying cigar in the ash tray, grabbed his overcoat, and stood up. "And it may take all three of us. But on our way—" He looked at his watch. "That doped bottle of whiskey. It might be that the one thing we want to know—" His face began to redden again. "All right, on our way down to von Flanagan's office, I'll stop off at the beauty parlor and talk to Ruth Rawlson. She'll tell me the truth, this time."

Jake made a rude noise through his nose. The little lawyer pretended not to have heard it.

"She will," Malone repeated, "or I'll wring it out of her. And," he added, looking at Jake, "from you, no comments!"

Chapter Seventeen

"FOR THE LUVVA Pete!" Madame Bettina said. "You can't see her now. She's having her facial."

Malone stamped out his cigar in the ash tray upheld by two glass cupids. "I'm a bad man to argue with, you know it. I'll see her now, or you'll give me back that thirty-two-dollar bottle of perfume I gave you in December 1939."

He wondered what he ever could have seen in a slightly chubby, round-faced brunette.

"But, Malone." She stared at him, shrugged her shoulders, and said, "Well, it's your funeral. What's all the rush about, anyway? Is she one of your precious witnesses?"

"Sure," Malone said, admiring the pale-grey upholstery of the waiting room.

"Okay," Madame Bettina said. "I'll take you in. What kind of a case is it?"

Malone stifled an impulse to swear at her; instead

looked carefully around the waiting room; then leaned over and whispered something in her ear.

Madame Bettina started, giggled, poked Malone in the ribs, and said, "You lawyers!" and led the way out of the waiting room.

The walls of the long corridor Malone entered were hung with highly imaginative and very sketchy paintings of lovely ladies between curtained doors. A sign above one of the doors read *"Gentlemen's Hair-dressing,"* and through the crack in the curtains Malone could see a lanky young man with a perma-nent-wave machine attached to his head. In a booth two doors down a bored young woman was fussing over the hair of a stout, pleasant-faced matron who was saying, "And I know it's the truth. She met this man at the house of a friend of mine—" Through the slightly parted curtains of another booth, Malone could see a bored little girl, about eight, her hair in curlers, reading a comic book.

At the very end of the corridor a pair of curtains parted to reveal the most ornate booth of all. The little lawyer took one step inside, and halted. For all that it was a triumph of interior decoration, he found himself remembering the more frantic scenes of Boris Karloff movies, and shuddered.

"Oh, Miss Rawlson," Madame said, coyly, "some-one to see you."

The figure on what looked like an ornamental operating table stirred slightly. Its hair was con-cealed behind a cloth. Its face was completely covered

with what looked like an African witch doctor's mask.
Its arms, instead of ending in hands, became shape-
less lumps of greyish clay just above the wrists.

"It's me—Malone," the little lawyer said hoarsely,
sniffing the odor that was a combination of perfume
and chemicals, and wondering what it was.

The white mask moved. "My dear man, what are
you doing here?" said the beautiful, throaty voice of
Ruth Rawlson.

Malone waved to the beautician to leave them
alone, and said, "I couldn't wait until tonight to see
you." He waited till Madame Bettina was out of earshot and added, "And besides, I did have something
I wanted to ask you." He cleared his throat, and
wished he were anywhere else in the world. "What
time did you have your drink in the midget's dressing
room?"

After a moment, "It was—Oh, it was late. After
two," said the mask.

Malone wondered if he dared light a cigar in this
sanctuary. "The coroner's office has established the
midget's death as being sometime before that. How
could he have invited you to have a drink if he was
dead?"

"Oh my goodness, he couldn't have! Did I say he
invited me? I must have been thinking of some other
time." There was a slightly volcanic movement of
the mask. "No, no, it wasn't last night that I saw him.
It was night before last. Last night—"

"Go on," Malone said. He made up his mind to be

firm if it killed him. "He didn't give you that doped whiskey."

"No, he didn't," Ruth Rawlson's voice said very slowly and deliberately, as though she were trying to remember. "Oh yes, I know. It was Angela. We were chatting, you know, and when we went down the hall she said, 'Oh, I wish I had a drink,' and I suggested we stop at the bar for one, but she didn't want to do that, with everybody staring at her—you know, Mr. Malone: one of the penalties you pay for being beautiful!—and so she said, 'Let's stop in the midget's dressing room. He always has a bottle on his dresser, and he won't mind.' So we did—and really, I felt terribly strange about it, since he wasn't there. Dear, if I'd known he was dead! Oh Mr. Malone, can you imagine anything so awful!"

"There, there," Malone said soothingly. He wished Ruth Rawlson had a hand, instead of a lump of clay. He'd have patted it.

"Dear Angela is such a thoughtless child," Ruth Rawlson murmured.

"She is indeed," Malone said, glad he had everything cleared up. He felt a little angry with Angela Doll. She might have told him that. Suddenly he started. "You must have been thinking of another time," he said quickly. "Because last night Angela Doll went home right after her last performance."

"Did she?" said Ruth Rawlson. "I don't blame her a bit. It must be a terribly tiring act, though goodness only knows, when I was with—"

"What I mean," Malone said in a subdued roar, "is that this matter of the doped whiskey—"

"You don't think it's done me any permanent harm, do you?"

"No, no, no," Malone said. "I mean"—he drew a long breath—"the midget was dead, and Angela Doll had gone home, and how did you happen to drink it?"

There was another faint movement of the white mask. "Oh Mr. Malone, you won't think I'm too terrible a person, will you? Especially since he told me to."

"Who told you to do what?" Malone asked. He wondered if the fumes in the beauty parlor were getting him down.

"The midget. The thoughtful little man. That time I did stop by and have a drink with him, he said, 'My dear Miss Rawlson, there's always a bottle of whiskey in my dressing room, and any time you want a drink and I'm not here, don't hesitate to come in and help yourself.' And you know, honestly, I never would have taken advantage of it, but last night I felt terribly upset, what with his death and all, and there wasn't a soul I knew backstage, and I felt too shattered—much too shattered—to go out to the bar with all those strangers, so I said to myself, 'Well after all, Ruth, he told you to help yourself,' and I just popped right in and took one quick little teensy-weensy drinkie and popped right out again, and that's all there is to it."

"Well," Malone said, "that clears that up. Do you know what time it was?"

The mask moved slightly from side to side. "I have *no* idea. My watch is being fixed."

Malone remembered the size of the teensy-weensy drink that had vanished from the quart bottle. He decided to light a cigar anyway, beauty parlor or no beauty parlor.

"You don't think I did anything wrong, do you, Mr. Malone?" said a faint, wistful little voice from behind the mask.

"Oh no," he reassured her quickly. "Just what I would have done, in the same circumstances. And now there's just one more thing—"

"Yes?" It was like a note played on a violin.

"About how you knew the midget was dead. You couldn't have heard it on the radio, because the news wasn't on the radio until after you woke up. So how did you know about it?"

"Did I say I heard it on the radio? I must have been thinking of something else. Oh Mr. Malone, you know how awful I felt this morning. I really wasn't thinking what I was saying. You know how that can be."

"Of course I do," Malone said, sympathetically. "But just how did you know about it?"

"Why, Annette Ginnis told me. How silly of me to have forgotten that! Poor child, she was so terribly upset about the whole thing! She's such a young thing, you know. It's no wonder she was upset."

Malone remembered what Helene had told him, and thought no indeed, it's no wonder at all.

"I felt so *sorry* for her," Ruth Rawlson's voice went on. "Things like that can be simply terrible when you're so—well, so juvenile. I don't suppose she even knew him except to speak to, but when a thing like that happens right under the same roof with you"— A sigh escaped from behind the mask. "I remember once, a long time ago—Oh, but no, I can't tell you about that. I remember it too, too vividly, even now."

"There, there," Malone said soothingly. "I'm sorry to have disturbed you like this."

"Oh, it's *quite* all right." A faint little giggle. "I know how you lawyers are. You always ask *so* many questions. Just so you don't ask me what this stuff on my face is, I won't mind."

"I won't," Malone said, from the bottom of his heart.

A white-clad beauty operator brushed her way between the curtains and said, "I'm afraid we must ask you to leave now. It's time for us to remove madame's mask. Madame is going to look very lovely."

Malone gulped, "I'm sure of it," took one more quick glance at the ghastly mess, shuddered, gasped, "Good by," and fled.

Chapter Eighteen

"Just what we figured out in the first place," Helene said coldly. "She peeked into the midget's dressing room, saw a bottle of hooch with no visible owner, and went in and helped herself." She swung her car around the turn into Michigan avenue, and added, "How in blazes can Ruth Rawlson afford to be having her hair done at Bettina's, anyway?"

"I don't know," Malone said miserably, looking out the window.

"Maybe she's found an admirer," Jake hazarded. "If she has, I hope it's one with money. What's the matter with you, Malone?"

"Me? Nothing," the little lawyer lied. "Just bit on a sore tooth." He remembered that, in addition to everything else he had on his mind, he had to wring some money out of some source, enough at least to spend on Ruth Rawlson.

Helene shot the big car expertly between two taxicabs and a bus. "Annette Ginnis. There's something funny there." She was silent a moment, concentrating on piloting the car through a bad patch of April slush. Suddenly the car leaped ahead. "I know!" It slowed down again, as quickly.

"Whatever you know," Jake grunted, "don't kill us before you tell what it is."

"She—I mean Ruth Rawlson—told Malone that Annette Ginnis told her the midget was dead. Well, Annette Ginnis left the Casino immediately after her last performance, and she didn't come back again. Ruth Rawlson was already groggy when we saw her leaving the Casino, and she couldn't have seen Annette during the time she was there, because Annette was already gone. And if you're trying to tell me someone woke Ruth Rawlson up from *that* sleep to tell her anything—"

Malone said, "But—" and shut up again.

The car traveled a block and a half, no one saying a word.

"I told you not to believe her," Helene said severely.

"All right," Malone said. "Next time, damn it—" He paused. "But if you think I'm going back to that infernal beauty parlor again, you're crazy." He relit his cigar and chewed savagely on the end of it.

"And what's more," Helene went on, "the way she found out the midget was dead may be important."

"I know where Miss Rawlson will be later in the afternoon," Malone said. He spoke slowly, and as though he were controlling his temper with a great effort. "I shall have words with Miss Rawlson later, and endeavor to learn how she knew that the midget was dead. In the meantime I have had no sleep, and I have things on my mind, and if you heckle me any more, Mrs. Justus, I am going to wring your damned neck." He tossed the cigar out the window and lapsed into a gloomy silence.

Helene giggled.

"By the way," Jake said suddenly. "Annette Ginnis. Where the hell was she while all these things were going on? She left the Casino early, and for an hour or so she was seen in and out of a bunch of night clubs with her intended victim. But where did she and the intended victim part, and why, and under what circumstances?" He drew a long breath. "There's a lot of things I'd like to ask Annette Ginnis."

"Me too," Helene said. "And I'm going back there after a little while, because I'm the person she'll give the answers to." She was silent while she turned off Michigan avenue. "I've a whole lot of things I want to know. For one, will we be able to talk von Flanagan out of this silly notion of holding Allswell McJackson?"

"For another," Malone growled, "are we going to be able to keep our part in last night's affair quiet, or am I going to end up as usual, running around bribing cops? And if I am this guy McJackson's lawyer, will I be able to get any dough out of him."

"For one more," Jake said unhappily, "what am I going to use to replace the midget in tonight's floor show at the Casino?"

"Malone," Helene suggested, "giving a lecture on legal ethics."

There was silence the rest of the way to von Flanagan's office.

At the homicide officer's door, Malone paused. "Let me do the talking, remember. He can't legally hold McJackson, but it may be hard to make him realize it."

"Making von Flanagan realize things," Helene said, "has never been child's play. But we'll keep our mouths shut, if that's what you're leading up to."

They passed through the anteroom. Malone tapped on the door to von Flanagan's office. A voice beyond it called, "Come in." The little lawyer opened the door just as a large white egg rolled across the floor and crashed against the leg of a chair.

Von Flanagan said, "Hell's bells!" in a voice that was more despairing than angry.

"You see, Captain," Allswell McJackson said mildly, "I told you that you should practice it with blown eggs instead of raw ones."

"Haven't time," von Flanagan growled. He glared up at the trio who had just come in. "Shut that door. What the devil do you want?" Before anyone could speak, he went on, "As a matter of fact, you're just who I wanted to see. Would you mind running out and getting me a dozen large, well-shaped eggs?"

"Not at all," Malone said calmly. He tossed his overcoat over the back of a chair. "How have you been feeling lately, von Flanagan?"

"There's a couple more eggs here," Allswell McJackson said.

"How do *you* feel, Allswell?" Helene asked, in a sympathetic tone.

Von Flanagan's desk was littered with a miscellany of string, handkerchiefs, playing cards, an upturned derby hat, and the ruins of another egg. Jake stared at the collection for a moment, then strolled across the room to where Allswell McJackson was leaning his six-foot-six against the wall, and looked at the title of the book in his hand.

"How to Become a Magician," he read aloud.

"Look, Jake," von Flanagan said. He picked up the playing cards. "Watch me very closely. Now pick a card. Any card."

"No, no, no," Allswell McJackson said. "You aren't doing it right." He took the cards from the policeman. "Now, Mr. Justus." He assumed all the airs of a great magician. "Will you be so kind, sir, as to take a card? Any card, any card at all. I thank you, sir. And now watch very closely"—The pack of cards he was carefully riffling suddenly seemed to explode in his hands and scatter over the floor. A look of comic despair came over the big man's face. "They slipped," he explained in a small voice, stooping to gather them up again.

"But the one I picked?" Jake said.

"You must have it in your hand," Allswell Mc-
Jackson said sadly, looking up from the floor. "That's
the only place it can be."

Helene giggled.

"This is serious," von Flanagan said sternly. "Never
mind the cards. I'll show 'em the egg trick." He took
one of the remaining eggs from the paper bag on his
desk. "Now you look what I'm gonna do." He pulled
the derby hat closer to him, and spread out the handkerchief. A look of almost devotional concentration
came over his large, red face. "This is gonna be good.
Now look." He slipped the egg into his pocket, and
said, "Hell, you guys know I've got an egg here. So I
ain't gonna act like it comes out of the hat by itself.
But just watch what happens." He began monkeying
with the handkerchief.

"Not like that!" Allswell McJackson exclaimed, in
the tones of a wounded artist. "Look, I'll show you
again. And show them, too." He took the remaining
egg from the paper bag and put it into his own
pocket. Then he made a new arrangement of the
string, the handkerchief, and the derby hat. "Ladies
and gentlemen: The question has long been debated,
which came first, the chicken or the egg. Tonight I
shall attempt to answer it for you, by producing an
egg without the aid of a chicken—indeed, with no
more than an ordinary derby hat and a handkerchief
borrowed from this gentleman in the audience." He
was making motions with the hat and the handkerchief as he spoke. "I will appreciate your watching

very closely." He took one corner of the handkerchief between his teeth. An unconcealed loop of string began to move slowly; he hastily tucked it out of sight. Suddenly a triumphant look came into his eyes. Still holding the handkerchief in his mouth, he cried out, "Kut-kut-kut-ka-*daw*-kut!" in a fair imitation of a Rhode Island Red hen with something to announce. The handkerchief fluttered slightly, the egg bounced lightly into the derby hat, and bounced out again, landing on Allswell McJackson's vest at the exact moment that the amateur magician lost his balance, tripped over the edge of the rug, and slid across the floor to land at Jake's feet.

"Wonderful!" Malone said. "I never saw a better trick in my life."

Allswell McJackson shook his head sadly. "I knew we should have used blown eggs. Or hard-boiled ones." He began dabbing at his vest with the handkerchief.

"Just the same," von Flanagan said indignantly, "it's a hell of a good trick, and with a little more coaching from my pal here, I can learn to do it."

"I've no doubt," Malone said. "But why?"

The big policeman sat down behind his desk and lit his pipe. "I don't know if I ever told you or not," he began slowly, "but I never wanted to be a cop. And it ain't my fault I turned out to be a cop."

"I know the story," Malone said wearily. "You never would have been a cop, only some politician owed your old man dough, so you got appointed to the force, and you've been trying to get off it ever since."

Von Flanagan looked hurt. It was his story, and he wanted to tell it.

"You were going to retire and run a mink ranch," the little lawyer went on mercilessly. "All you'd have to do, you said, was buy two mink and just wait. Then you were going to buy a Georgia pecan grove and raise nuts. And then it was to be a country news-paper. You wanted to be a journalist." He paused for breath.

"Look," von Flanagan said unhappily. "For any one of those things you have to have an investment. And with kids in school, and the kind of tastes my wife has, and with all my relatives, and all her rela-tives, and"— He sighed heavily. "But you don't have to have an investment," he finished, "to go on the stage."

"So that's it," Jake said.

"It's an easy life," von Flanagan said. "You don't have much work to do, you don't have to get up in the morning early, and you get to travel all the time. And when you travel, you don't have all your in-laws trailing along with you."

"I see exactly what you mean," Helene said sym-pathetically.

He beamed at her. "Only," he said, "I couldn't de-cide what to do. I can't be an actor, I'm not the type. I'm too fat to dance. And I can't sing."

"I don't know about that," Malone said, relighting

his cigar. "I've heard you do some surprising things with 'My Wild Irish Rose.'"

Von Flanagan ignored him. "And it takes too long to learn to be an acrobat. What was left?"

"A magician!" Helene exclaimed. "Just the thing!"

"Jake," von Flanagan said, with feeling, "you've got a wonderful wife. I hope you appreciate her." He drew a long breath. "I got this little book, and I been practicing. But it's hard to figure those tricks out for yourself. So when I found out the professor here is a magician—"

"For the hundredth time," Allswell said weakly, "I'm not a professor."

"You may not be a professor," von Flanagan said to him, "but you sure as hell are a magician."

The giant blushed. "I learned a lot of magic tricks once. Used to do them at the college shows. Only," his brow contracted, "I never seem to do them quite right."

"That's okay, pal," von Flanagan told him affectionately. "You know how, and that's the thing."

Malone cleared his throat. "Fun is fun," he said, "and all that. But we didn't come down here to watch a vaudeville show." He assumed his sternest look. "Now look here, von Flanagan," he said in a loud voice, "you can't hold this man in jail, and you know it."

Von Flanagan looked up, surprised. "Sure I know it. I don't need a lawyer to tell me that. The doc says that the midget couldn't have been killed later than two o'clock, from what was in his stomach, and what the headwaiter at that joint of Jake's says he ate last. Besides, he wasn't killed at his apartment. He was killed someplace else and took there. So it wouldn't have had to be someone with a key to the apartment, because there would be the midget's own key, right in his pocket. And that Doll dame gives the professor an alibi for all the time up to three in the morning."

He knocked his pipe against the side of the wastebasket. "Besides, a swell guy like the professor wouldn't murder anybody. He could have gone home a coupla hours ago if he'd wanted to, only we been busy."

Malone glanced around the littered office and said, "I hope you'll pardon us for disturbing you."

Helene settled herself on a corner of von Flanagan's desk, and smiled at him. "Do you have any idea who did murder the midget, or oughtn't I to ask?" Her voice was dangerously sweet.

"I ain't saying," von Flanagan told her. "Not yet. But I got my eye on somebody. One of the Hook's boys. Name of Johnny Oscar. He was mixed up with the midget someway, and he's the kind of a guy who *would* murder a midget."

Helene nodded slowly. "It's wonderful of you to be able to figure that out," she breathed.

Von Flanagan seemed about to purr. "Professor," he said, "show the lady that dollar-bill trick."

"Some other time," Allswell said modestly.

"Oh no," Helene said. "I'd love to see the dollar-bill trick. And I'm sure these gentlemen would, too."

"Very well," the giant agreed. "Has anyone here got a dollar bill?"

It developed that only Malone could oblige.

"I'll give it right back to you," Allswell promised. He took two Official Business envelopes from von Flanagan's desk, placed the dollar bill in one and a slip of paper in the other. Then he turned his back on them for a moment. When he turned around again only one envelope was in his hand. "Your attention, please. Do not take your eyes from me for even a second. But the flight of a dollar bill, ladies and gentlemen, can be quicker than the eye." He laughed hollowly, made a few quick motions with his handkerchief. "Money to burn, ladies and gentlemen, money to burn."

It was a familiar routine, and Allswell performed it expertly, complete with the burning of the envelope before their eyes, and ending with the mysterious reappearance of the envelope under Malone's coattail.

"See?" von Flanagan said triumphantly. "I told you so!"

"Like the phoenix from the ashes," Allswell McJackson said, "it returns, unharmed. Your dollar bill, Mr. Malone." He handed over the envelope with a flourish. "Of course," he added in his normal tones, "you had to see me fix the dummy envelope that I burned. But then you probably know how it's done anyway."

"You mystified me," Malone said.

The little lawyer tore open the envelope. It contained the blank slip of paper. "Is this part of the trick?" he asked.

Allswell McJackson's eyes bulged, almost filled with tears. He shook his head, his jaw dropping. "Oh my God!" he moaned. "I burned up the wrong envelope!"

It developed that the big amateur magician could not leave with them. Von Flanagan was going to keep him there for another hour's lesson if, he growled, he had to arrest him all over again.

As Jake closed the door after them, they could hear von Flanagan saying, "Now, professor, *you* take a card—"

"I haven't enjoyed anything so much in weeks," Jake said. For the first time that day, his voice sounded cheerful.

Malone snorted. "I'm glad you did."

"Why, Malone?" Helene began.

"Not only," the lawyer roared, "do you get me a client who probably can't ever pay me a cent. Not only do you do that: you have to get me one who burns up my last one-dollar bill!"

Chapter Nineteen

"I KNOW a good trick I'd like to see done," Malone said crossly, "and that's to make the whole damn shebang of you disappear, so I could go home and get some sleep." He lit a fresh cigar and tossed the match out the window of Helene's car. "As a matter of fact, my only interest in this mess was the client you wished on me, and he's in the clear now. So that's the end of it as far as I'm concerned."

"You can't do that to us," Helene objected. "How about who murdered the midget?"

"None of my business," Malone said.

"How about Pen Reddick's box?"

Malone said slowly, "Say, that's a thought. Maybe I can talk Reddick into bringing action against Jake for assault and battery. He's rich enough to be a first-class client, and," he added generously, "I'd even split the fee with Jake."

"You're a very wicked man," Helene said severely. "How about Annette Ginnis?"

"A charming girl," Malone said, "but not exactly my type."

"How about Ruth Rawlson?"

"You leave her out of this," Malone snapped. He added in a milder tone, "And you'd better leave yourselves out of this, too, or you'll get into more trouble."

"Malone's right," Jake said slowly. "There's nothing we can do except sit tight and say nothing. So we'll drop Malone at his office. He probably has other things to tend to besides our affairs. And I've got to see about tonight's show, and publicity, and a million other things. And you've got to get some sleep."

"Don't we all," Helene said bitterly. She sighed, swung the car into Clark street, and said, "Have it your way, but I've a hunch you're going to be sorry. Remember, von Flanagan knows the midget wasn't murdered in his apartment and that his body was moved there. And he isn't so dumb. Suppose he stumbles on the fact that we hid the midget's body in that fiddle case?"

"We'll tell him we were practicing a magic act," Jake said wearily, "and try to teach it to him. Don't bother me, woman. I've got things on my mind."

It was a worn and haggard Malone who left the car at the corner of Clark and Washington streets and walked the few steps to his office building. Losing a

night's sleep was nothing serious. It had happened
before and would happen again. But he was de-
pressed, puzzled, and worried. Not over the murder
of Jay Otto, the Big Midget, but over a little matter
of raising enough money to entertain Ruth Rawlson
in the style he'd dreamed of, back there in 1921.

He glanced at a clock in a shop window and realized
he'd have to work fast, too. The banks would be
closing in a couple of hours. Meanwhile—

"There's always a way of handling things," he told
himself sternly.

There was a heavy frown on his face as he rode up
to his office. But by the time he opened his office
door, he beamed at the plump little black-haired
office girl, and was brisk and businesslike.

"*Good* morning, Maggie."

She laid down her magazine and looked at him
disapprovingly. "Out all night again."

He pretended not to have heard her. "Maggie, I've
a little errand for you to do, if you don't mind. Take
a check out and get it cashed for me. Not at the bank,
but anywhere you can get it cashed."

She sniffed. "The bank called up this morning,"
she said coldly, "to say that the fifty-dollar check you
cashed at the Club Alabam night before last just
came in and bounced."

Malone looked mildly surprised. "Oh, it did, did
it? I forgot about that check."

He went into his office, threw his hat on one
corner of the couch and his overcoat on the other,

sat down at his desk, and rested his forehead on his hands.

This was what came, he told himself, of letting unscrupulous women play on his sympathies. Of going back again and again to a gambling joint he knew was crooked. Of being an easy touch. Of taking the fat fee he'd collected from that bookie he'd defended last week and lending it to a policeman's widow, instead of spending it extravagantly on himself. This was how things turned out. You worked and saved and drove a hack to send yourself through law school, only to end up twenty years later with a date with Ruth Rawlson, and exactly sixteen cents in your pants.

The little lawyer sighed and unlocked the desk drawer marked "Confidential" just as Maggie opened the office door and peeked in.

"And Mr. Malone, there was a man telephoned twice. He said it was urgent—"

Malone waved to her to shut up. "I don't want to talk to him."

She banged the door shut again, and he mopped his brow with a soiled and rumpled handkerchief. On top of everything else, someone calling up about that check that had bounced. He'd have to do something about that, too. Just because he'd met some charming people at a bar, at a time when he didn't have any cash with him, and had forgotten what his bank balance was—

From the drawer marked "Confidential" he drew

out a dingy sheet of paper which constituted his sole bookkeeping department, and began poring over it. Its record consisted of people who owed him money, people who had owed him money and had paid it and were therefore crossed off, people to whom he owed money, people to whom he had owed money and had paid it back, likewise crossed off.

The bookkeeping department didn't tell him anything encouraging. Still, there was one item—"Mr. Fairchild, $25, for services rendered." That would be better than nothing. He began looking for Mr. Fairchild's telephone number, just as Maggie reappeared.

"Mr. Malone, it's the same man, and he insists on talking with you."

"Tell him I'm not here," Malone growled. "Tell him I'm in Little America. Tell him you never heard of a Mr. Malone. Tell him to go to hell."

She shut the door again, and he went on looking for Mr. Fairchild's number. Finding it at last, he called and was told that Mr. Fairchild had not come into the office yet. He was expected any minute, the impersonal female voice at the other end of the line volunteered.

"Tell him to call me the minute he comes in," Malone said. "Tell him it's urgent." He added, "I don't suppose you have any idea how long it will be?"

The impersonal voice said that Mr. Fairchild should be in within the next fifteen minutes.

Malone hung up, and looked at his watch. One-forty-five. If Mr. Fairchild called back by two o'clock, Maggie could dash over and pick up the check and cash it by the time the banks closed.

Maggie returned to announce, "I told him everything you said, Mr. Malone, and he said he'd be right over here anyway."

"When he gets here," Malone said grimly, "throw him out. You're a good strong girl."

He dragged himself over to the closet, threw open the door, and stared at himself in the mirror. An eighteen-hour growth of beard was faintly blue on his chin, his eyes were red-rimmed and bloodshot, his cheeks were haggard. A fine-looking guy to be taking Ruth Rawlson out tonight!

"Call that a map?" he asked the mirror indignantly. "I've seen better ones in an extra edition of a two-cent newspaper." He peeled off his coat and tie, tucked in his collar, filled the bowl with hot water, soaked a towel, and held it against his face.

In a minute the phone would ring. Mr. Fairchild. Meantime—Malone sighed into the towel. Who could have killed that little guy last night? He ran over a list of names in his mind. *Artie Clute*. Would he have wanted to get back his bull fiddle badly enough to have murdered the midget? Yes, he would. But if he'd murdered the midget, he'd have carried away the bull fiddle. Or would he? It would have cast suspicion on him, if he had. *Allswell McJackson* and *Angela Doll*. They alibied each other. Allswell must have hated the midget who bullied him, and Angela was sore as a goat over the burlesque of her act. *Annette Ginnis.* She had motive enough. But at the time when the midget was killed, she was doing the hot spots with Ned Royal.

Do all these people have names beginning with "*A*"? Malone asked himself, looking at his lathered face in the mirror. Not forgetting *Al Omega,* the band leader, he thought. If the midget had stumbled onto the runnings-around of Al Omega and Lou Goldsmith's wife, that could have led to murder.

"Get on to the 'B's,' " he muttered, starting to shave. *Betty Royal.* Did she have reasons, and did she have the opportunity, or, more important, the determination? Who had a name beginning with "C"? Nobody. A, B, C, D, E, F, G— Malone, he told himself sternly, all this has obviously unhinged your mind. Or maybe you just need a good night's sleep.

He hummed the first twelve letters of the alphabet to the tune of "Skip to My Lu"—and paused suddenly. *Pendleton Reddick.* The midget had something in that box of his that Pen Reddick wanted, and wanted bad. Pen Reddick was supposedly out with Betty Royal, looking for her brother, at the time of the midget's murder, but you never could tell about those things. He went on humming. P, Q, R— *Ruth Rawlson.*

"She had nothing whatever to do with it," he said aloud.

The phone rang and he leaped to answer it, his face half-covered with lather.

It was not Mr. Fairchild. It was Jake.

Angela Doll was ill. Nothing serious wrong with her: just passed out. Apparently from shock, the hotel doctor had said. What was he, Jake, going to do about tonight's show if, on top of the midget's murder, he had to fill in an act to replace Angela Doll?

"Get von Flanagan to come down and do card tricks," Malone growled, and slammed down the receiver.

He glared at the phone for a moment; at last dialed Mr. Fairchild's number again. Mr. Fairchild was not in yet. Malone returned to his shaving.

A lot of questions bothered him. Why had the midget been strangled with eleven silk stockings, all different sizes? Did it mean that eleven members of the chorus had combined to carry out his murder, and if so, which one had been left out? There was a reason, an important reason, for those eleven silk stockings, but he couldn't figure it out. Then, who had moved the fiddle case, with the midget's body, out of the Casino, and put the midget carefully to sleep in his own bed, and left the fiddle case outside Jake's door?

The phone rang, and he dropped his razor to answer it. Mr. Fairchild must be in by now.

It was Helene.

"Malone," she said, "I can't get hold of Jake. He's busy somewhere. And I'm terribly worried about Annette Ginnis."

"Go to sleep," Malone snapped. "And if you've got

to worry about someone, worry about me." He hung up. After a moment's deliberation he dialed Mr. Fairchild's number again. After all, it was five minutes till two.

Mr. Fairchild had not come in yet.

Malone swore, kicked an inoffensive wastebasket, and went back to his shave.

There was another thing. The midget's body had been concealed in the fiddle case; then someone had carried it out of the Casino; then it had reappeared at the hotel in the early morning. But there was a whole collection of people who'd found out about the midget's murder before it had been officially announced. Angela Doll, Annette Ginnis, Ruth Rawlson, Artie Clute. How did they know?

Back of all the questions he asked himself and tried to answer, there was one he didn't ask because he didn't know what it was. Something that bothered him, that he told himself he knew, and yet couldn't just put a finger on. It was as important as hell, but he couldn't remember it. If he'd just once be able to think of it, he'd know who'd murdered the midget. He might not know the answers to the other questions that bothered him, but he'd know that one.

The little lawyer finished shaving, dabbed a little talcum powder on his cheeks, combed his hair, and put on his coat and tie. "You're still a terrible-looking guy to be taking Ruth Rawlson out tonight," he told the mirror. Taking Ruth Rawlson out! And with what?

The phone rang. There! That must be Mr. Fairchild now. He grabbed the receiver, looking at his watch. Five after two. Well, Maggie could still make it with the check.

It was not Mr. Fairchild on the phone. It was Maggie, calling from the outer office.

"Mr. Malone, the man who called you is here."

"Tell him to wait a minute," Malone said. He felt a sudden coldness of the skin as he dialed Mr. Fairchild's number once more.

"I'm so sorry, Mr. Malone, but I'm afraid that Mr. Fairchild isn't coming in today. No, I don't know where we could reach him. If he should call in at the office, I'll ask him to phone you. Otherwise, I'm sure he'll call you tomorrow."

Malone put the phone down gently and said, "Tomorrow I'll be in a better world, I hope."

Well, the man who'd come to see about the check could be managed. An apology—"Just an oversight, you know how it is"—a glance at the watch—"I'm afraid it's too late to get to the bank today, but"— and a promise—"I'll straighten it out first thing in the morning."

That wouldn't take care of the real problem, of course. Ruth Rawlson. Tonight.

Malone squared his shoulders, picked up the phone, and said to Maggie, "Send the gentleman in, please."

The gentleman was Pen Reddick.

"I hope you weren't busy," Pen Reddick said, "because this is really important."

"Me? Busy?" Malone said with a hollow laugh.

"I've been trying to reach you for the past couple of hours," Pen Reddick went on. He sank into the nearest chair. "But your secretary didn't seem to know where you were."

"Sorry," Malone murmured. He glanced at the young man from the corner of his eye, while he fumbled with the wrapping of a cigar. Pen Reddick's front tooth appeared to be back in place, but his face was pale and very weary.

"It's that box," Pen Reddick said. "I've got to get it, you understand. Not because of myself, but because—well, other people. That's why I came to see you. You do understand, don't you?"

Malone nodded as if he'd been paying attention. "Of course, of course," he said, in his best professional tone. He glanced at his watch and realized that if, by some miracle, Mr. Fairchild did call now, Maggie wouldn't be able to make it to the bank and cash his check unless she went on a rocket ship. And meantime he had to sit listening to Pen Reddick chattering about his damned box.

"I know a lot about you," Pen Reddick said. "I think that if anyone can get that box for me, you can. What's more, I think you can find out who murdered—the midget. That's more important than you think. I can't explain why, but it is."

"I'll take your word for it," Malone said. He wondered if Maggie had any money he could borrow, in a pinch.

"If you'll take the case," Pen Reddick said, leaning his elbows on his knees, "I'll pay you a thousand dollars if you find the box, and another thousand if you find out who murdered him—the midget, I mean." He stared at Malone for a moment and, getting no answer, said, "I know that isn't enough, not for a man like you. I'll double it."

Malone looked at him for a moment, laid his cigar down in the ash tray with exquisite care, wheeled his chair around and gazed out the window for several seconds, his arms clasped behind his head, and at last turned around to face Pen Reddick with a grave and scowling look.

"These cases are frequently difficult, Mr. Reddick," he said seriously. "I can't promise you anything. But I'll try. I'll do the best I can."

Pen Reddick said, "Oh, thank God!" He didn't say it to Malone.

"Of course," Malone said, "you understand there are bound to be expenses—"

"Yes, yes, I know that," Pen Reddick said hastily. "I'll want to give you a retainer. Will two hundred dollars be enough, for the present?"

Malone caught his breath and then said, slowly, "Yes, I think so." He looked at his watch. Maggie could still make it to the bank with a check, if she took a cab.

"Good," Pen Reddick said. He drew out an alligator-skin wallet, took out four fifty-dollar bills, and tossed them across the desk to Malone.

"I'll find your box," Malone said hoarsely, "if I have to dig it out of the subway excavations with my bare hands. And I'll find who murdered the midget if I have to wring a confession out of the mayor." He tucked the bills into his own wallet and stood up, a sympathetic smile on his face. "My dear young man, you've been through a bad time. What you need is a drink. Suppose we go out for one, and then you can tell me everything I'll need to know about this business."

"That's a very good idea," Pen Reddick said with a wan grin.

Malone picked up his hat and overcoat and opened the door for his new client. "Believe me," he said feelingly, "you couldn't be in better hands."

The telephone was ringing as he stepped through the office door. In the anteroom Maggie stopped him.

"Oh, Mr. Malone. A Mr. Fairchild on the wire."

The little lawyer beamed at her. "Tell Mr. Fairchild to go straight to hell," he said pleasantly. "And tell him I'll send him a greeting card there, sometime."

Chapter Twenty

"**G**O TO SLEEP, darling," Jake whispered. "Pretend it's night instead of day. Wash your face and brush your hair and take a big bath and climb into bed, and if you can't drop off right away, well—count sheep."

He looked at Helene through the half-open door and wondered how anyone could look so flawlessly beautiful at two o'clock in the afternoon, after missing a night's sleep. Her face was pale, but it was the pallor of flower petals. One shining strand of hair had slipped from its moorings and fallen across her cheek, and he resisted an impulse to become maudlinly poetic about it. There was a tiny smudge of soot on her right cheek. He felt that if he kept on looking at it he would burst into childish tears.

"Wash your face and brush your hair," he repeated gruffly. "You look like a hag."

He closed the door and went on down the hall

toward the elevator. No man had a right even to wish for a girl like Helene to fall in love with him and marry him, and if by a miracle one did—well, then he certainly ought to surround her with all the most wonderful things in the world. "At least," he said to himself grimly, punching the elevator button, "you ought to keep her in night clubs."

Something had to be done about tonight's show, and done fast.

But what? Substitute something for the midget's act, and ignore the whole situation? Call off tonight's whole floor show and make a publicity stunt of it? Or, he thought with a wry smile, interrupt the show for a minute of silence? In this case, perhaps, a half-minute of silence.

There was Max Hook's loan, that had to be paid back in a hurry. There was Angela Doll, having tantrums. There was the question of who murdered the midget—not that he, Jake, cared a hoot. There was Pen Reddick and his damned box. There was—

"I could do with a few sheep to count myself, right now," he said.

The elevator operator grinned at him as he opened the door. " 'Morning, Mr. Justus. We sure have a lot of excitement around here, haven't we?" He closed the doors but, before starting the car down, he turned around to Jake and asked in a quiet voice, "Say, just between us guys, is it the straight dope that one of his babes did him in?"

"I don't know," Jake said, fumbling for a cigarette, "but could be."

"Beats me," the operator said, shrugging his shoulders. He put one hand on the lever. "What would you imagine a babe would see in a little feller like that? You'd think"— He coughed, and started the elevator downward. "Maybe guys like us just don't know about the babes. Time and time again I've brought him up in the car with some gorgeous-looking dame. Betcha he's brought home every damn gal in the Casino chorus, one time or another. What he did with 'em when he got 'em home, I don't even wanna guess."

"Oh go ahead," Jake said. "Go on and guess. Don't be a reactionary."

The operator stopped the elevator two floors down, opened the doors and peered out. "False alarm," he announced. Then, his hand on the lever, he turned to Jake. "Can you imagine it? Beautiful babes like that, all foxed up in swell clothes and furs, and these fancy hair-dos, and figures like"—he whistled—"and this bastard, three feet tall if he stretched himself—" He shook his head. "Well, maybe we just don't know about the dames, Mr. Justus." He started the car down again.

"You certainly see what's going on," Jake said politely, thinking of everything else in the world.

"Listen," the elevator operator said in a low voice, "I could tell you more dirt if I wanted to!" He stopped the car at the fifth floor, without opening the doors. "I bet you any money this midget was putting the bite on Al Omega and Mrs. Goldsmith. Why? Because once when the midget and Al Omega were riding up in the elevator together, I heard the little feller say, 'If he knew about this, he'd kill her with his own bare hands, and you know it.' And I've taken Mrs. Goldsmith up to Al Omega's floor more'n once. For that matter, I've taken her up to the midget's floor more'n once."

"Well," Jake said, without conviction, and encouragingly, "it's none of our business."

The elevator shot down to the first floor. When it stopped there, the door still closed, the operator turned around and looked confidingly at Jake.

"Sure it's none of our business," he said in a low voice, "but Mr. Justus, I do wanna tell you one thing. You know a guy hears a lot that's being said, running an elevator up and down. Well, one night this midget said a very funny thing."

Jake said, "If it's funny enough, I'll laugh."

"This Mrs. Goldsmith was with him," the operator continued. "And just when she got in the elevator she was saying, 'Aren't you afraid of *anything*?'" He paused for dramatic effect.

"And was he?" Jake said.

"The little guy," the operator murmured, "he said, 'Yes, I am.' And she said, 'Oh, you are! What is it?'" He paused for breath, then went on. "You wouldn't believe how well I can remember everything I overhear in this elevator. Like what you said to Mrs. Justus the time she got arrested for speeding up near Waukegan. You said—"

"Never mind," Jake told him hastily. "I believe you. What did the midget say he was afraid of?"

"He—" The operator paused, scratched one ear, and then said, "I remember exactly the words he used. He said, 'I'm only afraid of one man. And he's closer to me than any other person in the world.'" He put one hand on the elevator door. "Who do you suppose he meant by that, Mr. Justus?"

"I don't know," Jake said, "unless he was referring to King Oberon."

The operator looked blank. "Never heard of him. Still a guy can't keep up with all these European countries. You won't tell anybody I been gabbing to you, I hope."

"I didn't hear a word," Jake said soulfully.

He stepped out of the elevator and stood for a moment in the lobby, lighting a cigarette. Maybe Mildred Goldsmith had murdered the midget. He hoped not, because it would be tough to find someone her height and weight to replace her in the Casino chorus. For the same reason, which had to do with the Casino, its music, and its floor show, he hoped Annette Ginnis hadn't murdered the midget, nor Al Omega, nor Artie Clute, nor Angela Doll.

But who had murdered the midget, and why? And who had carried his body out of the Casino? For a moment his mind whirled with speculation. Then for a second moment, he went into a terrific wrestle with his Midwestern conscience.

If he went down to von Flanagan's office right now, and confessed his part in the affair, and explained his reasons—von Flanagan might be sympathetic and helpful. He might say "Sure, Jake, I don't blame you for trying to get the little stiff"—Jake smiled wryly to himself—"out of your joint. And thanks for giving me the information." Or he might turn purple and yell something about obstructing justice, close up the Casino, and call out, "Open the jail doors for. Mr. Justus, coming in, not going out!"

"You've got a night club to worry about," Mr. Justus said grimly to Mr. Justus, "and tonight's floor show, and a loan from Max Hook. And the most beautiful wife in the world, who deserves the best of everything."

Maybe he could get hold of that comedy dance team who'd just closed at the State-and-Lake.

"It's none of your business who murdered the midget," Mr. Justus added to Mr. Justus. "You did nothing but try to protect your own interests, which is what any man would have done under the circumstances. Besides, you didn't move the body, you only hid it."

Jake finished lighting his cigarette, tossed the match into the nearest ash tray, and strode across the lobby, resolved to put the midget and his murder completely out of his mind. His mind refused to co-operate.

What could be in Pen Reddick's box, and who had

wanted it badly enough to knock him, Jake, on the head, and walk off with it? His head still throbbed, and he rubbed one hand over his brow. Why eleven silk stockings? How had Artie Clute known the midget was dead? What was he going to do about tonight's floor show? *And what had he overlooked?*

He stopped dead-still in his tracks, halfway across the lobby. Something. Right there, almost within the reach of his mind. But he couldn't coax it any nearer. And something important.

"What have I forgotten?" he said aloud.

"Your topcoat, Mr. Justus," the hotel manager said, with what was nearly a giggle.

Jake looked blankly at the little man for a moment; then said, "No topcoat. It's April. It's spring." He started to move on toward the door.

The manager moved in front of him. "I'm sorry to trouble you again, Mr. Justus," he said, "after all that's happened this morning. But Mrs. Justus said you'd just left the apartment when I phoned, so I took the liberty of stopping you in the lobby"— He paused and coughed apologetically. "I'm sure it isn't anything serious, but the doctor didn't quite seem to know what was the matter, and so I thought I'd better—"

Jake stared at him. "What the hell are you talking about?"

"It's Miss Doll," the manager said weakly. "Angela Doll. We called the doctor, and then we tried to call you, but Mrs. Justus said you were on your way downstairs, and so—" His voice broke off and he looked helplessly at Jake's back, which, along with the rest of him, was halfway to the elevator by that time.

Angela Doll's Irish maid met Jake at the door, one finger to her lips. "If she ain't dead, she's dyin'," she whispered, "and if she ain't dyin', she's a mighty sick woman. And the doctor's with her now, and don't you go speakin' in a loud voice."

"What happened to her?" Jake said hoarsely, leaning his back against the door.

"She fell on her face," the maid said, shaking her head sadly, "like she'd been struck by a bolt from heaven. When I came here the mornin', she was up and gay and lively as a cricket. Then all at once she got up on her feet and said to me 'Mary Margaret, I'm dyin', and down she fell on her face." She sniffed loudly. "And what's to become of me? Heaven knows where I'll find anyone so kindly and considerate as Miss Doll, the little darlin'."

"Now, now, now," Jake said absentmindedly and comfortingly. First the midget, then Angela Doll. Tonight's floor show. The Casino. Max Hook. Helene.

The house physician, looking professional and bored, came out from the bedroom, locking his case.

"She's dead, is it?" the maid moaned, sniffing again. "Should I be going in and closing her eyes?"

"No," the doctor snapped, "but you could be going in and putting cold towels on her head." He glared at Jake. "There's nothing the matter with her, Mr. Justus, except that she must have taken some kind of dope last night. One of those things that wear off, and then come back and hit you again. She'll be all right. All she needs is sleep." He started to open the door.

"Wait a minute," Jake said desperately. "Will she come to in time for tonight's show?"

The doctor opened the door. "She may," he said crisply, "and she may not. Time will tell." He closed the door quietly.

Jake dug his fingernails into his hat brim. "The next thing," he told himself, "is for the whole Casino chorus to come down with measles."

He tiptoed into the bedroom. Angela Doll lay in the exact center of the big bed, dead to this or any other world, looking like just what her name implied, a mixture of angel and doll.

The maid came in from the bathroom, a cold wet cloth in her hand, and looked down at the sleeping girl. "I've never seen anything so beautiful," she sobbed, "since my aunt Bridie's wake." She laid the cloth over Angela Doll's forehead.

"You take good care of her," Jake said. He drew a long breath and said, "You take damned good care of her." He tiptoed into the living room, picked up the telephone and called Malone to tell him what had happened. What was he going to do if, on top of the midget's murder, he had to fill in an act to replace Angela Doll!

Malone's answer, just before he hung up, was hardly helpful.

"All right," Jake said grimly to himself, going out in the hall, "I'll find two acts for tonight's show— one bad, and the other worse."

He hailed a taxi in front of the hotel and drove to the Casino. Al Omega's band was there holding rehearsal, and Artie Clute waved the bow of his bull fiddle at Jake as he passed by the door.

The overturned chair still lay on the floor in Jake's office. He picked it up, swearing under his breath. Someday he hoped to meet the guy who'd conked him on the head. But right now— He sat down in the chair, picked up the phone, and began dealing with the problem of tonight's show.

After a half hour of telephoning, he'd gotten nowhere.

Jake lit a cigarette and glared at the offending telephone.

"I'll have a show tonight," he said indignantly, "if I have to go out there myself and juggle plates." He rubbed the aching spot on his head with one hand. "Of course," he reflected, "Angela Doll may still be able to make it. The doctor said"— He paused in his thought, staring into space.

"Just one more thing," he said grimly to himself, "will be the camel that tries to grasp at a straw." He smiled wryly and thought, "Malone should have said that."

The phone rang.

Jake stared at it for a moment before he picked up

the receiver. He had a hunch that, whatever the message was, he didn't want to know about it.

It was a hoarse, ugly voice that spoke to him. "I'm calling for Max Hook," the voice said. Max Hook never talked on the telephone himself.

Jake cast one despairing glance around the Casino office and thought, "Well, it *was* a nice night club. I *did* enjoy owning it." He said, "Yes, this is Mr. Justus," as pleasantly as he could, into the phone, and waited.

Max Hook, the voice explained, would like to see Mr. Justus right away. And the matter was urgent.

Chapter Twenty-One

FOUR HUNDRED and ninety-nine sheep had jumped over the fence. The five hundredth, a particularly silly-looking old sheep with a long, sad face, balked and refused to jump.

Helene sat up in bed, ran her hands through her blonde hair, and said, "The hell with it."

Not that she wasn't tired. It seemed to her that her bones were fairly shuddering with tiredness. But that had nothing to do with dropping off into a nice, peaceful slumber.

"After all," she said to an imaginary Jake, "Lord knows I tried to sleep. I did all the things you told me to do. I took a bath, and washed my face, and brushed my hair, and went to bed just as though it was two o'clock at night and not two in the afternoon."

She hadn't slept, but she had dreamed. A restless, half-waking, half-sleeping dream made up of the past night's experiences, the anxieties of the present, and

the terrors still to come in the future. She'd thought
of Allswell McJackson and his dilemma, and suddenly
Allswell had appeared, a magician's cloak over his
shoulders, saying, "I couldn't have done this trick if I
weren't twelve feet tall." Then she'd turned over, trying to find a softer spot in the pillow and to think of
something else. The melody of "The Object of My
Affections" began to run insanely through her head,
and Artie Clute played it over and over on his bull
fiddle, which suddenly turned into Annette Ginnis
and, as suddenly, turned into a small grey kitten
which began to spin around like a top in the center
of the room.

Helene had turned over in bed and murmured,
"The object of my affection. But the kitten couldn't
have been Annette." Then she had been entirely
awake for a moment, wondering how soon Jake would
call. Her eyelids closed and she drowsed again. Allswell McJackson came into the room carrying a basket
of eggs which he turned into a multitude of small grey
kittens. He said, "The midget can't be dead. Because
I am the midget."

There hadn't been any dreams after that, only a
long period of lying with her eyes closed, pretending
she was asleep, while thoughts raced through her
brain. Jake. Tonight's show at the Casino. Annette
Ginnis. Eleven silk stockings, all different sizes. Allswell McJackson. Betty Royal. The fiddle case standing empty outside their door. Annette Ginnis. The
drugged whiskey. Annette Ginnis, Annette Ginnis.

She began counting sheep then, and the five-hundredth sheep, the one who'd refused to leap over the fence, leered at her and said, "I'm Annette Ginnis, and I'm probably dead by now."

That was when Helene sat up in bed, swung her feet down to the carpet, stared at her bare toes, and said, "The hell with it."

What on earth could be in that box Pen Reddick had to find? A secret in Pen Reddick's life, something too terrible to tell? If the midget had been doing a little fancy blackmail, it might have led to murder. But Pen Reddick had told Jake, "It wasn't blackmail. Something more damnable. Something deadlier."

Helene yawned, stretched, and said, "I can make up lost sleep any time. But to go to bed in the middle of the afternoon is downright silly."

She reached for a cigarette, lit it, stared at the pale-grey smoke curling up toward the lampshade, and tried to remember all of her half-waking dream. She had an uneasy feeling that it had told her something, reminded her of some one important fact that had been buried in her thoughts under the layers and layers of other thoughts. But all she could think of was the kitten, the grey kitten, and the sheep that had leered at her, and said, *"I'm Annette Ginnis. And I'm probably dead by now!"*

Helene gasped. That was it! Facts began to pile up in her mind. Annette Ginnis knew about the midget's racket. Annette Ginnis knew who'd been helping the midget. And there had been a look of mute terror in her eyes when Helene had left, after Mildred Goldsmith had arrived.

She picked up the phone and called the Casino. No one answered. She called Malone. He snapped, "Go to sleep. And if you've got to worry about someone, worry about me," and hung up before she could say another word.

It took Helene thirty seconds to make up her mind, and two minutes to dress. The last touch of lipstick was applied in the taxi.

At the door of Annette Ginnis's apartment, she paused. Suppose the whole thing had been her imagination running wild? Suppose she were to find Mildred Goldsmith and Annette having a pleasant little feminine chat, with everything quiet and serene?

In that case, she could always be looking for a lost cigarette case. She tapped lightly at the door.

There was no answer. She knocked again, louder, finally pounded. Still no answer.

For a moment she stood there in the hall, trying to convince herself that Annette and Mildred Goldsmith had gone out to the beauty parlor, or to lunch, or to the movies. But there was a cold, uncomfortable sensation at the back of her neck. Annette had been in no condition to go out. And there had been that look of terror in her childlike eyes!

One good thing about being the wife of a night club owner, she told herself grimly on her way down in the elevator, was that you know all the apartment-hotel managers on the near-North Side!

Miss Ginnis had been ill, she explained suavely to the manager, and now she didn't answer her door. There was probably no cause for alarm, but just in case—

The manager understood, and was politely obliging. He rode up in the elevator with her himself, carrying the passkey.

"Has Miss Ginnis had any visitors this morning?" she asked. Keeping one's voice steady wasn't such a trick, when you knew how to do it.

The elevator boy shook his head. "Not as far as I know. Just yourself. 'Course, I can't keep track of everybody gets off at the twelfth floor."

Mildred Goldsmith could have slipped up to Annette's room and slipped away again, unnoticed. She could have gotten off at another floor and walked up or down a few flights. And too, there was always the self-service freight elevator at the far end of the building.

But she, Helene, had seen her. Helene shivered, and wondered if Mildred Goldsmith was out gunning for her, right at this moment.

It was an unpleasant feeling to walk down the carpeted hall of an apartment hotel, chatting idly with the manager and knowing that you'd find a murdered girl at the end of your walk. They paused for a moment outside the door. The hotel manager knocked several times; finally looked questioningly at Helene.

"Of course," Helene said, between cold lips, "she might have gone out. But since she was ill, I thought it would be best to make sure."

"Yes indeed," the manager said uneasily. He slipped the passkey into the door, opened it, and stepped inside. Helene drew a long breath, and followed.

"She must have gone out," Helene said. The cold began to flow over her entire body. "I'm afraid I've bothered you for nothing."

"Quite all right," the manager said, smiling. Then, *"Mrs. Justus!"*

"I'm not going to scream," Helene said.

Through the half-open closet door she could see the feet in their absurd little suède shoes, hanging limp against a rose satin evening dress. She could see the noose and, even from where she stood, she knew it was made of long, honey-colored silk stockings.

"The other eleven stockings," she whispered. "The rest of them."

But where was the twelfth pair?

"I'd better call the police," the hotel manager said.

"Yes," Helene said quietly. "I think you'd better."

Suddenly she found herself staring at those dangling feet. Black suède shoes with absurd high heels, elaborately studded with nail-heads. But no stockings.

"Just a minute," she said hoarsely.

The noose was slender, delicate. Not like the knotted one that had suspended the tiny body of the midget.

"Please, Mrs. Justus!" the hotel manager said. "Don't distress yourself. I'll call the police, and—"

Helene didn't hear him. She swung open the closet door. The noose was not made of eleven silk stockings, but only two.

She felt a strange, cold spasm in her stomach as she spun the body around from where it faced the wall.

It was not Annette Ginnis. It was Mildred Goldsmith.

Chapter Twenty-Two

"**N**o, my boy," Malone repeated for about the tenth time, "you haven't a thing to worry about. You couldn't be in better hands."

He looked thoughtfully over the rim of his glass of rye at Pen Reddick.

"Of course," he added slowly, "you'd make it a lot easier for me if you'd tell me what's in that damned box."

Pen Reddick shook his head. "Outside of what I'm interested in, I don't know what's in the box. And as far as my personal interest is concerned, I told you, I'll show it to you as soon as the box is in my hands, and I won't tell you any more about it until then."

The little lawyer sighed. "You're a stubborn guy, aren't you? All right then, we'll do it the hard way." He frowned into his glass.

"I've told you everything I can," Pen Reddick said.

"The rest is up to you." He glanced at his watch, and reached for his hat.

"Just a minute," Malone said, motioning him to stay put. "One more, before you go." He raised his voice and called, "Joe. Two more ryes." As an afterthought, he said, "Two double ryes."

"One thing more," Pen Reddick said. "If the box doesn't come to me unopened, the deal is off."

"Oh, sure, sure, sure," Malone said quickly. He waited while the bartender brought the two more ryes to their table, and then said, "Under the circumstances, I guess the only way to deal with this is to put the cart before the stable door." He paused. "I mean lock the cart after the stable door is stolen."

"You mean——" Pen Reddick began.

Malone waved him to silence. "*I* know what I mean. The way to find this blasted box is to find who murdered the midget. Because whoever murdered the midget probably has the box."

"I don't see——" Pen Reddick began again.

"Shut up," Malone said amiably, looking into space. "That box must contain something the murderer wanted. Because the midget was blackmailing the murderer, and that's why——"

Pen Reddick interrupted him to say, "But as far as I know, the midget never blackmailed anybody."

Malone drew a long breath. "You sure do want to make it hard for me, don't you?" He looked moodily into his glass. "What time did you and Betty Royal join forces last night, to start in this wild-brother chase?"

"It was"—Pen Reddick frowned, thinking. "It must have been about two o'clock. I went to the Casino last night, but I went straight home after the late show. Then Betty called me from some all-night drugstore and asked me to come there right away, and I did."

"Fine," Malone said. "And when did you learn that the midget had been murdered?"

Pen Reddick blinked. "When I came into the hotel this morning," he said, "to see Mr. Justus. The elevator boy told me. But why—"

"Never mind why," Malone said. "Now, do you know where Betty Royal was last night, in the hour or two before she telephoned you?"

"No," Pen Reddick said in a puzzled tone.

"For that matter," the little lawyer went on mercilessly, "does anyone know where *you* were between twelve and two last night?"

The young man shook his head slowly.

"That's all I wanted to know," Malone said. "You can go home now."

Pen Reddick rose, picked up his hat, and stood beside the table, hesitating. "Look here," he said. "Do you think I—"

"I don't know," Malone growled. "I haven't the faintest idea. But if I do what you engaged me to do, and if I find out that *you* stole the box, and that *you* murdered the midget, then you still owe me that four thousand bucks—less two hundred," he added hastily. "And," he went on before Pen Reddick could speak, "if you did murder him, I'm the best defense lawyer who ever came down the pike, and we'll talk about the size of that fee later."

He sat in gloomy solitude for a few minutes after Pen Reddick had gone, hoping the young man hadn't murdered Jay Otto, the Big Midget, and wondering what the hell was in that precious box. He wondered even more what he was going to do about it.

Well, first he was going to talk to Ruth Rawlson, and find out how she had known the midget was dead. He glanced at the clock on the wall of Joe the Angel's City Hall Bar. Ruth Rawlson would be picking out a white evening dress about twenty minutes from now. Time for one more quick one. He signaled to Joe.

Then, after he'd talked to Ruth Rawlson—hell, he'd think about that later.

A shadow fell across the table, and Malone looked up to see the towering figure of Lou Goldsmith, the slot-machine king.

"I'm glad to see you," Lou Goldsmith said. "I was just coming over to your office." He raised his voice a trifle and said, "Joe! A double gin." Then he leaned his elbows on the table and looked at the lawyer. "Malone, I've decided I'm going to kill my wife."

Malone downed the rest of his drink, lit a cigar, and said very thoughtfully, "Well, I'm glad you have the foresight to see a lawyer first. It always helps in court if a lawyer has helped to plant the evidence."

"You think I'm kidding, don't you?" Lou Gold-smith said. "Joe, bring Mr. Malone whatever he's drinking." He added, "So you think I'm kidding."

Malone looked at the big man through a haze of cigar smoke. Lou Goldsmith's face was lined and haggard, his eyes were red-rimmed from lack of sleep. The last remaining wisps of greyish hair on the top of his head were all this-way-and-that. He needed a shave.

"No," Malone said calmly. "I don't think you're kidding. And"—he regarded the end of his cigar—"I don't know that I blame you much, either."

Lou Goldsmith seemed to relax a little. He lit his own cigar. "Good old Malone. I knew I could depend on you. So you'll defend me in court?"

"Sure," Malone told him, "if they catch you. And I never lost a client yet." He sipped slowly at the rye Joe had set before him, and told himself firmly that this would be his last drink before he met Ruth Rawl-son at the Casino tonight.

"That woman!" Lou Goldsmith said. He ran a big, short-fingered hand over his jowls, pinched the nape of his neck, and then scratched his back hair. "Malone, I always give her everything she asks for." He rested his head on his hand.

The lawyer looked thoughtfully at Lou Goldsmith, at his Finchley suit and his barrel stomach, at his seven-dollar necktie and his drawn face and thinning hair, and remembered the tough, gangling boy of the old bootlegging and gangster days, who'd risen to become an even tougher and just as gangling bookie, and finally rolled his dough down the right alley with the slot-machine control as the prize. Lou Goldsmith hadn't monkeyed around with women; he'd been too busy. Not until he met the hard-eyed and soft-faced, glittering blonde who called herself Mildred Montgomery, now Mildred Goldsmith.

Tough old Lou Goldsmith, who could lick—and had—his weight in gangsters, being led, or misled, around by a shrewd, conniving little blonde he could crush with one sweep of his big hairy paw!

"Well," Malone said, "before you take the step, tell me when and where and how."

"Last night," Lou Goldsmith began hoarsely. He gulped the rest of his gin, coughed, and said, "Strangle her. With"—He coughed again, rose to his feet, mouthed, "Pard'n me," and staggered off in the direction of the men's room.

For a moment Malone sat nursing his cigar, resisting the impulse to drop everything and look after Lou Goldsmith. It was an impulse that had nothing to do with preventing a probable murder. Probable, because when Lou Goldsmith said, "I'm going to kill so-and-so," he didn't kid. No, that wasn't it. Frankly, Malone explained to his cigar ash, he hoped that Lou Goldsmith would strangle his wife, with whatever came to hand. But in the meantime, someone had to look after Lou Goldsmith.

But also in the meantime, he reminded himself someone had to find out who'd murdered the midget, someone had to locate the midget's private strongbox, someone had to quiz Ruth Rawlson about how she'd known of the midget's murder. "And all of those guys," he added to himself, "are me."

He went up to the bar, called Joe the Angel off to one side, and pulled a fifty-dollar bill out of his wallet. "Take my check and what I owe you out of this," he said. "And wait a minute, Joe." His voice dropped to a whisper. 'When Lou Goldsmith comes out of the toilet, buy him about nine drinks on the house. When he passes out, call a cab, throw him in it, and shoot him over to my hotel. I'll call up and arrange to have the bellhop haul him up to my room and park him there."

"You betcha," Joe the Angel said. He added in a half whisper, "I thought he didn't look so good when he came in." He performed a quick adding operation on the back of a bar check and began counting out Malone's change. "You just leave it to me."

"Thanks, pal," Malone said. He scooped up his change, slid the silver into one pocket and the bills into another, dived into the phone booth and called his hotel to arrange for the reception of Mr. Goldsmith, and went out into the street.

The first thing to do was to talk to Ruth Rawlson and find out how she'd known of the midget's murder. Malone looked at his watch, and waved to a cab. This time, he told himself, he was going to be tough. All through the short drive he kept on giving himself a pep talk.

He hopped out of the cab, paid the driver, and

pushed his way through the glass doors into a bewildering vista of cut-glass perfume bottles, stockings, gloves, and knickknacks. Other men might have been awed or alarmed, but not Malone. He'd been there before. He waved familiarly at the girl at the stocking counter, and went on up to the third floor. Yes, Miss Rawlson was here, in the fitting rooms. Malone headed for them. He'd been there before, too.

"I'm afraid you can't see Miss Rawlson now, Mr. Malone. She's trying on dresses."

"Nonsense," Malone said cheerfully. "Which room is she in?"

"Number three. But you can't—"

"Since when?" Malone said. He knocked on the door of number three, and called, "It's me. Malone."

Ruth Rawlson said, "Oh!" in a startled voice, and then, "Wait a minute."

The little lawyer felt a sudden flash of excitement. By now *Bettina's* would have finished with Ruth Rawlson's face and hair. He could hardly wait to see how she looked.

She looked, when the door was opened for him, like something straight out of an illustration for "Amazing Stories". She had been between dresses when Malone knocked, and now she was wrapped in a white, sheet-like robe. Her face and hair were covered with what looked like a semi-transparent bag, through which he could only see the vaguest outlines and no colors.

"It's to protect Miss Rawlson's hair and make-up,"

the girl explained in answer to Malone's questioning look, "when she slips dresses over her head." She smiled tactfully, said, "I'll be back in a few minutes," and left.

"You dear man!" Ruth Rawlson said throatily. "I was just thinking about you." The head covering gave her voice an odd, muffled quality.

"Be tough, now," Malone reminded himself. He drew a long breath. "Ruth," he said firmly. "Miss Rawlson. You told Angela Doll the midget was dead, didn't you?"

She nodded. The head covering rattled faintly. "Not anyone else, just Angela. She's always been such a dear, dear friend. And I thought that after the take-off on her act, she'd be glad to know he was dead."

"Was she?" Malone asked very casually.

"She didn't seem to be interested," Ruth Rawlson said, shaking her head.

"Now," Malone said. "What time did you call her up?"

"Oh gracious," Ruth Rawlson said, in a small voice, "I haven't the faintest idea. I've always had such a poor sense of time. All my life. You've no idea how many times I've been late for appointments—"

"I'm sure you were forgiven," Malone said. "Last night"— He paused, looking thoughtful. "It must have been before Jake sent you home in a cab." She nodded, and he went on, "That means it was—quite a while before the murder was officially discovered. So how did you find out about it?"

There was a moment's silence before she said angrily, "Are you accusing me of murdering him?"

"No, no, no," Malone said hastily. "But it's damned important to know how you found out."

"Oh," Ruth Rawlson said. Her voice was very small. "Because the person who told me must have been the murderer."

"Something like that," Malone said.

"In that case," she declared, "I won't tell you who it was. I may be shielding a criminal from justice, but I simply couldn't do it. It would haunt me all my life if I did such a thing, Mr. Malone. All my life."

Malone sighed. "Now look here," he said firmly. "You wouldn't be turning anyone over to the police if you told me. All you'd be doing is help me out of a difficulty. I'm not a policeman: I'm a lawyer."

"Oh dear!" she said. "I don't know what to do. If I do tell you, will you promise and cross your heart and hope to die that you won't go right away and tell the police?"

"I promise," Malone said. "I won't tell them a damned word. Now, who was it?"

Ruth Rawlson said, "I don't know."

"Damn it," Malone began.

"It was a voice," she added.

"A—for the love of Mike!" He caught himself just in time, and went on in his gentlest voice, "I thought you trusted me."

"I do," she said unhappily. "Mr. Malone, I'll tell you the truth, the whole truth." Her tone was that of a worried child. "It was that bottle of liquor on the midget's dressing table. I knew he wouldn't mind if I went in and helped myself, but I felt funny about doing it without asking him. You can understand that, can't you, Mr. Malone?"

"Of course," Malone said sympathetically.

"So I went into the telephone booth and called him up at the hotel. At least I meant to call him up, but the most awful voice answered the telephone."

"What kind of a voice?" Malone asked. There was a sudden excitement in his eyes.

"Oh, a simply terrible voice. Crude, and hoarse, and—well, just frightful. And I asked to speak to Mr. Otto and the voice said, 'Mr. Otto can't come to the phone because he's been murdered,' and then laughed —Oh, horribly!" She shuddered. "Can you imagine what I felt?"

"I can indeed," Malone said. He wished that her hands weren't covered by the robe. He'd have liked to pat one of them.

"I just stood there and thought about it, and then I called up Angela. Oh Mr. Malone, that voice! I'm afraid it's going to haunt me, always." She gave a little gasp.

"Now never mind," Malone soothed her. "It's all over with. Try to forget it." He rose. "I'm sorry to have had to bother you again, but it was important. Remember—tonight, at the Casino."

"I'll remember," she breathed.

Malone stood for a moment in front of the store,

looking at the still cloudy sky, thinking the whole thing over. A hoarse, crude-sounding voice. That didn't tell him much. But it cleared up the matter of how Ruth Rawlson had learned about the murder.

Just the same—what next?

He took out a cigar and began slowly unwrapping it. There was one angle to this he hadn't followed up yet: Johnny Oscar, one of Max Hook's gunmen. He had been involved in the marriage-annulment scheme the midget had been working. Chances were that he hadn't murdered the midget himself, since he'd apparently been accompanying Ned Royal and Annette Ginnis at the time of the murder. Though of course the chronology of that trio's peregrinations was still uncertain. But in any case—he might be the lead for Malone to follow, straight to the murderer and to Pen Reddick's box, and to Malone's $4000 fee.

The thing to do was to see Max Hook. Johnny Oscar might not prove to be talkative, but Malone had a shrewd hunch that Max Hook wouldn't like it if he learned what had been going on. It was a cinch Max Hook wasn't mixed up in it himself, as it was entirely out of his line. He wouldn't like it, and he was an expert at making people talk.

At least, Malone reflected, it was something worth trying. He hailed a cab, and directed the driver to take him to the Lake Shore drive building that housed the gambling czar's palatial apartment.

On the way, he began thinking over what Ruth

Rawlson had told him. Unfortunately, he had gotten too far to turn back and question her again before he remembered that there hadn't been any telephone calls for the midget at his apartment before two o'clock.

Chapter Twenty-Three

"I'LL HAVE TO CALL the police," the hotel manager said, looking helplessly at Helene.

"It's customary," she said, between cold lips.

She sat down on the couch where, a few hours before, she'd talked with Annette Ginnis.

Annette Ginnis hadn't murdered Mildred Goldsmith. She was sure of that. Because Annette hadn't murdered the midget, and only the murderer of the midget—and Jake, Malone, and herself—knew that the midget had been hanged with a rope made of long silk stockings.

The manager reached for the telephone. Helene held up a restraining hand. "Wait a minute."

She frowned. "Before you call the police, call downstairs and find out if anyone here happened to notice Miss Ginnis leaving the hotel."

The manager stared at her for a moment, then obeyed.

No, no one had seen Miss Ginnis leave.

She could have slipped out by the freight elevator, Helene reflected. But there had been a third person in the room—the murderer of the midget and of Mildred Goldsmith. Somehow she doubted that Annette Ginnis had left that room of her own volition.

She picked up the telephone and called Malone's office.

Mr. Malone was out. No, the girl didn't know where he was, nor when he'd be back, if he came back at all.

She tried the hotel and the Casino. No one seemed to know where Jake was.

Meantime, something had to be done about Annette Ginnis. And done fast.

She slammed down the telephone, stood up, and picked up her purse.

"Call the police," she said, "and tell them about this."

"But," he said helplessly, "you can't leave here now."

"Oh yes I can," Helene told him, "and I've got to." She opened the door.

"But—the police—"

"Will raise particular hell," she finished for him. "I'll worry about that when the time comes."

The elevator boy was helpful, but vague. He hadn't seen Mrs. Goldsmith that morning. Nor had he noticed anyone getting off at Annette Ginnis' floor. A dozen people might have gotten off there, but he hadn't paid much attention.

She hailed a taxi in front of the hotel, and said, "Just drive slowly up Michigan avenue. I want to think."

Four people had known about the multiple-marriage racket of which Annette had been the key person, up to the time of the midget's death. Those four were Annette herself, the midget, Mildred Goldsmith, and Johnny Oscar.

The midget and Mildred Goldsmith had been murdered, hanged by long silk stockings—Mildred, by her own stockings. Annette was missing. That left Johnny Oscar.

She called to the driver, "Stop at the nearest place where I can telephone."

From a drugstore phone booth she called von Flanagan, using her extra-sweetest voice as she asked where Johnny Oscar lived.

He told her, naming an address on West Schiller street, before suddenly catching himself and saying, "Hey? What do you want to know for?" As she started to answer something about idle curiosity, he said, "Wait a minute, there's a call coming in."

Helene didn't wait. She hung up fast. That other call would be the word of Mildred Goldsmith's murder.

Again she tried to reach Jake, or Malone. Again she was unsuccessful.

She returned to the cab, her brows knit. "Just go on up the Avenue."

The driver grinned at her. "Still thinking, huh?"

The telephone call to von Flanagan had been a wild hunch, but her wild hunches in the past had been pretty reliable. If Johnny Oscar had intended to murder Annette, he'd have done it right there and then, at the same time as Mildred Goldsmith. Evidently, that wasn't his plan. Perhaps he meant to try and frighten Annette into keeping quiet about the affair, and maybe even go on with the racket, with him as the boss. He'd murdered Mildred Goldsmith, and forced Annette to leave with him. But where would he take her?

Why not to his own home?

"Drive west on Schiller street," she told the driver.

She had no idea of what she intended to do. Certainly, not walk right in and say, "Where is Annette Ginnis?" But she had to do something, at least to confirm her own suspicion if she could, and then call the police.

At the corner nearest the address von Flanagan had given her, she paid off the cab. Now what?

Perhaps if she walked very slowly past the house, she could see in through the windows, or hear or notice something that would tell her if the hunch was right.

It was the third building from the corner, an old-fashioned house which had been cut up into flats. She slowed down as she came to it, and groaned with disappointment. The windows were not only grated, but every blind in the house was down. There wasn't a sign of life around the place.

Still, the blinds might be down because Annette Ginnis—

"Don't move, Mrs. Justus," a voice said behind her, "and don't make a sound."

Something hard was pressed against her back.

"Just walk quietly up the front steps," the voice went on, "and no funny business."

Helene obeyed, filled with a cold fury rather than fear.

At the shabby door, an arm reached around her to unlock the door.

"Step right inside, Mrs. Justus."

The little hall was black as the bottom of a coal mine. Helene felt herself growing uncomfortably cold.

A light was switched on, and she turned around. The man with the gun was not hard to recognize, from the descriptions she had of him. It was Johnny Oscar.

"Where's Annette Ginnis?" she said impulsively.

"I haven't the faintest idea," the gunman said, "but I know where you are, and where you're going to stay. So Annette talked to you, did she? And now you're spying on me. Well, I can't have you running around loose with that much information in your head." He smiled mirthlessly.

"What are you going to do?" she asked.

"I don't know yet," he snapped. "I gotta figure something out. But you're gonna stay right here." Again he smiled. "Make yourself perfectly to home.

The place is yours. Only don't try to get out of it, because there's nobody lives upstairs, and you couldn't bust out through those windows in a lifetime, and all the doors is locked. And there's no telephone, and you could yell your head off here, and nobody'd hear a sound."

He opened the door.

"Wait," Helene began.

But Johnny Oscar had gone. She heard the key turn in the lock.

Of all ridiculous things to happen, right here in the center of Chicago! Helene leaned against the wall, her hands clenched at her sides. Damn fool, she told herself. You could have told the police, and let them break in and search here. Or you could have waited till you found Jake or Malone. But no, you had to rush right out and play detective. And look where it landed you.

It seemed odd to her that she wasn't afraid, only angry.

Well, she reflected, since you're here, you might as well explore. Annette Ginnis might still be here. And there must be some way to get out of this place.

It was a four-room flat, with a staircase leading down to the basement. There didn't seem to be any way of getting to the rooms above. At first she tried opening the blinds, only to find that they were nailed shut, save for one tiny window in what appeared to be the bedroom. Evidently Johnny Oscar liked his privacy.

There was a dusty little living room, furnished with a moth-eaten davenport and easy chair, and a few cigarette-scarred tables. There was a disordered bedroom, with dirty sheets on an unmade bed, and soiled and wrinkled clothing littering the floor. There was an equally disordered bathroom, and a kitchen where a few day-old dishes stood in the sink, and a half-empty bottle of cheap bourbon stood on the battered table. But there wasn't a sign of Annette Ginnis, nor anything to indicate she'd ever been there.

Helene lit a cigarette, dusted off a chair, and sat down to think it over.

She could hardly break down one of the doors, nor saw her way through one of the gratings on the windows. But—suddenly a light seemed to flash on in her mind.

People must be going up and down Schiller street. If she could possibly pry loose the blinds on one of the windows, and break the glass, then she could call for help!

She inspected the blinds at the front of the house. Yes, with a chisel, she could do it.

For a few minutes she searched feverishly through the house. There was a big kitchen knife—but no, it wouldn't be strong enough. Perhaps if she looked in the cellar—

She switched on the light at the top of the cellar stairs, and stood there for a moment, hesitating. It looked gloomy and uninviting, if not downright fearsome.

Come now, Helene, she asked herself, you know there's no one here. What are you afraid of?

Mice, she answered herself, truthfully.

This was no time to be afraid of mice. Not if, somewhere in that cellar, there was a chisel or any tool she could use to break out of the house before Johnny Oscar came back. She drew a long breath, and went slowly down the stairs.

The cellar was divided into two rooms, the farther one evidently serving as a furnace room and coal bin. In the room at the bottom of the stairs was a collection of trunks and boxes, broken furniture, a pile of kindling wood, and a bin full of empty bottles.

Helene stopped suddenly at the foot of the stairs, staring in front of her.

There was a table in the center of the room, and on it was what she had been seeking, a sturdy hammer and a chisel, both brand new.

Now, having found them, she didn't even look at them.

Because, there in the center of the table, stood a small, leather-covered, metal strongbox. She knew it immediately for the one Pen Reddick wanted, the midget's box.

She took two steps toward the table, and stopped again. Somewhere overhead a door closed.

She stood there for a long moment, listening, her stomach frozen into a lump of ice. There were faint sounds from overhead. Then suddenly she heard a soft click, and the cellar was plunged into darkness.

At almost the same instant the door closed at the head of the stairs.

How long she stood there, she never knew. There was silence now overhead. A long silence.

At last she found the courage to move again. Perhaps there was another light switch down in the cellar, or perhaps she could make her way back up the stairs and turn on the switch just inside the door.

She moved slowly and cautiously through the inky darkness, feeling her way with every step, holding her hands outstretched before her. Once she bumped against the table, and realized she'd been going in the wrong direction. She tried again, moving carefully, until her fingers touched a wall. It was, though, the wooden partition that divided the cellar into two rooms. She was lost, now.

She drew a long breath, and stood for a moment, trying to figure out in which direction to move. Perhaps by going along the wooden partition, using it as a guide, she could get back to the wall out of which the cellar stairs opened. She felt her way along, stumbling once over a box and getting splinters in her fingers, until she came to the door in the partition. She paused there a moment, and then moved on, her arms outstretched, feeling for the wall beyond the door.

Suddenly her hand touched something. Something warm. Something alive. A human face. There, within arms' reach of her, in the darkness.

She heard a faint little gasp, and something fell at her feet.

This was what people meant when they said "frozen with terror." This was what happened to you in nightmares. For a moment Helene wondered if she was going to drop dead, right there on the spot.

There wasn't a sound anywhere. Little by little Helene could feel the blood coming back into her face again. Instinctively she reached in her pocket for a cigarette, and immediately cursed herself for being, if not the biggest fool in history, at least the biggest fool in the world.

There had been a folder of matches in her pocket all the time. With four matches in it.

She tore out a match with shaking fingers, lighted it carefully, and bent down to inspect whatever lay at her feet.

The faint glow from the match fell on the tear-stained, soot-streaked, unconscious face of Annette Ginnis.

Chapter Twenty-Four

MAX HOOK'S living room, Jake observed, had been redecorated. The last time he had seen it there had been pale-rose taffeta curtains held back with enormous satin ribbon bows, a multitude of little decorative lamps, and delicately tinted pink walls. Now, the walls were done in an exquisitely designed paper, grey-white scrolls against a darker, purplish grey; the windows were covered with what he suspected to be light-mauve chiffon in thick, billowing folds; the lamps had been replaced by chromium indirect-lighting fixtures. But the frail, beautifully carved, satin-covered furniture remained—now upholstered in violet—as did the cut-glass vases, the enameled cigarette boxes, the white jade statuettes and the painted china ash trays. One more thing remained: the big painted-pine rolltop desk, scarred and dented, which Max Hook had brought with him from his first tiny office on the West Side.

"Pretty, isn't it?" Max Hook said. He had a voice

like a radio announcer advertising a facial cream. "I always like to have things nice." He swung around in the specially built swivel chair at his desk and faced Jake. He was a mountain of a man, six feet tall and still twice too fat for his height, a jelly-like, quivering fat. His face, with its big, sad eyes, was deceptively gentle and friendly. His head was as bald as an orange. Even his fingers were fat, and they were covered with rings.

"It's beautiful," Jake said, wondering how he was going to talk Max Hook out of wanting his money back.

The big man beamed. "You have excellent taste, Mr. Justus." He carefully fitted a tinted cigarette into a slender jade holder. "I'm sorry to have had to trouble you today—"

"It was no trouble," Jake said. He sat down on one of the silk-upholstered chairs and dropped his hat on the floor. "Now it's like this—"

Max Hook pushed a buzzer beside his desk. "You'll have a drink?"

"Thanks," Jake said. "Rye." He waited until a sallow-faced young man had come in, taken Max Hook's order, and gone away again. "Look here. You know the Casino only opened last night, and you promised me more time than that. And you know that you'll get your money—"

"Money?" Max Hook raised that portion of his forehead where his eyebrows should have been. "Who's talking about money? Me?"

"Well, but—" Jake began.

He was interrupted by the sallow-faced young man bearing a tray with his rye, and a tall glass of some pinkish stuff. Then the Swiss chimes above the door sounded, the young man slid open the peephole, and turned to announce, "Mr. Malone."

"Good!" Max Hook said. "Ask him in."

Jake thought, "Thank God!" and drank his rye, fast.

"I'm glad you got my message," Max Hook said, as Malone came in the door, "but I didn't even hope you'd be so prompt."

"Message?" Malone said. "I didn't get any message. I came to see you on business of my own." He glanced at Jake, said, "What the hell are you doing here?" bounced across the room, and picked up Max Hook's glass. "What in blazes are you drinking? Pink lemonade?" He sipped it, set it down, and said, "Holy mahogany, it's pink champagne." He sat down, fanned himself with his hat before he dropped it on the floor, and said to the sallow-faced young man, "Since I'm invited, I'll take gin. A big one."

"Is it any wonder that I like him?" Max Hook said admiringly to Jake.

Jake waited until Malone's drink had arrived, and then said, in the hope of tipping off Malone, "You say it isn't the money you want to see me about, Mr. Hook?"

"Ah," Max Hook said, "since Mr. Malone didn't

get my message asking him here, let's wait and learn what he wanted to see me about."

"Well, it's like this," Malone said. He lit a cigar and looked disgustedly at the tiny ash tray. "I'm going to open up a night club, pal, and I thought I'd ask you to lend me— Now, you tell us what you wanted."

"A great joker, isn't he?" Max Hook said. "Well gentlemen, since you insist—" He swung his chair around to face them.

"It's too bad you went to night school and studied speaking," Malone growled. "You sounded a lot better when you ran that joint on West Madison."

"Let us not speak of the past," Max Hook said gently, laying his perfumed cigarette aside.

"Oh yes, we shall," Malone said, "the immediate past anyway. What was the tie-up between you and the midget?"

"There was none," Max Hook murmured. "I never saw the midget in my life until last night. A great entertainer, too. Too bad that he was called to such an untimely end."

Malone scowled. "The best thing I can say about you, Max, is that you don't tell lies. But"—he puffed at his cigar—"I heard a certain musician in a certain orchestra now performing at a certain night club declare that he and the other band boys hung out at your crooked joints, because the midget—"

"That's perfectly true," Max Hook said. "But I didn't learn about it until this morning. The rake-off,

if I may use so coarse a term, went to a young gentleman who has been in my employ, and who was, so I
understand, splitting the proceeds with the midget."

Jake shivered involuntarily. He didn't like the way
the Hook had said "who *has* been."

"You can readily understand," Max Hook went on,
"that I could not tolerate anything of the sort."

Malone said, "But that hasn't been all—"

"Please!" Max Hook looked at him gravely. "I
thought you wanted *me* to tell *you*." He paused.
"Then you know about this"—he paused again, his
eyes blazed, and suddenly he snarled—"this God-
damned racket these stinking rats have been working
behind my back." He pinched out his tinted cigarette between two pink fingers.

"We know all about it," Malone said, "or almost all
about it. I came up here today to find out if you did."

"I do now," Max Hook said. "That's why I sent
for Jake Justus here today, and why I tried to reach
you. Because in the first place I won't stand for any of
the boys going into rackets of their own, and in the
second, this business, it's—it's as bad as blackmail."
He drew a long breath, turned purple, and said, "It's
criminal!"

Malone thought of Max Hook's assorted gambling
and vice interests, and of the homicides that had been
unofficially chalked up to his boys, and said nothing.
After all, every man was entitled to his own opinion
about what was criminal.

Jake said, "How did you find out about it?"

Max Hook beamed at him, his composure regained. He picked up another cigarette, this one tinted pale blue. "My dear Mr. Justus, don't you suppose I keep a watch on my boys?" He paused long enough to light the cigarette. "I know all about the marriages and annulments; I know that the midget had a little box containing papers that someone could have used for blackmail purposes; I know that while Mr. Justus was getting the box out of his safe, Johnny Oscar came in and hit him over the head and took the box. I learned all this from the young man who had informed on Johnny Oscar a little earlier in the day and who was following Johnny Oscar."

There was a moment's silence before Malone murmured, "You do get around, don't you?"

"I suggest," Max Hook said, "that you go to Johnny Oscar's and get back the box." He pressed the buzzer again and, when the sallow-faced young man came in, he said, "Give these gentlemen a duplicate key to Johnny's apartment." He beamed at Jake and Malone and said, "I like to keep a check on my boys."

"I see you do," Malone said. "Did Johnny Oscar murder the midget?"

Max Hook shrugged his enormous shoulders. He didn't know, and it wasn't important. Malone knew better than to press him for more information. He tucked the key into his pocket.

At the door, Jake paused. "But what about Johnny Oscar?"

"I think"—Max Hook smiled, a wide, magnificent smile—"I will be able to handle that problem."

Malone walked halfway down the hall to the elevator before he growled, "Well, there goes two bucks for flowers to send to Johnny Oscar's funeral. But at least we know what happened to that damned box." He poked savagely at the elevator button.

"But who killed the midget?" Jake demanded. "Johnny Oscar?"

"Possibly," Malone said. "In which case, all I've got to do is prove that he did, before Max Hook gets around to taking steps." He told Jake about Pen Reddick's visit.

Jake said, "But at the time the midget was murdered—"

"Johnny Oscar is supposed to have been roaming around the city with Annette Ginnis and Ned Royal. We don't know that for sure."

The elevator interrupted further discussion. Out on the sidewalk Malone peered around for a cab and muttered, "I find a guy who might have murdered the midget, and Max Hook is likely to beat me to the draw and do me out of two thousand bucks. What did I ever do that everything should happen to me?"

"Everything doesn't happen to you," Jake said. "I still have tonight's show to worry about." He told what had happened to Angela Doll, just as a cab arrived. Slamming the door, he said wearily, "Well, at least Helene's getting some sleep."

"Schiller street," Malone said to the cab driver.

"What are we going to do when we get there?" Jake asked. "Walk in barehanded? Not," he added, thinking of the bump on his head, "that I wouldn't like to beat him to a jelly, with my bare hands."

"We're going to ring the doorbell, like little gentlemen," Malone said. "And if Johnny Oscar is home, we're going to tell him we've heard that the Hook has designs on his life, and that we just dropped in to tip him off. And we're going to act as if we hadn't the faintest idea he'd ever heard of the midget's box, and sit and have a drink with him, and hope that he'll inadvertently drop us some helpful piece of information. And if he isn't home, we'll go in and search the place."

"Very nice, master mind!" Jake said scornfully. "Especially since, if he isn't there, it's likely that the box isn't there either. And if he is there, we just pay a pleasant little social call and go away again." He frowned out the cab window. "And he probably didn't murder the midget. Johnny Oscar would never have thought up a refinement like those eleven silk stockings."

"My pal!" Malone said bitterly. "Always encouraging. I thought of that myself. But if he didn't murder the midget, he might know who did."

"You don't think he'll tell you," Jake said.

"I'll do magic tricks," Malone said, "and hypnotize him."

The cab dropped them in front of the shabby house on Schiller street. Malone said, "Cheerful-looking place, isn't it?" rang the doorbell, and added, "Let me do the talking."

He rang the bell half a dozen times before he gave up and used Max Hook's duplicate key.

"He may be just inside the door, waiting for company," he warned Jake in a whisper.

Stepping to one side, he gave the door a sudden push. Nothing happened. He led the way into the hall slowly, looking to right and left. After a few steps he paused.

"I guess there's no one home."

The little lawyer peered into the four rooms.

"Nope. Nobody home. Listen for anybody at the door, and we'll take a look around."

"Wait a minute," Jake said. "There's a light in the basement. I can see it through the crack of the door."

Malone tried the door. It was locked, but the key was there. He unlocked it, opened the door, peered down the stairs, and then called, "Who's there?"

There was a moment's silence, and then from the depths below, "Oh good Lord! Malone?"

"*Helene!*" Jake was down the stairs in one bound, Malone at his heels.

They saw Helene sitting on the cellar floor, her face streaked with dirt, her hair disheveled, a small scratch on one cheek. Annette Ginnis was lying on the floor, her head in Helene's lap. The leather-covered metal box was on the table beside them.

"Don't ask questions," Helene said. "Just get us

out of here." She bent over Annette. "You can walk all right, can't you?"

"Yes," Annette said faintly. She struggled to her feet.

"But—" Jake said. He gasped, "Helene, are you all right? What happened? How did you get here? I thought you were—"

"I said, don't ask questions," she said. "Get us out of here first." She struggled to her feet, pulling Annette up with her.

"The box—" Malone said.

Helene said, "Bring it along, and don't *you* ask any questions, either."

Malone took a quick look at her white face, tucked the box under his arm, and said, "I'll run out in the street and get us a taxi. You come on up the stairs."

"No," Helene said. "We'll all run out in the street and get a taxi. I'm not staying here another minute."

Annette Ginnis began to cry. Helene pulled a handkerchief out of her pocket and began an expert nose-wiping job on her as they started up the stairs.

"Johnny Oscar—" Jake began.

"He isn't here," Helene said. "I don't know where he is. I'm not even sure I want to know where he is."

Jake said, "But Helene, tell me—" and Malone said, "Shut up, Jake," in the next second.

Malone had been leading the way up the stairs. Reaching the top, he saw something that he hadn't been able to see coming down the little hall in the other direction. The door of a small closet, near the entrance, stood open.

He said, "Wait a minute," and went on to investigate.

Helene said, "Malone, what is it?" She gasped, and said, "While I was down there, I heard a noise—"

Annette Ginnis moaned faintly.

Malone came back out of the closet. His round face was pale.

"Well," he said, "I know where Johnny Oscar is. And I know where the other eleven silk stockings are, too."

They looked toward the closet. Even from where they stood, they could see the heels of a pair of shiny black oxfords, against the closet wall, six inches from the floor.

Chapter Twenty-Five

"**Y**OU CAN WALK NOW," Helene said firmly. "Just make a little tiny effort."

"I'm sure I can," Annette Ginnis whispered. She reached for Malone's outstretched hand and slowly pulled herself to her feet. For a moment she stood there, swaying; then she managed a very small, very wan smile. "I promise I won't faint again."

A taxicab would be out of the question, Malone had explained. No cabdriver would forget two girls looking the way Helene and Annette looked, especially after Johnny Oscar's murder was made public. And it might possibly be just as well if nobody could prove, later, that they'd been on the scene of the crime.

Malone had been silent, staring into space. Now he said unexpectedly, "Then Johnny Oscar didn't murder the midget. I never really thought so. But I still don't know who did."

"I thought you didn't care," Helene said.

"I care now," Malone told her. "I care two thousand dollars' worth." He told her about Pen Reddick's visit, and the deal they had made.

Before Helene could comment, Jake arrived with the car. For once, Helene let him drive. She sat in the back seat, one arm around Annette.

"We're taking the freight elevator," she announced. "We've already created enough sensation in the lobby for one day. Come to think of it, we ought to send them a bill for entertaining their guests."

Upstairs, she stared around the living room. It had never looked so beautiful to her before.

It looked beautiful to Annette, too. She gave a quick glance around her, and began to cry again.

"I was so frightened," she sobbed. "I never should have gone there."

Helene gasped. "You *went* there?"

"Let her tell it," Jake said. Malone was already in the kitchenette, making coffee.

"I had to," Annette said. "It was the box. I knew I had to get it."

Jake and Helene looked at each other over the girl's head.

"Why?" Helene asked very gently.

"My marriage certificate. To the midget. It was in the box, and I had to get it before anyone saw it. I begged Mildred to tell me where the box was, and she laughed at me and said that if Johnny Oscar didn't already have it, he'd have it—pretty damned quick." She paused to blow her nose.

"Take your time," Jake said.

"I knew they'd keep it and hold it over me—the certificate, I mean. And I knew Mildred had a key to Johnny Oscar's house. So when she was in the bathroom I got the key out of her purse, and went down the hall real quick before she knew I'd gone. And then I went out the back way, and got in a cab, and went right to Johnny Oscar's house."

Malone had returned from the kitchenette. Now he said admiringly, "I wouldn't have thought you had it in you. What would you have done if Johnny Oscar had been there?"

"I don't know," Annette said. "I didn't think of that." A fresh set of tears began to flow.

"Never mind," Jake said. "Helene here hasn't any sense either."

"But he wasn't there," Annette went on. "So I searched, and I found the box. It was down in the cellar, right where you found it, with a hammer and a chisel beside it. And then I heard someone at the door."

"That was us," Helene said. "Me 'n' Johnny Oscar."

"We'll get to you later," Malone told her. "Go on, Annette."

"That's all," Annette whispered, "except that I went up quick and turned off the cellar light, and went back down again. And after a while the light went on again and I heard someone open the cellar door—I didn't know it was Helene—so I ran and hid behind the coal pile, and then someone came downstairs and then the light went out. And I don't know anything else."

"Well anyway," Jake said, "we've got the box. If we can get it open. Maybe we should have brought along that chisel and hammer."

Malone scowled. "We've got the box," he agreed, "but we can't open it, because part of my arrangement with Pen Reddick is that it be delivered to him unopened."

Annette gave a faint little moan.

"Now wait a minute," the lawyer went on. "I'll be present when it's opened. That's part of the agreement too. Pen Reddick isn't even remotely interested in your marriage certificate. So when the box is opened, I'll get the certificate and bring it to you, and you can burn it up with your own little hands."

The first gleam of hope came into Annette's big, tear-filled eyes.

"See?" Helene said cheerfully. "You haven't a thing to worry about. And Jake, you heat a glass of milk while I wash Annette's face and tuck her into bed."

Annette murmured something about going home. Helene shook her head quickly. "You're staying right here for a while." She led Annette into the bedroom.

Jake put the milk on to heat and returned to the living room.

"Max Hook," he said. "Max Hook said he was going to take care of Johnny Oscar. And Johnny Oscar's been murdered."

Malone rolled his cigar between his fingers. "Very nice," he said. "But he said he **was** *going* to, he didn't say he *had*. Johnny Oscar must have been murdered about the time we were talking to Max Hook. And a silk-stocking strangling has never been one of the Hook's methods."

Jake groaned. "It's a mess," he said, "and no matter how hard we try to get out of it, it seems to be our mess." He paused. "It keeps coming back to who knew the midget was dead before his body turned up here at the hotel. If we had the straight dope on who knew, and how—" He paused again. "Did you talk to Ruth Rawlson?"

Malone nodded, a faint flush creeping into his cheeks.

"Well, damn it," Jake said. "Did she tell you anything?"

"She did," Malone told him. "A very interesting story." He went on with Ruth Rawlson's explanation of the "terrible voice" that had answered her call to the midget's apartment.

Jake scowled. "Who has a voice like that—" He stopped and stared at Malone. "But the midget had a couple of calls around three o'clock, and nobody answered. There weren't any calls before that. And Ruth Rawlson couldn't have called up anybody, after two."

"I know," the little lawyer said miserably. "I figured that out for myself. But too late to go back and talk to her again. Don't worry," he added, "I'm going to talk to her tonight."

Jake drew a long breath, swore at Malone, at Ruth Rawlson, at the memory of the midget, and at the world in general. He ended with, "Oh hell, the milk's boiling over," and dashed into the kitchenette.

When fresh milk had been heated and delivered to Helene through the bedroom door, he came back to the living room and sank down in a chair.

"Meantime," he said gloomily, "I still don't know what I'm going to do about tonight's show." He picked up the phone and called Angela Doll's apartment.

Miss Doll was still sleeping. Very soundly.

Malone frowned. "From the symptoms," he said, "it looks to me as if——"

Helene interrupted him, coming in from the bedroom and closing the door quietly behind her. She'd changed her soot-stained dress for one of soft beige wool with an immense gold clip at the throat, washed her face and made it up, and brushed her pale, shining hair.

"Annette's asleep," she reported. "I gave her a sedative and some hot milk, and by the time she wakes up, she'll feel all right again."

"That's just dandy," Malone said, "because I still had a lot of questions to ask Annette, and now you've gone and put her to sleep."

"You'll ask them after six o'clock then," Helene said firmly, "because that's about the time she'll wake up." She lit a cigarette. "And now, I've got something to tell you two. Mildred Goldsmith—"

A thunderous knock at the door interrupted her. Jake opened the door to admit von Flanagan and a thin, sour-faced policeman.

"Well, well," Jake said. "Have you brought a hat and a rabbit with you?"

The big police officer was in no mood for gaiety. His moon face was pink. He stood just inside the door, arms akimbo, and glared reproachfully at Helene.

"It's bad enough to be a cop," he began slowly, "it's worse to be an inspector in the homicide division. But when everybody sets out to make things hard for you, then it's—it's—" He paused, tried to think of a word superlative to "worse," and finally said, "It's awful."

"What's the matter?" Malone said quickly.

Von Flanagan ignored him. He went on looking at Helene. "I don't expect no consideration from common criminals," he continued. "But when somebody you think is a pal goes out of her way to do you dirt"—his face began to turn red, and his voice began to rise in volume—"then it's too damn much, and when a guy gets good and mad he's gotta do something about it, and I hope being tossed in the clink for obstructing justice is going to be a good lesson to you. And I hope—"

"Wait a minute," Helene said. "I can explain everything."

"You'll explain it to a judge," von Flanagan said.

"Helene," Jake said desperately, "what have you done?"

"Ask her what she's done," von Flanagan shouted. "Ask *me* what's she's done." His face had now reached the purple stage. He advanced a few steps across the floor, and shook a forefinger under Helene's nose. "What was the idea," he bellowed, "of walking in and finding that Goldsmith dame had been murdered, and then running out before the cops had a chance to get there?"

Jake said, "*Helene!*"

"It's true," Helene said, in a small voice.

Malone glared at her in his turn. "Why the hell," he demanded, "didn't you tell us about it?"

"When the hell," she answered in simple truthfulness, "have I had a chance?" After a moment's pause she turned to von Flanagan, looking helpless, appealing, and extremely beautiful. "I wasn't trying to—run out. You don't think I'd do a thing like that, do you?"

Von Flanagan looked at her for a moment; then looked down at the carpet. He said, "Well—" making three syllables of it.

"I went to see Annette Ginnis," Helene said, in a hurt voice. "When she didn't answer her door, I got worried about her, and I asked the manager to let me in. I was afraid she might be sick. And then we found—the body. That's all there is to it." She took

out a tiny wisp of lace handkerchief and pressed it
delicately to her nose.

"There, there," von Flanagan said automatically,
in a quieter tone. Then he remembered his errand,
and roared at her, "But why didn't you stay there
until the cops arrived?"

Helene gazed at him with stricken, violet-blue eyes.
"I was so frightened," she whispered. "I wanted to
find Jake. As soon as I found him, I was going to come
right down and see you."

The big police officer stared at her for a moment,
melted under her gaze, and sat down on the sofa, fan-
ning himself with his hat.

"This is the damnedest thing," he said. "Imagine
hanging a dame with her own stockings! Nobody but
another dame would think of that. So now we got to
find this Annette Ginnis, and the Lord only knows
where she might be." He looked up at Helene. "I
don't suppose you have any idea where she might
have gone to, have you?"

"Don't you think I'd tell you?" Helene said innocently.

Von Flanagan sighed. "Nobody ever tells me anything," he said sadly. "I always have to find out everything for myself. And everybody tries to make it hard
for me."

"In another minute," Malone said softly, "I'm going to burst into tears."

Von Flanagan didn't hear him. He looked up at

Helene. "You know you hadn't ought to have done that," he told her, in a tone he might have used to a misbehaving child. "You caused me a lot of trouble. I ought to have you arrested for it, just to teach you a good lesson."

"I'm terribly sorry," Helene said. "I'll never do it again."

Jake said quickly, "How's the magic getting along?"

"Say!" von Flanagan brightened up. "That guy taught me a wonderful trick, just before he left. If you folks had stayed about five more minutes, you'd have seen it." He drew a long piece of string from his pocket. "He made some mistake in it when he was showing me, and damn near took my finger off, but he showed me how to do it right." He advanced toward Malone. "Now hold out your hand and lemme make a loop around your forefinger—"

Malone held out a hand, casting a reproachful glance at Helene, as if saying, "See what I'm doing for your sake?"

"Now," von Flanagan said, "I tie another loop around like this—"

The telephone rang; Jake answered it. It was the desk clerk, asking if Captain von Flanagan was there. His office was trying to reach him.

" 'Scuse me," von Flanagan said, tying one more knot. "Finish this when I get back."

When he returned from the phone, however, he had forgotten all about the trick. "That's what I mean when I say everybody tries to make things hard for me. Some guy called up from a drugstore phone booth to say there was a dead guy at an address on West Schiller street. So it turns out the dead guy is Johnny Oscar who I'd figured out had murdered the midget. And what's more, *he's* been hanged with a bunch of silk stockings." He stood glaring at the trio, as if they were responsible for the whole thing.

"Monotonous, isn't it!" Malone said feebly.

"Imagine a frail little dame like her—like Annette Ginnis—strangling a guy like Johnny Oscar!" von Flanagan said, as though he admired her for it. "Well, we'll pick her up." He walked to the door, paused with one hand on the knob, and said, "If you hear anything from her, lemme know," opened the door and said in a melancholy voice, "And all this when I haven't had a good night's sleep!"

"All this," Malone muttered after the door was closed, "when I haven't had any night's sleep! And how in hell do I get this string off my hand?"

"Call von Flanagan back," Jake said unfeelingly, "or call in Allswell McJackson who seems to be running around loose. Oh—here's a pair of scissors."

Malone's remarks, as he cut his hand free, were almost unnecessarily to the point.

"You don't suppose by some wild chance von Flanagan could be right?" Jake asked slowly. "You don't suppose that instead of just walking out on Mildred Goldsmith this morning, Annette hanged her first?"

Helene said, *"Annette Ginnis?"*

"She isn't strong enough," Malone said, "to have hanged a mouse. And she certainly didn't hang Johnny Oscar."

"Well," Jake said, "it was the only idea I had."

Malone relit his cigar and stared out the window. "At least," he said, "that accounts for all twelve pairs of stockings. All twenty-four of them. Eleven for the midget, eleven for Johnny Oscar, and two for Mildred Goldsmith. There's some reason for those stockings being used, and especially, for their being used in that order. If we knew the reason, we'd know everything we needed. They were used that way deliberately, possibly to point out something that we're too blind to see."

"We're not blind," Helene said, "but we don't have X-ray eyes, either."

"What do you mean?" Malone asked.

"I mean," she told him, "that Jake's going out to the nearest hardware store to buy us a hammer and a chisel. And you, Malone, are going to get on the phone and get Pen Reddick over here in a hurry."

"But—" Jake began.

She shut him up with a gesture. "I've waited this long to find out what's in that box," she said firmly, "and I'm not going to wait any longer, if I have to open it myself, with my teeth and fingernails!"

Chapter Twenty-Six

JAKE WENT OUT and got the hammer and chisel. Malone reached Pen Reddick by phone, and told him to come right over. Helene went into the kitchenette and made a big platter of sandwiches that would have done honor to Oscar of the Waldorf.

Halfway through a sandwich, Helene said suddenly, "The thing Pen Reddick wants out of that box! It wouldn't be Annette Ginnis's marriage certificate, would it?"

Malone scowled. "Why the hell would he want that?"

"Maybe he's the nice young man she married after she married the midget."

"But the nice young man," Jake objected, "didn't know anything about the previous marriage. That was the hold the midget had over her."

"The midget might have told him," Helene said. "You can't tell what he might have done."

"It's true," Malone said slowly. "The midget might have told him, to make sure he wouldn't go running after Annette Ginnis. And when Pen Reddick found out how the midget was using Annette, he'd have known what hold the midget had over her. Now, with the midget dead, he'd want to get that certificate and destroy it to protect her."

"Well," Helene said, "we'll soon know." She began clearing away the remains of the sandwiches.

Suddenly Malone jumped as if he'd been shot. "Lou Goldsmith!" It was almost a yelp.

Helene put down the empty dishes and came back into the room. "You don't have to startle people like that," she complained. "What about Lou Goldsmith? Somebody'll have to break the news to him that his wife's been murdered, but—"

"That isn't it," Malone said. "That isn't it at all. He's lying in my hotel room right now, dead to the world, and he said he was going to murder his wife."

"Give Malone another cup of coffee," Jake said disgustedly, "and an aspirin. Or maybe he needs a drink."

"Damn you," Malone said. "He is there, and he did say so."

Helene sat down, lit a cigarette, and looked at the lawyer. "When did you see him?"

"About"—he looked up, blinking. "About the time Mildred Goldsmith was being murdered."

"Well then," she said sensibly, "he didn't murder her."

Malone mopped his brow with a wrinkled handkerchief. "No, but I should have asked him more questions. If I'd known she was being murdered, I would have."

"If you'd known she was being murdered," Helene pointed out, "you could have trotted up there and found out who the murderer was. And then you could have given Pen Reddick the box and the murderer both, and collected the whole fee all at once."

"I wish I had some sleep," was all Malone said.

There was a knock at the door, and Helene sprang to answer it. It was not Pen Reddick, however. It was Betty Royal and her brother.

Ned Royal was a slender, limp-looking young man with light-brown hair, watery blue eyes, and a pleasant, if blank, face. He looked pale and a little shaky, but he managed a weak smile at Jake and Helene.

"How do you feel?" Jake asked sympathetically.

"Terrible," Ned Royal said. "I'm suffering from delusions."

Helene raised a slender eyebrow. "Delusions?"

The young man nodded. "I suffer from a delusion that a cold bottle of beer when you wake up is the best thing in the world for a bad hangover." He sank into a chair and managed to light his cigarette on the third try.

"I brought Ned over," Betty Royal said firmly, "as soon as he could make it, because I knew you wanted to get everything straight. And so did I. So here you are, and here he is." She planted her little brown oxfords firmly on the floor in front of her chair, and looked very determined, and very young.

"I didn't marry that girl, you know," Ned Royal said sheepishly. "Close shave, wasn't it? If I had"— he paused and shuddered.

"If you had," Helene said severely, "it would have been hell."

Malone asked, "But why didn't you? Or better, why were you going to in the first place?"

"Well—" Ned Royal wrinkled his brow. "I met this awfully nice woman somewhere. Mrs. Goldsmith. And she suggested that I come to the Casino some night and go out with some friends of hers, and have fun. I didn't see anything wrong with that." He looked up appealingly.

"Naturally not," Malone said helpfully. "Go on."

"So yesterday she phoned, and suggested I meet these friends of hers for a drink before the show. I said, swell, and she introduced me to this very nice chap—can't think of his name to save my life—" He paused.

"Never mind it," Jake said.

"Well, anyway. She had to go back and get dressed for the show, and he and I hung around the bar and had a few drinks—well, quite a few. Then this really very nice girl came out and joined us and said Mrs. Goldsmith was tied up and couldn't be with us, so the three of us started out going places. I guess we went quite a lot of places."

"I guess you did," Betty Royal said unfeelingly.

He reddened. "Well, anyway. This really was an awfully, very nice girl. I don't know how the idea of our getting married came up exactly, but it did, and it seemed like a good idea at the time."

"So many things do," Malone commented.

"Well, anyway. We went to a few more places and all I remember is this. One place we went to, the bartender said there was some guy had tried to reach Annette there a few minutes before, and then another place we went—the last place—some guy did call Annette while we were there, and when she came back to the table she was laughing like everything. She said, 'I'm not going to marry you,' and then she laughed, and then she said, 'The midget's dead, the midget's dead,' and then she laughed and laughed." He frowned. "She must have had a laughing jag."

Helene said, "Something like that. Or maybe she just thought it was amusing."

Ned Royal thought that over in silence for a moment. "Well, anyway. The last thing I remember is this guy—wish I could think of his name—getting a cab for me and I guess he put me in it, and that's all."

He looked up at them like a child who wonders if he's done his recitation correctly.

"You see?" Betty Royal said. "I thought you'd want to know about it."

"We did," Malone assured her. "We did very much."

She rose. "I guess that's all, then. Come on, Ned. Only, what ought we to do now?"

"Nothing," Malone said. "There wasn't any marriage and nobody knows anything about it except us five and Annette Ginnis, and none of us are going to say a word."

Ned Royal blinked. "What about this chap who was with us?"

"He won't say anything either," Malone said. "Not ever."

After they had gone, the little lawyer lit a fresh cigar, walked to the window, and stood looking out.

"Well," he said at last, "we know how Annette Ginnis found out about the midget's murder. Somebody called her up and told her. And we know Ned Royal didn't murder the midget, because from the hangover he has today, last night he couldn't have murdered a gnat with a Flit gun. And Annette and Johnny Oscar evidently were with this guy all the time, so they couldn't have murdered the midget either. Not that we didn't know that already."

"What we don't know," Jake said, "is who called up Annette."

"The murderer, no doubt," Helene said.

"But why?" Jake asked. "Why go to all the bother of calling up all the saloons in Chicago until he happened to hit the one where Annette was, just to let her know that the midget was dead?"

Malone said, "Maybe the murderer thought she'd had her quota of marriage ceremonies." He looked thoughtfully at his cigar. "Maybe he wanted to spare her this one more. Maybe he was trying to give Ned Royal a break."

Helene shrugged her shoulders. "Ask the murderer that at the same time you ask him why he used silk stockings for his weapon." She paused. "While we're asking questions, who called up the police and told them they'd find a murdered man in a house on Schiller street?"

"I don't know," Malone said scowling, "but I have a pretty good hunch. And it won't take me more than a minute to find out."

He went to the telephone and dialed Max Hook's number.

"Ask Mr. Hook," he said to the male voice on the other end of the wire, after identifying himself, "if any friends of his called today on a gentleman he was discussing with me this morning, and if his friends subsequently talked to the police on the telephone." He waited a moment, said, "Thank Mr. Hook for me," and hung up.

"Well?" Helene demanded.

"It was," Malone said. "I thought so, because— unless the murderer himself telephoned, and of course that was possible—somebody had to get into the house and find the body. Max Hook had one key to the house, so he might have had others, for emergencies. His gunmen went in, found Johnny Oscar already dead, went out again and made an anonymous call to the police."

"Then how did the murderer himself get into the house?" Jake asked.

Malone frowned. "Unless he also had a key, he must have come in with Johnny Oscar."

"I can't be sure," Helene said, "but while I was down there in the cellar, I only heard the door open and close once."

"The more I think about this whole damn business," Jake said, "the more I think Malone was right about his first theory. Little elves. Eleven silk stockings. The midget is carried back to his hotel in the fiddle case and put carefully to bed. Everybody in the world seems to know about the murder before the body is found. Mildred Goldsmith is hanged with her own silk stockings at a time when her husband is telling Malone *he's* going to murder her. Then Johnny Oscar is murdered with eleven silk stockings. Ruth Rawlson tells some of the most wonderful stories in the world, and Allswell McJackson is teaching von Flanagan how to do magic tricks." He groaned.

"I'll add to the confusion," Helene said. "Eleven pairs of stockings, and there were twelve girls in the show. I'll bet you any money that the twelfth pair— the one that wasn't included—belonged to Mildred Goldsmith."

"Because she had them on?" Jake asked.

"You're a very stupid man. Those eleven stockings were a special kind, worn only in the show. No, her stockings were left out deliberately." Her eyes began to flicker with excitement. "And I think it was in order to call attention to her, for some reason. To point to her."

"Very nice theorizing," Malone said. "Why?"

"That," she said, "is what I left for *you* to figure out."

Pen Reddick arrived just then, a trifle breathless. "Sorry I took so long. I was way up on the North Side when you reached me." He took off his hat and shoved back his hair. "Have you got it?"

Malone pointed to the box, to the hammer and chisel.

Pen Reddick gasped, sat down on the nearest chair, and said, "I never was so glad to see anything in my life. I'll write your check right away, Mr. Malone."

"Wait a minute," Malone said. "Open the box first, and see if what you want is there. I want to make sure I don't cheat you."

Pen Reddick smiled. "It's there, all right. But I'll open the box first, if you insist."

He inspected the box and said, "This won't be so hard to bust." Then he looked dubiously at Jake and Helene.

"Now look," Helene said firmly. "We're all in on this, together. If you trust one of us, you've got to trust all three."

"Besides," Jake said, "you said this morning—"

Pen Reddick nodded slowly. "All right," he said. "I do trust you, God knows. But when we've opened the box—you'll understand—"

It took both Jake and Pen Reddick a good fifteen minutes to break the lock. At last a combined effort with both the hammer and the chisel did the trick. The lid bounded open.

"He sure got himself a good strong box, while he was about it," Jake said, wiping his brow.

Helene repressed an insane impulse to recite, "When the box was opened, the birds began to sing—"

Pen Reddick dumped the contents of the box into his lap. They were few. A thin bundle of letters, tied with cord. A legal paper of some kind, which he also laid aside. A single paper with a few lines written on it in ink. And a second legal paper, which Pen Reddick glanced at, said, "This isn't mine," and handed to Malone.

It was Annette Ginnis's marriage certificate. Malone stared at it, gave it to Helene, who signaled to Jake.

Written across it, in jet-black ink, was, "In the event of my death, kindly return this to Miss Ginnis, who will doubtless be delighted to learn that it was a forgery, which I arranged to have made."

Helene gasped, "Then she wasn't—" and stopped at a warning "Sh!" from Jake.

"The little bastard!" Malone growled under his breath. Then he looked again at Pen Reddick.

There was a look of almost incredible relief on the young man's face as he sat there with the papers in his hand. "They're all here," he announced. "Everything."

"But what are they?" Helene began. She stopped herself and then said, suddenly, "No. If it's something—if you don't want us to know—"

"It's all right," Pen Reddick said. "I do trust you." He held up the legal document. "This is the midget's birth certificate. This," he held up the packet, "are letters from his mother. And this—appears to be a will. I hadn't known about it." He handed the single sheet of paper to Malone.

Helene and Jake crowded close to read it. There was only a brief sentence, written in the same jet-black ink.

> "*Everything that I possess in this world I leave to my beloved brother, Pendleton Reddick.*
>
> *Signed, Jay Otto, the Big Midget.*"

Chapter Twenty-Seven

"I GUESS that explains why I felt the way I did— about the box," Pen Reddick said.

"Yes," Malone said. "Yes, I guess it does."

There was silence for a moment, broken by the sharp scratch of a match as Helene lit a cigarette.

"I remember," she said very slowly, "you—had an older brother. He died when he was very small."

"No," Pen Reddick said. "He didn't die. He grew up on a farm, without knowing anything about his family. That was—after they found out he—what was wrong with him."

Again there flashed through Jake's mind that picture of the Reddick family. The Reddick millions. The Ambassador to England. The leader of New York society. The famous Virginia belle who had been Pen Reddick's mother—and the midget's—who had written that little packet of letters Pen Reddick held in his hand.

"He didn't know—anything about himself," Pen Reddick said, "except that the farm couple were very well paid for taking care of him, and that—he was a midget." He drew a long breath. "The farm couple had a son who was a very famous mimic in his day and who came back to visit every summer. The midget learned his tricks from him, and grew up to be—the Big Midget."

Jake remembered the biographies of the midget, that always began, unaccountably, with his being about twenty-one years old.

"His mother—visited him as often as she could," Pen Reddick whispered, "without ever telling him who she was. He became—quite fond of her. She was very lovely, you know. And she wrote to him. He kept —a few of her letters."

Helene said gently, "You don't need to tell us anything more, if you don't want to."

"I do," Pen Reddick told her. "You know this much: I want to tell you the rest." He paused. "He grew up, hating everybody. Because he was a midget, and—other people weren't. By the time he was twenty-one, he was an orphan, and a—very handsome trust fund had been set up for him. The lawyer who informed him about it—didn't tell him who his parents had been. Just that they had left the money to him—and that it would come to him every month."

He paused to light a cigarette. "That made him worse than ever. To realize that he came from a rich, and probably prominent family—who'd hidden him away, and not even let him know who they were, because he was a midget. He went on the stage. He didn't need to, he had plenty of money. But he wanted to. It was an outlet for his—hate. His imitations—you know. They were cruel as hell."

"Decidedly," Malone said.

Helene asked, "But how did he find out who he was?"

"He set himself out to," Pen Reddick said, "devoted himself to the job. He had a few clues. He knew his family had been rich, and he knew how his mother had looked. And he knew how old he was. It wasn't hard to fit a description of his mother to—the late Mrs. Pendleton Reddick II—who'd had two sons —of whom the elder had died when—quite small."

He smiled wryly. "He got a copy of his birth certificate. Jay Reddick. And he had those samples of his mother's handwriting."

"But"—Jake frowned—"what was his idea? Just curiosity? You said he never blackmailed you."

Pen Reddick shook his head. "It wasn't money he wanted, it was revenge. Revenge for—having been a midget. He wrote to me, and told me what he'd learned. He told me that he didn't want a thing from me. And he told me that someday—he didn't know just when, but someday—he'd tell the world who he was. And that in any event—when he died, the world would know who he had been.

"I'd been told about him, of course. I knew that

he'd been well provided for. And—I'd promised both my parents—that I would never let people know.

He got up and began to pace the floor.

"He did that—for the same reason that he did everything else. For the same reason that he worked out this elaborate marriage-annulment scheme. He didn't need the money it brought him. He was—getting his revenge. It was for the same reason that he had an oversize bed and elaborate silk pajamas and an enormous limousine and the tallest man he could find to work in his act. The same reason that—his secretary jumped out of a New York hotel window, and no chorus girl that he dated would ever go out with him twice."

He paused. "He was the most completely evil creature I have ever known. The very incarnation of evil." He slipped his hand in his pocket. "I'll write your check, Mr. Malone. For finding the box."

He sat down at the desk, wrote the check, gave it to Malone and walked to the door. "I'll give you the other check," he said, "when you find out who murdered him."

Malone said, "Wait a minute." He looked at the check, blew on it, and put it in his pocket. "If he was all those things—why are you so anxious to find out who murdered him?"

Pen Reddick smiled. "Because after all," he said, "he *was* my brother." He opened the door, said, "I'll see you at the Casino tonight. Hope you have a good show," and was gone.

Helene stared at the door for a moment. "The poor little guy," she whispered.

"Little!" Jake said. "He's five-foot ten if he's an inch."

"I don't mean Pen Reddick," she said. "I mean— the midget."

"Yes," Malone said. "I know exactly what you mean."

The phone rang. It was the hotel manager. What was to be done with the furnishings of the midget's suite?

Jake said, "Oh hell, I don't know. Wait a minute." He left the phone and said, "Malone, run down the hall and see if you can catch Pen Reddick by the elevator, and bring him back here." Returning to the phone, he said, "I'll call you back in a few minutes."

Malone, a little breathless, came back with Pen Reddick.

"Look," Jake said. "He left you everything in his will. What's to be done with all that stuff in his suite downstairs? The bed—the pictures—"

"Oh Lord," Pen Reddick said. "Do anything you like with it. Keep it yourself. Burn it up. Give it to the Salvation Army. I don't want to hear of it again."

After he had gone, Jake called the manager back. "Put it all in the storeroom for the time being," he said. "I'll be responsible for it. Yes, you can store it under my name." He hung up, came back, and said, "It'll probably stay there for the rest of our lives."

"Oh Jake," Helene said. "Do you mean you aren't going to hang up those lovely pictures in here?"

He blushed. "That's the last I want to hear of those lovely pictures."

Malone strolled to the window and pulled back the blinds. It had begun to grow dark outside, the snow had stopped falling, and the sky had cleared. It promised to be a warm, mellow April evening.

"Nightfall," he reported.

"Damn," Jake said. "Tonight's show at the Casino—" Again he called Angela Doll's apartment.

Miss Doll was somewhat better, but it was still uncertain as to whether or not she could appear that night.

Jake looked at his watch. "My interest in murder is ended for the day," he reported. "From now on, I'm a business man." He began putting on his coat.

"Where are you going?" Helene demanded.

"To make one last stab at getting something good to replace the midget. You stay here and look after Annette. One member missing from the Casino chorus is enough."

"And take very good care of her," Malone added, "because I've questions to ask her, and they're important."

"You've questions to ask Ruth Rawlson, too," she reminded him, "and they're just as important."

"I will," Malone said crossly. He too put on his overcoat, and said, "I'll go downstairs with you, Jake."

"And as Pen Reddick said," Helene called after them, "see you at the Casino."

Left alone, she wandered restlessly about the apartment for a few minutes. Annette Ginnis was still asleep, looking like a kitten curled up in a basket. She would be awake, and feeling like herself again, in time for tonight's show.

Helene yawned, carried the ash trays into the kitchen, emptied, washed, and replaced them. She tried to read, but her mind persisted in wandering. She turned on the radio, and turned it off again in thirty seconds.

At last she turned down the lights and stretched out on the davenport, lit a cigarette, and lay staring at the ceiling. It had been more than twelve hours now since she and Jake had come home, to find the empty fiddle case leaning against their door. Twelve crowded hours.

Her mind kept returning again and again to the fiddle case. What had been the idea of moving it from the midget's dressing room? And especially, what had been the idea of bringing the midget's body home and putting it to bed?

Suddenly she remembered another thing. Who had called the desk at four o'clock that morning and left a call for the midget, for seven-thirty? And, in heaven's name, why—when certainly, whoever called knew that the midget was dead?

She put out her cigarette, closed her eyes for a moment, and opened them again. Perhaps a little nap was the thing right now. Then a big leisurely bath and a little work on the face and hair. Same recipe for Annette, when she woke up. If Jake didn't get back in time, she'd have a tray of dinner sent up for Annette and herself. Annette's clothes were in pretty bad shape, but she'd change into costume as soon as she got to the Casino. She yawned, and told herself that everything was taken care of very nicely.

Again she closed her eyes.

Half asleep, she opened them again. There was something—something she knew, and yet couldn't quite remember. It was there, just beyond her mind's reach. Perhaps if she went to sleep, she'd dream of it. Whatever it was, she had to bring it back to mind. Because when she did, she'd know who murdered the midget.

Chapter Twenty-Eight

JAKE PUNCHED the elevator button and said, "Things aren't so bad. I've seen worse." His voice was gloomy.

"You mean," Malone said, "things are never so bad that they can't get worse."

"Hell," Jake said. "You have two thousand bucks that you didn't have this morning. You probably won't have it by day after tomorrow, but you've got it now. Pen Reddick has his box, and he's happy. Betty Royal's brother isn't in any trouble, and she's happy. I still own the Casino and all I have to do is find something to replace the midget in tonight's show."

"And all I have to do is find out who murdered the midget," Malone said, "and I have another two thousand bucks." He glanced at his watch. "I can probably catch Ruth Rawlson now. And this time, I'll get the truth out of her."

Jake said, "If I hurry"—he paused to step into the elevator—"I can still fix up tonight's show. Al Omega won't like this last-minute business, but it can't be helped."

"Sure," Malone said reassuringly. "Everything's okay now."

Down in the lobby Jake said, "Where are you going? Oak street? I'll drop you there on my way downtown—"

"Oh, Mr. Justus," the switchboard girl called. As Jake walked over, she said, "A call came in for you, just this minute."

Jake picked up a phone and said, "Hello?" hoping for the best.

It was von Flanagan. Jake would please come down to his office right away, and no monkey business. Yes, and bring that lying Irishman Malone, if Jake could lay his hands on him.

"But damn it!" Jake said. "I've got important things to attend to, right now."

If Jake didn't hustle right down to the office, he'd attend to those important things in a better world, courtesy of von Flanagan's bare hands.

"But wait a minute," Jake said. "What's it all about?"

If Jake had any questions to ask, he'd ask them down in von Flanagan's office. But he'd better be there to ask them pretty damn quick.

Jake swore, slammed down the receiver, rejoined Malone, and told him what was up.

"I wonder what the hell has made him mad this time," Jake said.

Malone muttered, "He probably found out you tried to hide the midget's body last night. Or that we were romping out of Johnny Oscar's house a few minutes before his body was discovered. Stop trying to look so innocent, and call a taxi."

They rode down to von Flanagan's office in a dismal silence.

"If he asks you anything you can't answer," Malone said outside the door, "just keep your mouth shut and let me do the talking."

There was a strange sound from the other side of the door. Malone swung it open, to have a large, enraged Rhode Island Red hen fly up in his face. He sheltered his face with his arms and yelled, "Help!"

Jake slammed the door shut and batted at the hen, who retired indignantly to the corner behind von Flanagan's desk.

"I told you," Allswell McJackson said patiently, "it's no good unless you use a trained hen. Or at least a tame one."

"This was the only hen I could get," von Flanagan growled.

The hen, from her corner, stated plainly what she thought of them both.

Jake threw his hat on the floor. "Listen," he said, "if you dragged me all the way down here to watch a lousy vaudeville act—"

Von Flanagan glared at Jake. "Sit down," he said,

"and shut up. The professor here just came down tonight to teach me the hen-in-the-basket trick."

"Only," Allswell said, "it *has* to be a tame hen."

"All right," von Flanagan said. "We'll try it again tomorrow. I'll get one of my sister-in-law's hens. Now you can take that wild buzzard out of here."

"Right away," Allswell said.

They had reckoned, however, without the hen. Jake forgot his own troubles while he watched the chase. If Allswell McJackson had not been so large and so clumsy, or if the hen had not been so unco-operative, it would have been just another man catching a hen. But twice Allswell fell on his face, and once the hen lit on his head, adding her vituperative comments to the confusion. By the time von Flanagan's office had been reduced to a shambles, Allswell McJackson was standing in the center of the room, triumphantly holding the protesting hen by one leg.

"Got her!" he exclaimed. Then, evidently touched by her protests, he managed to get her into an upright position in his arms, stroked her back, and, in an excess of sympathy, chattered a moment's baby talk to her.

The hen looked up at him and let loose a cackle that was almost a coo.

"What shall I do with her?" Allswell McJackson asked.

"Anything," von Flanagan bellowed, "but get her out of here."

"If I were you," Jake said, "I'd keep her for a pet."

After the door was closed behind Allswell Mc-Jackson and the hen, Malone mopped his brow, looked at von Flanagan and said, "That hen should be on the stage, not you. What the hell did you bring us down here for, anyway?"

Von Flanagan blew a couple of feathers off his desk blotter.

"I'm a very patient man," he began quietly, "in spite of all the troubles I've got"—he scratched violently at one ear—"in spite of all the people who go out of their way to make life hard for me." He scratched behind the ear. "I try to make allowances for human weaknesses, like it said in a book I read once, but when my own friends—" He whisked his hand past his ear. It came up with a chicken feather caught between two fingers. Von Flanagan stared at it for a moment, turned a light cerise, and for the next two minutes talked forcibly and colorfully to God about Allswell McJackson's hen.

When he paused for breath, Malone said, "As the professor said, you should have used a trained hen. And what does that have to do with whatever you dragged us all the way down here for?"

Von Flanagan drew a long breath, with the expression of a man who is counting, slowly, to ten. Then he picked up where he'd left off. "When my own friends hold out on me—" He drew another breath, this time a quick one, and said, "I've got the Commissioner after me. I've got the D. A.'s office after me. I've got the newspapers after me. And then my own friends—" He rose to his feet and shook an indignant forefinger at Jake. "Damn it!" he roared, "I'm perfectly justified in closing up your joint, and if you don't like it, you can—"

"Wait a minute," Jake said quietly. "What's this about closing up the Casino? What's the idea? What does the Casino have to do with this business?"

"Everything," von Flanagan said, breathing hard. He sat down again and glared at Jake from behind the desk. "Look, Jake. This little guy, the midget—the doc tells me he took some kind of dope before he was killed. All right. He works at your joint. Now, this dame, the Goldsmith dame, she was hung with a couple of silk stockings. All right. Your wife went in and found her body. Then Johnny Oscar, he was hung with a bunch of silk stockings. All right. Now the doc says he was full of the same kind of dope as the little guy. And just to make it one nice big package, I was tipped off that there was some kind of tie-up between Johnny Oscar and the little guy. So the whole thing has to do with your joint, and by God, I'll have it closed up until I find out what the blue-bang hell is going on—" He snorted. "I mean, pending further investigation."

"But you can't do that," Malone said.

"That's one man's opinion," von Flanagan said.

There was a long silence. Then Jake began, "Look here. You wouldn't do a thing like that to me—"

"I would," von Flanagan interrupted him, "and I will." He looked sadly and reproachfully at Jake. "I know you guys are holding out on me. I don't mind that so much. Your business is your business. But maybe you know who murdered the little guy and those other two, and you aren't telling. I mind that because the Commissioner and the D. A.'s office and the newspapers are all on my tail. So, since the whole damn shebang is tied up with your joint, why I'm closing it up until I find out who did murder those guys and that dame. I don't give a hoot what else has been going on, I just have to find out who bumped them off, because while I don't like being a cop, this is all the job I got."

Jake had a sudden vision of hordes of cash customers turning away from the locked doors of the Casino. The vision had sound effects with it: Max Hook asking for his money, and Helene as the wife of the press agent of an ice-skating troupe.

"For the love of Mike," he said, "give us a little time."

"Time?" von Flanagan demanded. "For what?"

Malone stepped up to von Flanagan's desk. "Time to deliver the murderer to you. That's what you want, isn't it?"

The big police officer beamed. "Now you're talking," he said in a happier tone. He paused, grew serious, and looked fixedly at Malone. "Who is he?"

"I don't know," the little lawyer said. "I don't know any more than you do. But"—he took out a cigar and slid off the cellophane jacket—"I think *I* can find out." He blew into the cellophane jacket. It soared up near the ceiling and floated down gracefully to rest on one end on top of von Flanagan's inkwell.

"Now *there*," von Flanagan said admiringly, "is a trick. Can you do it again?"

"Sure," Malone said. "Only I've got a superstition: I never use the same cigar jacket twice." He lit the cigar with an airy gesture.

Jake, sensing a change in the atmosphere, said, "Say, pal, why don't you drop in at the Casino tonight?" He added hastily, "As my guest, of course. You know, a guy who's going on the stage ought to get around and see a few shows."

A gleam came into von Flanagan's eyes. "I'd like to do that. What's the show tonight?"

"I won't tell," Jake said, "because it's going to be a surprise. But it's going to be terrific."

"Yes, I'd like to do that," the police officer repeated. "Tonight, you say? Sure, I'll drop around."

"Swell!" Jake said heartily.

Malone picked up his hat and said, "In that case, we'll be seeing you later."

"Wait a minute," von Flanagan said quickly. "I ain't through yet. These here murders. And closing up the Casino until I get them settled." He paused. "Well, I won't close it up tonight yet. But"—he looked at Malone—"you think you can find out who did these murders, huh?"

"Easiest thing in the world," Malone said, blowing a smoke ring.

"Well, in that case," von Flanagan said, "I'll tell you what I'll do." He paused, thought for a moment, and a near-angelic smile spread over his face. "After all, you two guys are pals. And I like your wife, Jake. So I'll tell you what I'll do. I'll give you twelve hours. I won't touch the Casino tonight. But," he added grimly, "if Malone here don't do what he says he can do inside of those twelve hours, I'll close up the joint so tight that you won't have any more customers than—than—"

"Than a hen has teeth," Malone said helpfully.

Von Flanagan leaped to his feet. "Don't talk about hens to me!" he roared. "Get the hell out of here, the pair of you."

Out in the hall, the door closed hastily behind them, Malone muttered, "Twelve little hours. Sixty little minutes to an hour. What does that guy think I am, a magician?"

"No," Jake said, "he's the magician. Do you know who the murderer is, Malone?"

Malone said, "I haven't the faintest idea."

Jake groaned. "Do you think you can find out, inside of twelve hours?"

"Sure," Malone said. "If during those twelve hours I'm suddenly struck with second sight." He puffed at his cigar and snapped, "Leave me alone! I'm trying to think."

Jake was silent until they reached the sidewalk. There they paused.

"Von Flanagan won't close up the Casino tonight,"

Jake said miserably, "because he's going to be a guest there. But tomorrow night"— He gulped, and said, "Tonight's receipts won't be enough to settle with Max Hook, if the place is closed up even for a couple of days."

"Shut up," Malone said. "I'm still thinking." He waved at a cab. "Toward the Loop," he told the driver.

As the cab crossed Van Buren street, the little lawyer turned to Jake. "Twelve hours. I think I can make it." He leaned forward and told the driver to drop him at his hotel. "Where are you going, Jake?"

"I'm going to an agent's office on Randolph street," Jake said. "And if after that I'm still stuck with tonight's show, I'm going out to the end of Navy Pier."

"The water's damn cold for jumping," Malone said. "It's April. But give all the little fish my love."

The cab stopped in front of Malone's Loop hotel. Malone got out.

"Wait a minute," Jake said. Malone leaned in through the window. "You said—you thought you could make it. Do you have any idea—"

"I've got plenty of ideas," Malone told him, "but none of them have to do with the midget's murder." He glanced at Jake's drawn face, and added quickly, "But all I need is a good, quick hunch, and everything will be okay. If I could only remember what"— He paused, and said, "Don't worry, it'll come to me."

"I hope you aren't referring to second sight," Jake said.

"The thing I've forgotten," Malone said. "The hunch. The tip-off. If I just sit down and review the whole thing in my mind"— He stood upright, still resting one hand on the cab door. "Don't forget you have a guest coming to the Casino tonight, to see the show. And he's expecting a surprise."

"The surprise," Jake said sourly, "will be if there is any show."

Chapter Twenty-Nine

THE TIP-OFF, Malone told himself, riding up in the elevator. The give-away. The one thing that would tell him what he needed to know.

He had to think of it. He had to remember it. Because it was going to lead him right to the man or woman who had murdered Jay Otto, and Mildred Goldsmith, and Johnny Oscar. Because it was going to keep von Flanagan from closing up Jake's Casino. Because it was going to give Jake enough time to pay up what he owed Max Hook. Because of Helene.

He paused outside his door. Lou Goldsmith was in there, sleeping off his drunk. And Lou Goldsmith, who wanted to murder his wife, didn't know that his wife had been murdered. He, Malone, had to wake him up and tell him.

The worst of it was that he was going to have to probe Lou Goldsmith for information about the murdered woman. It was going to be like going into an open wound with an iodine swab.

He relit his cigar, fumbled in his pocket for a key, and opened the door.

Lou Goldsmith was sitting up in a chair by the radio, wide awake. The room was full of cigar smoke. There was a crumpled newspaper on the floor.

"Sorry to have been so long," Malone said cheerfully, as though he'd been late for a luncheon engagement. He glanced at the front page of the newspaper, took off his coat and hat, and flung them over a chair, crushed out his cigar in the nearest ash tray, and said, "I see you've heard all the news."

Lou Goldsmith looked up at him through the blue smoke. His face was perfectly composed. "Sure, I heard about it."

"Well," Malone said, in the same cheerful tone, "that saves me the trouble of telling you about it then. How about a drink?"

"Okay," Lou Goldsmith said.

Malone located a half-empty bottle of gin on top of a pile of soiled laundry in the closet, rinsed out two glasses in the bathroom, and carefully poured two drinks, keeping a watchful eye on Lou Goldsmith. He handed the big man his drink, lit a fresh cigar, and sat down on the edge of the bed.

"Thanks," Lou Goldsmith said.

Malone sat perfectly still, holding his glass in his hand, watching Lou Goldsmith's impassive face. He was remembering an afternoon back in the old days, when Lou Goldsmith's speakeasy had been the focal point of a little trouble over territorial jurisdiction.

There had been that same look on Lou Goldsmith's face when the first gun barked.

"I had a good sleep up here," Lou Goldsmith said. "Thanks, Malone."

"That's all right," Malone said. "Glad to do it."

There was another long silence.

"When I woke up," Lou Goldsmith said, "about an hour ago, I turned on the radio to see what time it was. I hit a news broadcast. So then I had a newspaper sent up."

"Well," Malone said noncommittally, "that's one way of finding out what's going on."

Suddenly Lou Goldsmith put down his empty glass, leaned forward, and ran a big, hairy hand over his forehead.

"Tell me, Malone. When I talked to you today— you didn't know about it?"

"How could I?" Malone said. "It hadn't happened. Or," he added grimly, "it was just happening." He downed his gin, fast. "Happening just about that time." He eyed the big man closely.

Lou Goldsmith had been in love with his wife, and his wife was dead. Lou Goldsmith had wanted to murder his wife, and someone else had murdered her. What the reaction would be, Malone reflected, was anybody's guess. He sat tight, and waited.

It was a long time before Lou Goldsmith looked up and said, "Well, somebody saved me a lot of trouble and a lot of lawyer's fees." His eyes were puffed and red-rimmed.

"That's the way to think about it," Malone said, looking at his cigar.

"If this hadn't happened," Lou Goldsmith said, "what I told you—would have still held. You know what I mean? Last night—"

Malone twirled his cigar in his fingers. "What about last night?" he asked very quietly.

"Right after the show," Lou Goldsmith told him, "we went backstage. Milly said she had to go in her dressing room for a minute. So I waited a few minutes and then I knocked on the door, and she wasn't there. So I started looking for her. I went in one place and it was this damn midget's dressing room."

"Was he there?" Malone asked, feeling a sudden quickening along his spine.

"Sure, he was there. Standing up in front of his dressing table, just pouring himself a big slug of liquor. I said, 'Pardon me, pal, I was just looking for my wife.' He took his drink and turned around and said, 'Pardon *me*, pal, but if I were you, I'd kill my wife.' "

Malone continued to look at his cigar. "Why?"

"Because"—Lou Goldsmith looked at the floor, talking like a man in a trance. "Well, he told me all about—what she'd been doing. This racket of getting some rich young dope to marry a cheap chorus girl when he was full of liquor, and then hitting him for the big money to put through a bribed annulment. It seems the midget had got wise to the whole scheme somehow."

"He had, had he?" Malone murmured.

Yes, that would be one of the midget's tricks. The midget, who hated big men. Lou Goldsmith was a big man. Tell Lou Goldsmith about the whole works, leaving himself out of it, of course, and putting the whole blame on Lou Goldsmith's wife.

Lou Goldsmith went on, "He poured himself another drink—it seemed funny as hell to see a little bastard like that drinking liquor—and then he told me how she—Milly—had teamed up with one of the Hook's boys to work this racket. Then all of a sudden he passed out. You know, a little guy like that shouldn't drink. I would have stayed and looked after him, but so help me, Malone, I had other things to think about. And I figured that big guy who worked for him would be along any minute. So I just left him there, sprawled out over his dressing table, and I beat it back to the men's room to think it over. Finally I decided I'd better have it out with her— Milly—and I started looking for her again. I looked all over the place for her—I didn't go back in his dressing room again—and all of a sudden she turned up, right by the door that led out front."

"You don't know where she'd been in the meantime?" Malone interrupted.

Lou Goldsmith shook his head. "No idea. I said 'Milly, I want to talk to you,' and she said, 'Not now.' That's all I could get out of her all the rest of the evening: 'Not now!' So finally we went home and I figured then I could have it out with her. But she ducked into her room and changed her clothes and ducked out again, and that's the last I saw of her."

Malone sat silent, puffing at his cigar. Mildred Goldsmith hadn't murdered the midget, because she herself had been murdered by the same method. All the time Lou Goldsmith had spent looking for her, she'd been arranging the last details of Annette Ginnis' elopement with Ned Royal. And she'd changed her clothes and gone out to make sure that nothing would go wrong.

But Lou Goldsmith had probably been the last person to see the midget alive, save the murderer.

"I didn't mind her staying on in the chorus," Lou Goldsmith said, "though she didn't need to. And I knew she was running around with Al Omega now and then, and I didn't mind that. After all, I guess I'm no patent-haired movie lover. As long as she came home to me, I didn't kick. And when she'd get sore at me, I never talked back. But a business like that—" He drew his breath in between his teeth, stood up, and said, "Whoever did it, she had it coming to her. I'm sorry it wasn't me."

He peeled off his coat, vest, and shirt, and said, "I'm going to have to talk to the cops about this, I suppose. Mind if I stick my head under your shower, pal?" He vanished into the bathroom, closing the door.

Malone sat on the edge of his bed for a while, still looking at his cigar. He was thinking of big, tough Lou Goldsmith, and of Mildred Goldsmith, cold as ice and hard as nails. Then at last he began to think of the midget, of the Casino, of Jake, and of what he still had to do.

There were things he had to learn from Ruth Rawlson. Things that couldn't wait until tonight. And maybe he could be a little more firm over the phone than he could be in her presence.

He searched through his coat for the telephone number he copied down from the hall phone in her rooming house, found it, and called her.

Her voice over the phone was the voice of Ruth Rawlson as he remembered it from twenty years ago. He steeled his mind against the picture of ivory skin and rippling, red-gold hair, and said, as sternly as he could, "No funny business this time. How did you learn that the midget was dead?"

A faint little gasp came over the wire; then, "Why *Mister* Malone!"

"Can anybody overhear you where you're talking? No? Fine. Then pay attention. Nobody telephoned the midget's apartment last night until three o'clock, and by then you weren't telephoning anybody."

"Oh!" she said. A pause, and, "I must have been thinking of another time."

"You must have been," Malone said. He hated to do this, but it was the only way. "Remember, I know something about this business too. How did you find out the midget was dead? And this time, tell me the truth."

There was just a tiny wait before she said weakly, "I saw him."

"You—saw him?" Malone said.

"Please," she whispered over the wire. "I didn't want anybody to know. I didn't want to be involved. I knew a girl once in the East who got involved in something like that, perfectly innocently, and her whole career—"

"Never mind that," Malone said hoarsely. "You won't be involved. Where did you see him, and when?"

"I went in his dressing room. I—you know, he'd told me—anytime I was looking for a drink, to walk in—and help myself—"

"Yes, yes, yes," Malone said. "Go on."

"I knocked, and he didn't answer. So I went in. And he was there." She paused, and said in a very small voice, "Mr. Malone, he'd been hanged."

Malone said gently, "I know all about that. So what did you do?"

"I shut the door. I went into the ladies' room and thought about it. Then I went into the phone booth and called up Angela. I thought she'd want to know, and I thought she'd know what to do. Dear Angela, she's been such a friend to me! But she didn't seem to care about this. Then I went back in the ladies' room and sat there a long while, wondering what I ought to do. Finally, I decided I had to have a drink —just to steady my nerves, Mr. Malone—and the only thing I could think of to do was go back in *his* dressing room and help myself. So I went back there, and Mr. Malone, he was *gone.*"

"You don't say!" Malone said.

"So I took a drink—well, I guess a couple of drinks. Really, Mr. Malone, my nerves were *badly* shattered —and then I came out and Mr. Justus got me a cab and sent me home, and that's all I know."

Malone said, "Thanks." He counted ten, and then said, "Of course, the whole thing could have been a hallucination, you know."

There was a little gasp. "Oh, do you really think so?"

"I really do," he assured her. "You dreamed the whole thing. Don't ever think of it again, and," he added pointedly, "don't ever tell another soul."

"Never," she breathed, "I never, never will!" He could hear her relieved sigh over the wire. "I'm so glad it was all just a bad dream."

"I'm glad you're glad," Malone assured her. "And tonight—"

"Tonight!" she said.

He hung up the phone and relit his cigar. There was no doubt that this time he had the straight story. Ruth Rawlson couldn't have made up that bit about the midget being hung. But that didn't help him with the problem of who'd murdered the midget. It only made it tidier.

And in the meantime—twelve hours. Suddenly he was plunged in gloom.

Lou Goldsmith came out from the bathroom, his

face still glistening, his hair wet, and began putting on his shirt and tie.

"Well," he said. He fastened his tie and reached for his vest. "Well, that's that." He buttoned his vest and put on his coat. "Thanks for everything, Malone." He put on his overcoat and picked up his hat. "I'll go home now, and let the cops and the reporters talk to me."

"That's the stuff," Malone said, with false heartiness.

The big man paused at the door, one hand on the knob, his face a mask. "Malone, if they find out who murdered her, I want to talk to you. I want you to defend him. And I'll pay the bills."

Malone looked up at the first ray of sunshine he'd seen for hours.

"Now," he said, cheerfully, "now you're talking sense!"

Chapter Thirty

Everything was okay, Malone told himself. Everything was going to be swell.

He glanced at himself in the mirror beside the entrance to the Casino. A fine figure of a man, he told himself. That new Finchley suit really did him proud. The wallet in his pocket was a reassuring bulge against his ribs. And he was meeting Ruth Rawlson, any minute now.

It was true, there were a few odds and ends of things to settle. Just a little matter of finding out who'd murdered the midget. A mere trifle. And making sure that Max Hook didn't decide he was going to own the Casino, not Jake. Or that von Flanagan didn't close up the Casino, at this crucial time. Nothing, really, for a man like himself, who had a date with Ruth Rawlson, to worry about. Why, there was the nice fat fee he'd get from Lou Goldsmith just as soon as he'd attended to the item of finding the defendant. Everything was hunky-dory.

He took one more glance at himself in the mirror and wished he could convince himself that all those things were true. His tie was beginning to creep toward one ear, and there were cigar ashes on the vest of the Finchley suit. Von Flanagan had said twelve hours, and nine of them were left, now. He wondered what Jake had been able to do about tonight's show.

"I'm expecting a young lady to meet me," he told the headwaiter. "A Miss Rawlson."

The headwaiter's eyebrows didn't even quiver, let alone lift. "Yes, Mr. Malone."

"Show her to a table—" he hesitated—"a corner table"—rosy lights, and a secluded corner—"and then page me."

He went on into the Casino. It was early, but the crowd was there. Far across the room he saw Helene, sitting alone, and headed for her.

She looked up at him, smiled, and both of them said simultaneously, "Where's Jake?"

Malone sat down, ran a finger under his collar, and this time both of them said, "Don't *you* know?"

The lawyer waved to a waiter and said, "Let's start this dialogue from the beginning. You're supposed to say 'Where's Jake?' and I'm supposed to say 'I'll give you three guesses.' Or I'm supposed to say 'Where's Jake?' and then you"— He paused to say to the waiter, "A double rye, a glass of water, and a soda cracker."

The waiter said, "Yes Mr. Malone," without any

sign of surprise, and went away. Helene raised one eyebrow.

"The soda cracker?"

"Dinner," Malone said. "I haven't had time." He looked hopefully toward the door. Any minute now, when that headwaiter came in, he'd usher a red-gold blonde in a white dress to a corner table, and start looking over the room for him, Malone.

"Jake called up at the hotel," Helene said. "He said to come on down here tonight, and he'd meet me. He said everything was okay."

"He's right," Malone said. "Everything's going to be swell."

He nibbled the soda cracker, took a sip of the water, and then looked at Helene over the glass of rye. Her pale-green silk-jersey dinner dress reminded him, somehow, of Lake Michigan on a clear day. Her perfectly composed face was pale and exquisite and smooth, and her corn-silk-color hair was like satin.

"He's a very lucky guy," Malone said, "even if he does lose this joint."

"But he mustn't!" Helene said. "Malone—"

"I know," Malone said. "I've got to find out who murdered the midget." And in a little less than nine hours, too. "How's Annette Ginnis?" There were still those important questions he had to ask her.

"She's backstage dressing," Helene said. "She still feels a little shaky, but I think she'll hold out." She puffed at her cigarette and said, "I wish I knew where Jake could be."

"Shut up," Malone said. "The show's starting."

He'd promised himself he wouldn't watch the door, but he took one more glance.

Oh well, Ruth Rawlson would be along any minute now.

He lit a cigar, leaned back in his chair, and looked over the Casino. If Jake could keep this up for just a few more nights, he'd be in the clear.

There was a crowd again tonight, and scattered through the crowd, he saw familiar faces. Pen Reddick, sitting at a table by himself. Betty Royal, her eyes sparkling, surrounded by five adoring young men. Ned Royal, at another table, in deep and earnest conversation with a slightly overdone brunette. Through the doors that led to the bar—Malone looked, started, and looked again. Hunched over the bar, a pair of heavy shoulders that could belong to no one but Lou Goldsmith. He looked away quickly and saw Max Hook, at a shadowed table near the wall, wearing a tuxedo which appeared in this light to be a deep violet, three shadowy and indistinguishable figures lined up against the wall behind him. Malone turned his head again only to see, at a special floorside table, von Flanagan, viewing the floor show with the critical eye of a fellow artist.

The chorus—including Annette Ginnis, still looking a little pale, and a hastily recruited girl to fill the place left vacant by Mildred Goldsmith—finished the opening number. The lights changed, and Al Omega's band struck up the melody that announced Angela Doll.

She too seemed a trifle pale. Still, she'd recovered in time for tonight's show, Malone reflected, and that was something Jake had to be thankful for.

He cast one more wistful glance toward the entrance. Oh well, it was still early.

The chorus came back for its second routine, the South American number. Malone glanced at the long silk stockings, and glanced away quick. Good thing they'd had plenty of spares. Eleven members of the chorus there, and one substitute. Eleven pairs of silk stockings, and one pair—

That wasn't the thing he was searching for in his mind, he told himself. That wasn't the tip-off. It was something else.

Helene said, "Jake!" in a breathless voice.

Malone looked up to see the tall, red-haired man sitting down at their table. He hadn't changed his clothes and his face was pale and haggard from lack of sleep, but there was a hopeful gleam in his eyes.

"Everything's okay," Jake announced. "Everything's going to be swell."

"The show—" Helene said.

"It's all set," Jake said. "At least I hope it's all set." He ran a hand through his tousled hair. "Don't ask me questions now. I'm still out of breath." He looked at Helene and said, "How anyone has the right to look so beautiful, with so little sleep—"

"How anyone can get away with looking so terrible," she said affectionately, "just because he's lost a night's sleep—" She looked at him critically and said, "Jake, you're wonderful! And straighten your tie."

Jake straightened his tie, ordered a drink, and looked around the room. "A nice house." He looked at Max Hook, at von Flanagan, and then, hopefully, at Malone.

"I'll fix it," Malone promised, wondering how he'd do it and when Ruth Rawlson would arrive.

The chorus finished the South American number and vanished. The lights dimmed a little.

Jake downed his drink, leaned forward, and whispered, "Now, watch!"

The orchestra was silent. Then the pianist began to play, simply, and not too well, "The Skater's Waltz."

The curtains parted, and from between them appeared Allswell McJackson, in a full-dress suit that didn't fit him any too accurately, carrying a silk hat which was obviously too small. He stood there for a moment on the tiny platform just above the dance floor, blinking at the audience as though he were wondering what to do next.

Helene said, *"Jake!"*

Malone didn't trust himself to speak.

Von Flanagan, at his floorside table, applauded wildly.

"I shall try," Allswell McJackson said, in his pol-

ished accent, "to entertain you with a few tricks."
He came down onto the floor, almost tripping over
the step, and drew a pack of cards from his pocket.

The audience giggled.

Allswell McJackson picked a plump gentleman at
a floorside table. "Will you be so kind, sir, as to select
a card? Any card at all, sir, any card."

Obviously, he was sweating to perform the trick
exactly as the book had directed him. Somehow,
though, when he was riffling the cards, they seemed
to explode in his hands, spraying across the floor, and
landing him, stomach-side down, across the plump
gentleman's table, one card still in his hand.

"That's the one," the plump gentleman said loudly.

The audience howled. All save von Flanagan, who
looked on in a disapproving silence.

Allswell McJackson ducked backstage, returning
with a derby hat. "Ladies and gentlemen, the question has long been raised as to which came first, the
hen or the egg. Tonight—"

By some miracle the egg, bouncing from the hat,
just missed the piano player, who continued to play
"The Skater's Waltz."

Allswell said, "The wrong kind of egg."

The audience howled again.

The act of burning up the dollar bill turned out
even better, especially when Allswell McJackson not
only burned up the wrong envelope, but nearly set
fire to his coattails in doing so.

The climax came, however, when Al Omega's band

struck a lóud chord, and Allswell McJackson announced that, having produced an egg without the
aid of a hen, he would now produce a hen without
the aid of an egg. The hen—the same Rhode Island
Red—was still unco-operative. Halfway through the
trick Allswell paused to apologize that it really should
be done with a tame hen. And by the time the hen
had gotten away, been chased about the dance floor
by the tall, gawky man, finally caught by one leg, and
then lulled into an amiable clucking, the crowd was
helpless, gasping, and applauding.

"Jake," Helene said, "you're a genius!"

Allswell McJackson took his curtain calls with the
hen in his arms. Al Omega's band vanished backstage,
and Ramon Arriba's band began to play. The crowd
began to spill onto the dance floor.

"He may never be able to repeat himself," Jake
said, lighting a cigarette, "but it sure solved the
problem of tonight's show."

Malone finally caught his breath. "He couldn't do
it," he said, "if he weren't about twelve feet tall."

Helene stared at him. "I dreamed that."

"You what?" Malone said.

"Allswell McJackson. I dreamed of him doing a
magic act, and stopping in the middle of it to say,
'I couldn't do this trick, if I weren't twelve feet tall.' "

Malone started to speak, but there was an influx
of congratulatory customers around Jake's table. Pen
Reddick, a sports reporter from the *Times,* Betty
Royal and one of her young men, a City Hall hanger-

on, a society woman from Highland Park, and, at the tail of them, von Flanagan. The little lawyer took advantage of the moment's confusion to slip away for a word with the headwaiter.

No, the lady hadn't arrived yet. Yes, he would inform Mr. Malone immediately.

By the time Malone returned to the table, the customers had vanished, and Jake and Helene were alone.

"Well, that's that," Jake said. He lit a fresh cigarette and said, "Now, Malone, if you'll only"— He paused. "You know, von Flanagan wasn't fooling." He paused again. "If you don't—"

"Don't worry," Malone said confidently. "Just leave everything to me. I'm not just your lawyer, I'm your pal." He emptied his glass and said, "We're like brothers. We're closer than brothers." His voice seemed to catch in his throat on the last word.

His eyes met Helene's across the table for a long moment.

"What the hell," Jake said. "What's the matter with you two?"

"Nothing much," Malone said very quietly. He turned to look at Jake. "Except that Helene and I know who murdered the midget."

Chapter Thirty-One

WHEN MALONE said a thing like that, he didn't fool. Jake said "Who?" and, "How do you know?" all in the same breath.

Malone answered the last question. "You may not remember it, but you told me." He drained his glass and stood up.

"What are you going to do?" Helene asked.

"I'm going to collect my other two thousand bucks," Malone said. He lit a fresh cigar, and looked around the room. Suddenly he said, "I'm afraid we'll have to move fast. I've got a hunch—" Without another word, he headed for the door that led backstage.

Jake and Helene followed him, Helene flinging a dark-green woolen cape over her pale shoulders.

At the door to what had been the midget's dressing room, the lawyer paused. "I may be wrong about this," he said. "I hope that I am." He threw open the door.

Allswell McJackson lay sprawled on the floor, just below the spot where the midget's tiny body had hung. There was a noose of ordinary rope around his neck, and another strand of rope was fastened to the overhead bar.

"The rope broke," Malone said. "He was too heavy." He knelt down beside the big man.

Jake said, "Damn it, it's a conspiracy against me. As fast as I get a good entertainer for that top spot, somebody comes along and murders him."

"This time, it was a failure," Malone said, getting to his feet. He examined the piece of rope he had removed from Allswell McJackson's throat. "Helene, get Annette Ginnis here, right away."

Helene nodded, her face white as chalk, and darted out the door, closing it after her.

"Malone," Jake began desperately, "what do you think?"

"I don't think," Malone said laconically. "I know."

There was a gentle knock at the door. Jake opened it a crack. It was a waiter, with a whispered message for Malone.

"Show the lady to her table," Malone whispered back. "Tell her to order whatever she likes, and that I'll be with her as soon as I can." He shut the door again.

"Two thousand bucks is a lot of dough," Malone said grimly, "but I'm beginning to think I'd have done this for free."

Before Jake could ask a question, Helene returned

with Annette Ginnis. The chorus girl's face was pale under her makeup. She had thrown a coat hastily over her garish costume. She looked at Allswell Mc-Jackson and gave a frightened little gasp.

"He's all right," Malone said. "He'll come to any minute now."

"Malone," Helene said, "Pen Reddick's outside in the hall."

"Ask him in," the lawyer said. "He's paying for this party. He might as well attend it."

Pen Reddick came in, stared, and said, "What—"

"I'm collecting the rest of my fee," Malone said. He looked at Annette Ginnis. "My dear, everything hangs now on two questions I must ask you." He used the same gentle tone he would have applied to a nervous witness in a courtroom.

She nodded, her wide, terrified eyes fixed on his face.

"The very nice young man you married," Malone went on, "after the marriage to the midget—which you didn't remember. What was his name?"

There was a death-like stillness in the room before her lips managed to form the words, "Al Omega."

Malone gave an almost imperceptible start. For a moment he seemed lost in thought. Then he nodded, and said, "We'll invite him to this party, too." He opened the door an inch, called to a passing waiter, and said, "Ask Mr. Omega to step in here, right away."

"Listen," Jake said. "If you think, Malone—"

"Shut up," Malone said, almost absentmindedly. He waited until Al Omega came into the room before he spoke again.

The handsome young orchestra leader said, "You wanted"—caught sight of Allswell McJackson, looked around the room, and said, "Oh God!"

"Yes," Malone said, "another one. But this one lived." He knelt down for a moment beside Allswell and said gently, "How do you feel?"

Allswell moaned faintly and moved his head. "What—happened?"

"That," Malone said, "is what I want you to tell me."

"I—" He moaned again, and put a hand to his throat. "I—don't know. I—came into the dressing room—something hit me—I don't know—"

Malone nodded. "There wasn't time for knockout drops in the whiskey tonight." He rose, spied a big towel on the dressing table, wadded it into a pillow, and put it under Allswell McJackson's head. "Just lie there. You'll feel all right in a few minutes."

Helene said, "But, Malone—"

He ignored her. "My other question now, Annette. Last night—someone telephoned all over town to find you—and when finally the call reached you— told you that the midget was dead."

"Yes." It was the faintest of whispers.

"Now, my dear," he went on, "if you'll tell me who made that telephone call, I'll know everything I need to know. You must have recognized the voice."

She stared at him for a moment, while the last color faded from her face. She opened her mouth to speak, but no sound came, and then, with a little, choking breath, she slid to the floor at his feet.

Helene flew to her side, looking accusingly at Malone. "You didn't need to do that."

"No," Malone said, "because I knew the answer." He looked down at the unconscious girl. "She's been tortured enough," he said very quietly, "and there's nothing more I need to learn from her. Is there a place where she can lie down, while we get this over with?"

"There's a couch in the chorus girls' dressing room," Jake said.

Malone nodded. "You carry her there, Jake. Get someone to look after her. And there are two more people I need here, so we'll have a quorum. Send a waiter to bring Lou Goldsmith here from the bar. And get Angela Doll."

During the interval that followed, the little lawyer paced back and forth across the floor, chewing savagely on his cigar, his face grey, not saying a word. Allswell McJackson moaned again, struggled up to the one chair in the room, and sat down heavily, his head resting on his hands. No one else moved.

When Jake had returned, and Lou Goldsmith and Angela Doll had arrived, Malone stopped his pacing, and stood, half-leaning against the dressing table.

"Daniel von Flanagan of the homicide division is out front," he began. "I could ask him in to hear this, but I won't. Because what is said in this room to-night is never going to be repeated outside its walls." The words seemed to be forced from him by some great effort.

He looked around the room, at Helene standing, pale and motionless, in one corner; at Al Omega, whose forehead glistened with sweat; at the big, thick-shouldered Lou Goldsmith, his eyes dark and tortured; at Allswell McJackson leaning his head on his hand; at Pen Reddick; at the wide-eyed Angela Doll; at Jake.

"I can say that," he began again, "because every person in this room tonight has a good, sound, and entirely private reason for not wanting what is going to be said here to be repeated, anywhere, ever." He looked down at his cigar. "Please be assured, I'm not going to give away those reasons."

Jake burst out, "Malone, for the love of Mike! Who—"

"Don't rush me," Malone said. He looked beyond them all, somewhere into space. "There was a man," he began slowly, "who loved a certain girl, very greatly. And who discovered that she was being cruelly victimized by three people who were—as someone else has said—the very incarnation of evil. The girl was one of the twelve members of the chorus of the Casino. One of the three people was another member."

He paused for a moment in which everyone in the room looked surreptitiously at Lou Goldsmith. The slot-machine king's face was as impassive as concrete.

"This man," Malone went on, in the same, dreamy tone, "murdered those three people, by hanging them with silk stockings worn by the chorus girls. But for the two men that he murdered, he used only eleven stockings. The woman he murdered was hanged with her own stockings."

He drew a long, sighing breath. "He didn't do that in order to point to the woman's part in the past—crimes. It wasn't that he wanted the world to know the truth. Rather, it was—a strange, fantastic notion of justice." He paused, and said, "Of course, he must have been mad."

Helene said suddenly, "No, Malone!"

The lawyer said chidingly, "Yes, Helene. Or at least, if I can't make a jury think so"— He puffed at his cigar and looked at Lou Goldsmith. "I hope the offer that you made this afternoon still holds good."

Lou Goldsmith nodded and said hoarsely, "You're damned right it still holds good."

"Fine," Malone said. He was silent for a moment while he thought over a few details of finance.

"*Go on*, Malone," Jake said.

"I'm guessing, now," Malone said. "If I don't guess right, I hope—someone here will correct me." He crushed out his half-smoked cigar in the ash tray, and put his hands in his pockets. "I think that this man put dope in the midget's whiskey bottle here in the dressing room before the show last night. I think that, because the dope that was used takes a long time to act. It had to be an expert bit of timing, so that the midget wouldn't collapse until he got back to his dressing room. Then this man came back here, and strung up the midget with the stockings he'd previously stolen from the chorus girls' dressing room."

Allswell McJackson looked up. "You mean—Mr. Otto was murdered—here?"

"Right here," Malone said. "I have the proof of it—from someone who happened in here, and saw him." He wondered how Ruth Rawlson would look on a witness stand. "How he was moved from here has nothing to do—with his murder. That's one of the things—that will probably never be discovered." He added mentally, "I hope."

He began unwrapping a fresh cigar. "This morning, he traced Mildred Goldsmith to Annette Ginnis' apartment. He waited, I think, somewhere outside her apartment, planning to pick up the trail there, but as luck would have it, he saw Annette Ginnis leave. So—remember, I'm still guessing—he knocked at the door, and when Mildred Goldsmith let him in, he struck her over the head—the medical report on her will probably show that: I'm saying it because that's the only thing he could have done—took off her stockings, and hung her in Annette Ginnis' clothes closet.

"Then he came to Johnny Oscar. He probably made an appointment with Johnny Oscar—who was probably a pretty nervous man about that time— very likely on the pretext that he had some information for him. They had a drink together, and he doped the drink with the same stuff he had used on the midget—and on one other person. Then the two of them went to Johnny Oscar's apartment—again, the knockout drops must have been very carefully timed —went in together, and when Johnny Oscar suddenly keeled over, this man strung him up with the other eleven stockings."

He bit off the end of the cigar, lit it, and said, "That's all pure guesswork, but I'll bet you any money it's right. Because that's the way it *must* have been."

"Wait," Helene said. "Last night. Annette Ginnis. The telephone call."

Malone nodded slowly. "That's my proof," he said. "This man knew—that last night Annette Ginnis was to go through another meaningless marriage ceremony, with a young man who would be held up for a stiff fee for a quick, quiet annulment. He knew that the procedure would call for a great deal of night-spot visiting. He wanted to prevent that marriage, and so he called up every night-spot in town until he managed to catch up with her. Then he told her that the midget was dead."

Al Omega said suddenly, "You'll never be able to prove any of this."

"I could," Malone said, "by telling the police just what I've been telling you now. But the murderer loves Annette Ginnis enough to want to keep this whole story out of the newspapers. He knows I can give the police proof that won't involve this story. And he knows too," he said in almost a roar, "that he has the best damn lawyer in seven states, if not the whole civilized world, who can get him off on an insanity plea." He smiled. "Ladies and gentleman of the jury, this man murdered Jay Otto, the Big Midget, and Mildred Goldsmith, and Johnny Oscar, because his poor, sick brain had conceived the notion that they were persecuting him. You intelligent citizens, who are giving your valuable time to serve on a jury, can you honestly believe that a sane man would murder his supposed persecutors with—*silk stockings?*" He paused, mopped his brow, and said, "it will be as easy as that. And God knows, the man must have been mad." He wondered how big a fee he could stick Lou Goldsmith for.

"No," he said very quietly, "I don't think that the murderer will give away any secrets. Because if he did—he'd have to give away a secret of his own." He knocked a half inch of ash off his cigar, and said, "Jake, will you go and ask von Flanagan to step back here?"

Jake walked to the door, put a hand on the knob, paused, turned around, and said, "Wait a minute. Before we turn this meeting over to the cops, how did you know? What tipped you off?"

"You did," Malone said, examining the end of his cigar. "You should have guessed it yourself, from what a certain elevator operator told you. Remember? 'I'm afraid of only one man, and he's closer to me than any other person in the world'?"

Jake stared at him for a minute, blinked, shook his head, and muttered, "All right, I'm just a dumb guck. I'll get von Flanagan." He opened the door and went out.

There was a little flurry of movement in the room. Helene ran a hand over her smooth hair, took out a cigarette and lit it. Allswell McJackson moaned and rubbed the back of his neck. Lou Goldsmith fumbled in his pocket for a cigar, found one, looked at it, and put it back. Angela Doll straightened up and pulled her coat closer around her shoulders.

"It was a swell show," she said, "but why did you drag *me* in here to watch it?"

Malone smiled at her admiringly. "Because, sweetheart," he said, *"you're* the proof I need."

She started to speak, he frowned at her, and she was silent.

Lou Goldsmith said suddenly, "But how do you know?"

"That," Malone said, "is what I'm going to tell von Flanagan."

Chapter Thirty-Two

JAKE PAUSED for just a moment at the door leading out front, and looked over the Casino. Ramon Arriba's band was tearing off an impassioned samba, and the floor was jammed. There didn't seem to be an empty table in the place.

He hoped Malone knew what he was doing.

Halfway across the room, a gentle voice called to him. "Mr. Justus!"

He wheeled around, to see that Max Hook was signaling to him.

Feeling in his pocket for a cigarette, he strolled casually up to the table. "Good evening. Hope you liked the show."

"Delightful show," Max Hook said. "Don't know when I've enjoyed a show so much. But I didn't ask you over here to tell you how much I liked the show."

"No?" Jake said, as though he didn't have the faintest idea what Max Hook was talking about.

"No," Max Hook said, on the downbeat. "You know, I think it's about time for us to talk business, if I may be so coarse. About the Casino—"

"Oh yes," Jake said. "Listen. I'll be delighted to talk business with you, about fifteen minutes from now. Right now, I've something important to attend to. Do you mind?"

"Mind?" Max Hook said, waving his perfumed cigarette. "There's nothing I enjoy more than sitting here, watching all these charming young people having a good time. Make it whatever time is convenient for you. But"— he looked at his wrist-watch—"make it before twelve, Jake my dear boy, because I'm always in bed by one."

"Sure," Jake said. "Before twelve."

If Malone did know what he was doing, if he could turn up the murderer of the midget and Mildred Goldsmith and Johnny Oscar, then it would be possible to keep von Flanagan from closing the Casino. But Max Hook was another matter.

Malone wanted to see him backstage, Jake explained to von Flanagan. The big police officer finished his drink, cast a last wistful glance at the dancers on the floor, and followed Jake.

Malone was outside the dressing room, talking to a waiter. As Jake opened the door for von Flanagan, he heard the little lawyer say, "Tell her I'll be with her in just a few minutes. Does she have everything she wants?"

"Oh yes, Mr. Malone," the waiter assured him. "And she's talking with Mr. Bullock."

Jake thought that Malone's face paled as he said, "You don't mean Harrison Bullock, the broker?"

"Oh yes, sir," the waiter said.

Jake grabbed Malone by the arm. "With all the girls there are in the world—" he began indignantly.

"You were too young to see the Follies," Malone said, "back in '22."

"Damn you," Jake said. "Listen, Malone, there's some trouble—"

"Another murder?" Malone asked pleasantly.

"Worse. Max Hook wants his dough back."

Malone chewed his lower lip. "When?"

"Now."

"Well," Malone said, "we've met everything else. We can meet this, somehow. How much do you owe him?"

"Only thirty-five hundred bucks," Jake said. "But I can't take that out of the Casino receipts, what with—"

Malone said quickly, "Never mind." He was thinking fast. There was that check from Pen Reddick in his wallet, for two thousand bucks. There would be another check from Pen Reddick for eighteen hundred bucks—if he was guessing right about the midget's murderer. "Never mind," he repeated, "we can meet it." He'd still have a few hundred dollars left, to spend on Ruth Rawlson.

"Oh sure," Jake said bitterly, "we'll meet it! We meet everything." He opened the door for Malone, his heart sick.

Helene smiled at him from across the dressing room. That didn't help much either. She was pale and tired, and still smiling. "I wanted to make this place a success for you," he tried to tell her with his eyes.

Von Flanagan had stopped dead in his tracks in the middle of the room, staring about him.

"What the hell is this?" he asked suspiciously.

"Just a little quiet celebration," Malone said, smiling, "to celebrate my handing over to you the murderer of the midget and Mildred Goldsmith and Johnny Oscar."

The smile faded from his face. "I hate to do this, von Flanagan," he said, "because the guy's crazy. He didn't have a reason in the world for committing the murders, except that his poor, sick brain cooked up a notion that they were persecuting him."

Von Flanagan had heard Malone talking to juries in the past. He said, "Yeah?" and looked around the room. "Which one is it?"

"Imagine a sane man," Malone went on, "drugging his victims, and then strangling them with silk stockings. Imagine the conflict that must have been going on in his poor, tortured mind. Think of it, von Flanagan."

"Let a jury think of it," von Flanagan said. "I'm

just a cop." He paused, shook his head, and murmured, "The guy must have been nuts."

"That's what I've been trying to tell you," Malone said.

"Okay," von Flanagan said. "Maybe I'd better call a squad car."

"You won't need one," Malone said. "He'll go quietly."

Von Flanagan said, "I'll take your word for it. But which one?"

"Do you mean you don't know?" Malone said, in a hurt, surprised voice.

Von Flanagan's eyes followed Malone's. *"You're* nuts," he said. "He has an alibi—"

"The alibi," Malone told him, "is what proves I'm right." He turned to Angela Doll. "My dear, before you left the Casino last night, did you have a drink?"

She nodded. "Several drinks."

"Here? In this room?"

She nodded again. "Yes. He said—it would be all right—there was a bottle of Scotch—"

"And then you went home," the lawyer went on. "Do you remember what happened after you got home?"

"Well—" She paused. "Ruth Rawlson called me up. I remember that. But I don't remember—much else."

"No," Malone said, "because you'd been doped with the same drug that laid out the midget. I know, because you woke up this morning feeling swell, and then, all of a sudden, you passed out cold as a clam. The dope that was given to the midget worked that way." He turned to von Flanagan. "There goes the alibi. She doesn't know what time she went to sleep last night. And who in the world would be able to whip up a drug like that, except a man who'd studied to be a chemistry professor?"

Allswell McJackson struggled to his feet.

"Wait," Malone said. He went on mercilessly, "At the last minute, he decided to save himself. So he faked a murder attempt, in which he was to have been the intended victim." He picked up the strand of rope from the floor and handed it to von Flanagan. "Only, when he frayed the rope so that it would break and drop him to the floor unharmed, he had to use a razor blade on a few of the strands."

"Wait," Allswell McJackson said.

"The poor, helpless madman!" Malone said. "There isn't a jury in the world who would send him to the chair."

Allswell McJackson stared helplessly around the room, at von Flanagan, at Malone. "I must have been —I was crazy."

"*Was!*" Malone said. "You *are*." He walked up to the stricken man and laid a hand on his arm.

"I'll confess," Allswell McJackson said. "I'll confess everything."

"You do," Malone told him, "and I'll break your neck. Don't you dare say one damned word unless

I'm dictating it. What do you have a lawyer for?" He tightened the hand on Allswell's arm. "Don't worry, pal. When I get you before a jury, I'll save you from the chair." *

"A damn shame," von Flanagan rumbled. "He was a swell magician."

"He was a lousy magician," Malone said, "and a worse actor. That phony faint of his here tonight would have tipped off anybody with a discerning eye. A man who's just missed being hung by the snap of a rope doesn't lie peacefully on the floor with his eyes closed." He took out a fresh cigar.

Von Flanagan took the giant by one unprotesting arm. "Come along, professor. While you're waiting trial, maybe you can teach me that coin-and-glass-of water trick."

He walked to the door with his prisoner, everyone in the room watching and trying to pretend that he wasn't. At the door he paused and turned around.

"How the hell did you know, Malone?"

"An elevator operator told Jake," Malone said. He unwrapped the cigar. "He'd overheard something the midget said once. It was—" He paused, squinted at the ceiling, and quoted, " 'I'm afraid of only one man. And he's closer to me than any other person in the world.' " He lit the cigar, slowly and with exquisite care. "For a while, I thought that meant someone else. Then I realized. Who was closer to the midget than Allswell McJackson, who stooged for him in his

*Author's note: He did, too.

act, and drove his car, and put him to bed at night, and got him up in the morning, and looked after his accounts, and—read his mail?" He looked thoughtfully at the end of the cigar. "And who was as much a giant as Jay Otto was a midget. They were—closer than brothers." He met Helene's eyes across the room in a casual glance. "That's how I knew."

Allswell McJackson laughed hoarsely. For a moment Malone wondered if his analysis of the case had been right.

"Come on, professor," von Flanagan said gently.

The door closed behind them.

Malone slumped down against the dressing table. "I guess that ends the show," he said. Suddenly he looked up, a half-smile on his face. "I could have given another proof, if I'd needed to. The thing I've been trying to remember, and couldn't." He glanced up at the bar over the closet. "Helene had a dream about Allswell McJackson in a magician's cloak, saying, 'I couldn't have done this trick, if I hadn't been twelve feet tall.'"

"That's it," Helene said excitedly, "that's the thing I've been trying to think of—"

Malone interrupted her. "There wasn't any chair in this dressing room when the midget was hung. Jake's a fairly tall man, yet he couldn't have reached up to that bar where the noose was tied. Only a man as tall as Allswell McJackson could have done it. We should have guessed that—hours ago." Suddenly he looked very tired. "Will you call a waiter, Jake? I want to send a message." He ran a hand over his face, covering his eyes for just one moment.

Pen Reddick had been bending over the dressing table, busy with a fountain pen. Now he straightened up and handed a check to Malone.

"I guess that squares us," he said.

Malone stuck the check in his pocket without looking at it. "I guess it does," he said. He smiled. "Betty Royal's out front. Now that you've got the midget off your mind, there's no other reason why you can't manage a proposal, is there?"

"Not a reason in the world," Pen Reddick said. He put his fountain pen back in his pocket and ducked out the door.

Angela Doll pulled her furs around her shoulders. "I guess there'll be pictures, when the story breaks tomorrow," she said. "Maybe I'd better go and get a good night's sleep."

"You'd better," Jake said. "And have a facial before the reporters get to you."

She smiled wanly. "Leave it to me," she said, and was gone.

Then Lou Goldsmith roused himself from what had seemed almost to be a trance. "What I said still goes, Malone," he rumbled. "Defend the guy, and send me the bill." He picked up his hat, stood silent by the door for a moment, waved a good night, and took his leave.

The waiter Jake had called arrived at the door. Malone stepped outside to whisper to him. "Tell

Miss Rawlson I'll be with her in just a few minutes now. Is she having a good time?"

"Yes, sir," the waiter said. "Yes, sir, she's having a very good time. She's still chatting with Mr. Bullock, sir."

"Damn Mr. Bullock!" Malone said, stepping back into the dressing room.

"*Annette*—" Al Omega said.

"She never was married to the midget," Malone said. "The marriage certificate he showed her was a fake. She's had a hell of a time, and she needs a good strong arm around her. Her husband's, for instance."

"Thanks," Al Omega said. He paused at the door. "You know—Mildred Goldsmith—"

"I know," Malone said. "She didn't mean a thing. She ran after you. You were sore and hurt because you couldn't understand why Annette had left you the day after your marriage. You didn't give a hoot in hell about Mildred Goldsmith, but she was— available. And then the midget confided in you about his fake marriage to Annette, only he didn't tell you it was a fake. And Mildred confided in you that Annette was working this marriage-annulment game, only she didn't tell you it was someone else's idea, not Annette's. And you couldn't guess that the midget had put her up to it." The little lawyer shook his head. "He didn't miss a trick. He saw how tortured Annette was when she saw you with Mildred Goldsmith, he saw how tortured Lou Goldsmith was when he saw Mildred with you, and he saw how tortured you were, when you believed Annette was a grafting little gold-digger with a new approach." He picked up his cigar. "At least, I'm glad you two came out of it with your skins whole."

"Thanks," Al Omega said. He opened the door and said, "I'll look after Annette."

"He will, too," Jake said after the door was closed. "He's a good guy."

Malone stared at the closed door. "I should have guessed."

"After all," Helene said gently, "no one even pretends you're psychic, in addition to your other talents." At Jake's questioning look she went on, "Malone thought the nice young man Annette had married was—Allswell McJackson."

"It was the logical conclusion," Malone said. "But as a matter of fact, it all fitted together better this way. Remind me never to trust logical conclusions again." He lit his cigar. "Well," he said, "that winds up damn near everything."

"No it doesn't," Helene said. "I still don't understand about those silk stockings."

Malone passed his hand wearily over his eyes. "I explained it. There were eleven, because he wanted to use Mildred Goldsmith's own stockings on her—"

"That isn't what I mean," Helene said. "Why use stockings at all?"

"Revenge. Symbolism. Making the punishment fit the crime." Malone shrugged. "Remember, these murders were committed by a man who considered them acts of vengeance—not for the wrongs he'd suffered himself, but because of other people. You've heard enough about the midget's exotic personal life to realize that every member of the Casino chorus—except Mildred Goldsmith—could have killed him with pleasure." He sighed. "Well, Allswell fixed it so they practically did. That boy sure has a sense of justice."

Jake said, "Smart, too. He almost stumped you, Malone—for the first time."

Malone thought for a moment, then said, "There's always—just one key thing you need to know. The key that unlocks a door—or a mystery, or"—he paused suddenly, staring at them—"a fiddle case."

"Yes," Helene said excitedly. "A fiddle case. Malone, who moved the midget's body? And why?"

"Do you know?" Jake put in.

The little lawyer nodded. "Yes, I know. And I'll tell you in a minute. Jake, get Artie Clute in here."

Chapter Thirty-Three

FOR JUST A MOMENT, while Jake went to get the bass
fiddle player, Malone permitted himself the luxury of thinking about Ruth Rawlson. She'd be there
waiting for him, right at this very instant. The snow
queen of that twenty-years-ago ballet, all in dazzling
white, save for the red-gold hair that flowed over her
pale arms like a flame. Just a few minutes now—

"I don't feel as old as I look," he told himself,
"and by golly, I bet I don't look as old as I feel."

"What are you muttering about?" Helene asked.
She lit a cigarette with fingers that still trembled.

"Truth," he told her solemnly. "Truth is the key
that unlocks all doors, and all fiddle cases."

Helene said sternly, "Malone, you're drunk."

"Not yet, I'm not," he hold her happily. "But—"
What if he did have to turn over most of the fee he'd
gotten from Pen Reddick to square Jake with Max
Hook? He'd get it back from Jake later. Meantime,
Ruth Rawlson was waiting for *him*—

He could hear Artie Clute protesting by the time Jake had dragged him within six feet of the dressing room door.

"—honest, Mr. Justus, just a couple of quick ones before the show tonight. You know how it is, standing up there beating that ole bass fiddle, nothing to look at but the pretty girls in the chorus, a guy gets bored—" He came in through the dressing room door on the last word, looked around, and turned white.

"You're not going to get fired," Malone said sternly. "You're not going to have to talk to a cop. You're not in any trouble. But"—he drew a long breath—"why in hell did you carry the little guy out of here last night?"

"I didn't know I was," Artie Clute said, his round face unhappy. "Honest, Mr. Malone, I thought—say, Mr. Malone, how the hell did you know?"

"Truth," Malone said gravely, "is the key that—" He paused, cleared his throat, and said, "Nobody could have gotten the midget's body out of the fiddle case without having a key to the case. There was one key—the one the midget had—and it was"—he paused—"not available. So another key must have been used. And nobody in the world would have had that extra key to the fiddle case except—the man who owned it."

Artie Clute said, "Gee, I didn't mean to do anything wrong." He sniffed, like a small boy staving off the tears. "After all, hell, it had been my fiddle, and if I couldn't get it back Al Omega wouldn't give me

my job again, and I owed sixteen bucks at the hotel
and four bucks at the liquor store, and the—"

"So you *did* carry him out of here!" Jake said.

Artie Clute scratched the underside of his nose
with the back of his forefinger. "After Al Omega told
me I could have my job back, I thought I'd come in
and try to make some kind of a deal with the midget.
So I came back here and knocked on the door and
then I came in, and he wasn't here. But there was the
fiddle case leaning up against the wall. So I thought
what the hell, I'll take it along with me and make a
deal with him later. What would you have done?"

"Exactly the same thing," Jake said calmly.

"So I took it back to my place at the hotel, and I
got my key and opened it up and Jeez, instead of my
fiddle, there's a dead midget." He looked up appealingly. "Can you imagine how I felt about that?"

"We can imagine it," Helene said. "Easily."

"So I thought, Jeez, what the hell am I gonna do
with *this*? And I decided I'd better have a drink, only
all I had left was forty cents, so I went over to the
drugstore where you can buy an under-the-counter
pint for forty cents." He shuddered reminiscently.
"So I drank about half of it, and then I began to feel
sorry as hell for the little guy. Here he was, and not
even in his own bed. So I drank the rest of the pint,
and then I went through his pockets and found the
key to his apartment, and took him down there, and
undressed him, and put him to bed just as nicely and
carefully as I could." He sniffed again. "Honest, I

meant to fold his hands, but I'm afraid I forgot to.

"Don't apologize," Malone said hoarsely. "You did a beautiful job. And I suppose you called up the desk and left a 7:30 call for him, too?"

Artie Clute nodded. "Was that wrong?" he asked anxiously.

"No," Malone said, "but I hope you didn't think he'd hear it."

The bass fiddle player looked indignant. "Do you think I'm dumb?" He turned appealingly to Jake and Helene. "I thought if I left a call for him, when he didn't answer somebody would go up and see what was wrong. You wouldn't have wanted to leave that poor little guy there all by himself, and nobody to come up and find him, would you?"

"Perish the thought," Helene said.

Artie Clute smiled at her. "And then I meant to take the fiddle case back to the Casino and find the fiddle itself, but Jeez, I began to feel groggy as hell, so I decided just to take the case back to the Casino, and then I felt too groggy for that, so finally I thought well, Mr. Justus owns the Casino, so I took the fiddle case up and leaned it against your door. And I guess I got to bed all right after that, because that's where I woke up this morning." He looked anxiously at Jake. "You don't think I've done wrong, do you?"

"N-o," Jake said, dragging it out.

"That's swell," Artie Clute said, brightening up. He scratched his nose again, and said, "I gotta get back out there or I'll be in trouble again. Mr. Justus, have a heart! Please don't tell on me. I don't want to lose my job again."

"I wouldn't dream of it," Jake said.

"That's wonderful of you," Artie Clute told him, "and I want you to know I appreciate it. Because if Al Omega knew I'd been drinking that forty-cent whiskey again, he'd—" He started to open the door.

"Wait a minute," Malone said. "I thought you meant—you didn't want any of us to tell—you'd carried the midget's body out of here, in your fiddle case."

"That?" Artie Clute said, "Who the hell would care about *that*?" He stared at them and said, "Sure, I won't tell anybody about that, because if I did I'd have to tell about that forty-cent liquor, and then Al Omega would fire me again, and I couldn't let that happen because I just borrowed ten bucks tonight from the headwaiter and put up my fiddle for security." He opened the door, started out, and said, "Oh Mr. Justus, I bought a suit of clothes on time payments this afternoon, and forged your name as a reference. I hope you don't mind." The strains of Ramon Arriba's closing theme came in from the bandstand. Artie Clute said, "Gotta go. Good by," and closed the door.

"Well," Jake said at last, "he *is* a damn fine bass fiddle player." He glanced around the room and said, "Let's get out of here."

The three left the dressing room without a backward glance. Back in the Casino, Malone strained his eyes to see, in the farthest corner, two figures with their heads together. One of the figures wore a white dress. Well, he'd chase that Bullock guy away fast enough, even if he did own half the real estate on the near-North Side. Surely Ruth Rawlson wouldn't mind having been kept waiting, for such a little while.

"Now," Jake said in an undertone to Malone, "one thing more. Max Hook." As Malone nodded, he seated Helene at the table they had left such a short time before, leaned over her, and said, "You'll excuse us for a minute? Business."

She had never looked more beautiful, her pale hair smooth and gleaming around her face, her lovely eyes violet-edged with weariness.

As they threaded their way through the tables, Malone felt for the reassuring crackle of the checks in his pocket. The office rent could go for another month. That little matter at the bank could be taken care of. Apologetic notes could handle those February and March bills in his desk drawer. There would be the fee for Allswell McJackson's defense coming along. No, he didn't really need the money Pen Reddick had given him.

Max Hook looked up and smiled at them blandly. "Sorry to trouble you, Jake, my dear boy. Will you join me in a drink? No? Very well, shall we get right down to business?"

"Sure," Jake said. "Let's get it over with."

Max Hook glanced around as though to make sure no one was listening. "Jake, my boy, I let you have the use of certain money, to remodel and redecorate the Casino. You put up the Casino as security. Frankly, my dear fellow, I don't want the Casino. But"—he paused.

Malone thought, "Here it comes!" He felt again for the checks.

"Also, frankly," Max Hook whispered, "I don't want the money either. But I'd be glad to cancel the debt—" Again he looked cautiously around.

Malone withdrew his hand from his pocket and thought, "What the hell?"

"Jake, my dear young friend," Max Hook said, "I'll be glad to call it square, if— The midget: I understand he had some pictures in his room." He cleared his throat. "If you can arrange it—I'd be glad—I'd be delighted to take those pictures instead of the money or the Casino—"

Jake stared at him, and said hoarsely, "It might be arranged."

"Good, good, my dear boy," Max Hook murmured. He fitted a thin cigarette into his rose-quartz holder, leaned across the table, and breathed, "Are those pictures really as—"

Halfway back to his own table, Jake said to Malone, "I knew I'd find a use for those pictures, sometime."

Malone glanced at him. It was as though the weight of the world had dropped from Jake's shoulders. He watched while Jake sat down beside Helene, took one of her slender hands in his, and brushed his lips over the finger tips. He looked up towards the band-

stand where Al Omega had just appeared, bright-
eyed and smiling, keeping one eye on the table near
the door where Annette Ginnis sat watching him
adoringly. He started across the floor and passed Betty
Royal's table, her basketball team of admirers gone
and Pen Reddick at her side, just in time to hear Pen
Reddick saying, "There's a reason why I couldn't
tell you before, but now——" He glanced at his watch.
Oh well, Ruth Rawlson had only been waiting a little
over two hours. He threaded his way through the
crowd to her table.

It was empty. There was a little litter of cigarette
stubs and empty glasses which a busy waiter was rapidly clearing away.

"Miss Rawlson?" Malone said, with a sudden anxiety in his voice.

"Miss Rawlson? Oh yes, Mr. Malone. She left a
message for you."

Malone said, "*Left——*"

"Miss Rawlson left just a few minutes ago," the
waiter said, "with Mr. Bullock. She asked me to tell
you they were driving to Crown Point to be married,
sir." He sighed. "A very lucky young lady, if I may
say so. Mr. Bullock——"

"I know," Malone said hoarsely. He stood there
for just a minute, looking at the deserted table. Then,
"Tell me, how did she look?"

The waiter rolled his eyes heavenward. "Beautiful,
sir, simply beautiful! She wore a white dress, trimmed
with—I believe they're called gold nail-heads, sir.

And her hair—frankly, sir, I've never seen more gorgeous hair. Like red sunshine it was, I give you my word. And her face, Mr. Malone, was like the face of an angel."

"It was, eh?" Malone said. "I hope they'll be very happy." He handed the waiter a five-dollar bill.

The waiter stared at it and at Malone. "What's this for, sir?"

"Never mind," Malone said. "You wouldn't understand."

He took one more glance at the table, strolled out past the bar, through the lobby, and into the street.

Well, twenty years from now, perhaps—

He hailed a passing taxi, yawned, and climbed in.

"Home," said John J. Malone.

Craig Rice (1908-19570), creator of madcap murder mavens Jake and Helene Justus and John J. Malone, was Georgiana Ann Randolph Walker Craig Lipton DeMott Bishop in private life. The first mystery writer to grace the cover of *Time*, she was hailed by the issue of Jan, 24 1946 as virtually the only woman" of what the magazine deemed a distinctively American genre, "apt to mix the pleasures of the wake and the moment in a combination of hard drink, hilarity and homicide." This Rice did in high-spirited, Chicago-based spoofs like *8 Faces at 3*" (1939), *The Big Midget Murders* (1942) and *Knocked for a Loop*(1957).

Her life was less a laughing matter, The Dorothy Parker of detective fiction, Rice wrote the binge but lived the hangover. Rice's father was a painter, her mother a "cosmopolite," while her parents sojourned in Europe, divorced, married and remarried, Georgiana was raised by and aunt and uncle. She ran away from Miss Ransome's School in Piedmont, California, to become a "Bohemienne" in Chicago. There she went through a succession of five marriages of her own, providing two daughters and a son.

When *Time* got hold of her, Rice was living in Santa Monica and had written 15 books, including mysteries under the pseudonyms Michael Venning and Daphne Sanders. She would ghostwrite for stripper Gypsy Rose Lee and actor George Sanders. She scripted two entries in the *"Falcon"* film series and other creditable B movies.

She was deaf in one ear, blind in one eye and threatened with glaucoma in the other, In 1949 she was committed to Camarillo State Hospital for chronic alcoholism. Rice twice threatened suicide.

She was found dead in her Los Angeles apartment Aug. 28, 1957, "apparently," reported *Newsweek,* "from natural causes."

Rice was 49.

—William Ruehlmann
Series Consultant

THE LIBRARY OF CRIME CLASSICS®

Nine—and Death Makes Ten
The Peacock Feather Murders
The Plague Court Murders
The Punch and Judy Murders
The Reader Is Warned
The Red Widow Murders
The Skeleton In the Clock
The Unicorn Murders
The White Priory Murders

HENRY CECIL
Daughter's In Law
Settled Out of Court

LESLIE CHARTERIS
Angels Of Doom
The First Saint Omnibus
Getaway
Knight Templar
The Last Hero
The Saint in New York

EDMUND CRISPIN
The Case of the Gilded Fly

CARROLL JOHN DALY
Murder from the East

LILLIAN DE LA TORRE
Dr. Sam: Johnson, Detector
The Detections of Dr. Sam: Johnson
The Return of Dr. Sam: Johnson, Detector
The Exploits of Dr. Sam: Johnson, Detector

PETER DICKINSON
Perfect Gallows
The Glass Sided Ants' Nest
The Sinful Stones

PAUL GALLICO
The Abandoned
Love of Seven Dolls
Mrs.'Arris Goes To Paris
Farewell To Sport
Too Many Ghosts
Thomasina
JAMES GOLLIN
Eliza's Galliardo
The Philomel Foundation

DOUGLAS GREENE & ROBERT ADEY
Death Locked In

DASHIELL HAMMETT & ALEX RAYMOND
Secret Agent X-9

A.P. HERBERT
Uncommon Law

REGINALD HILL
A Killing Kindness

RICHARD HULL
The Murder of My Aunt

E. RICHARD JOHNSON
Cage 5 Is Going To Break
Case Load Maximum
Dead Flowers
The God Keepers
The Inside Man
The Judas
Mongo's Back in Town
Silver Street

JONATHAN LATIMER
The Dead Don't Care

Headed for a Hearse
The Lady in the Morgue
Murder In the Madhouse
The Search for My Great Uncle's Head
Red Gardenias
Solomon's Vineyard

VICTORIA LINCOLN
A Private Disgrace
Lizzie Borden by Daylight

MARGARET MILLAR TITLES
An Air That Kills
Ask for Me Tomorrow
Banshee
Beast in View
Beyond This Point Are Monsters
The Cannibal Heart
The Fiend
Fire Will Freeze
How Like An Angel
The Iron Gates
The Listening Walls
Mermaid
The Murder of Miranda
Rose's Last Summer
Spider Webs
A Stranger in My Grave
Vanish In An Instant
Wall of Eyes

BARRY MALZBERG
Underlay

WILLIAM F. NOLAN
Look Out for Space
Space for Hire

WILLIAM O'FARRELL
Repeat Performance

STUART PALMER
The Penguin Pool Murder

STUART PALMER & CRAIG RICE
People VS Withers and Malone

BARBARA PAUL
Liars & Tyrants & People Who Turn Blue

ELLERY QUEEN
Cat of Many Tails
Drury Lane's Last Case
The Ellery Queen Omnibus
The Tragedy of X
The Tragedy of Y
The Tragedy of Z

PATRICK QUENTIN
Black Widow
Puzzle for Players
Puzzle for Puppets
Puzzle for Wantons

S.S. RAFFERTY
Cork of the Colonies
Die Laughing

DAMON RUNYON
Trials and Tribulations

CLAYTON RAWSON
Death from a Top Hat
Footprints on the Ceiling
The Headless Lady
No Coffin for the Corpse

CRAIG RICE
The Corpse Steps Out
8 Faces at 3
The Big Midget Murders
The Right Murder
The Wrong Murder

GEORGE SANDERS
Crime On My Hands

WALTER SATTERTHWAIT
Miss Lizzie

HAKE TALBOT
Rim of the Pit

ROBERT TAYLOR
Fred Allen
His Life and Wit

DARWIN L. TEILHET
The Talking Sparrow Murders

P.G. WODEHOUSE
Full Moon
If I Were You
Plum's Peaches
Service with a Smile
Tales From the Drone's Club
Who's Who In Wodehouse
Wodehouse On Crime

Write For Our Free Catalog:
International Polygonics, Ltd.
Madison Square, P.O. Box 1563
New York, NY 10159